THE SPIRIT WELL
LUTESONG BOOK TWO

R.K. ASHWICK

The Spirit Well

Copyright © 2024 R.K. Ashwick

RK Ashwick Books

rkashwick.com

All rights reserved. No part of this book may be reproduced or used in any manner without the prior written permission of the copyright owner, except for the use of brief quotations in a book review. To request permissions, contact ash@rkashwick.com.

ISBN (Paperback): 979-8-9855819-7-3

ISBN (E-Book): 979-8-9855819-6-6

LCCN: 2024900339

First edition March 2024.

Edited by Kim Halstead

Cover art by Patrick Knowles

Map by Lucia Vázquez de Prada

Illustrations by Tristan Voronov

Chapter icons by R.K. Ashwick

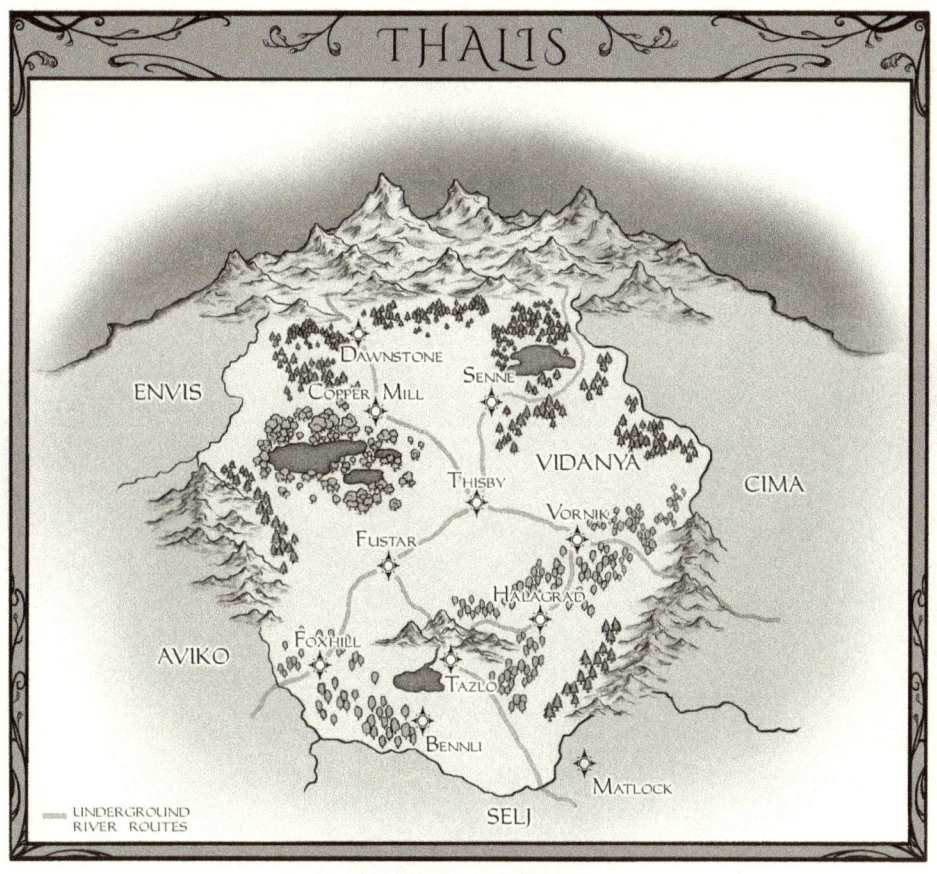

CONTENTS

Chapter 1	1
Chapter 2	15
Chapter 3	25
Chapter 4	33
Chapter 5	47
Chapter 6	51
Chapter 7	55
Chapter 8	77
Chapter 9	91
Chapter 10	103
Chapter 11	115
Chapter 12	127
Chapter 13	131
Chapter 14	143
Chapter 15	155
Chapter 16	167
Chapter 17	181
Chapter 18	189
Chapter 19	197
Chapter 20	201
Chapter 21	207
Chapter 22	215
Chapter 23	223
Chapter 24	235
Chapter 25	247
Chapter 26	255
Chapter 27	265
Chapter 28	269
Chapter 29	281
Chapter 30	289
Chapter 31	297

Want More?	303
Acknowledgments	305
About the Author	307

CHAPTER ONE

EMRY

IN THE WEAK light of morning, a bard and a farmhand surveyed the withered orchard around them. The farmhand said nothing, slouched in gloom and silence. The bard, having a personal distaste for the former and a professional distaste for the latter, wouldn't stand for it.

"Look, it's not that bad," he tried.

The farmhand gave him a sideways glance. "It's half dead."

"It's half alive."

"Granville's farm down the road doesn't look like this," the farmhand muttered, folding her burly arms. Emry Karic, the bard on duty, was unsure how to respond.

Technically, she wasn't *wrong*. Emry had visited Granville's farm last week with Cal and Aspen. The place had been glistening with greenery and ripening fruit, a veritable celebration of life returning after last year's deadly wave.

This orchard here was, well...surviving, at the very least.

Not that all of it looked terrible—roughly half the trees still stood. The grass boasted a greenish-yellow tint here and there. The smell of spring apples wafted feebly under gray clouds.

But the other half of the orchard stood blackened and barren, a stark reminder of what had happened six months ago.

"And it's been like this since the wave?" Emry asked the farmhand, who nodded.

"The wave took whatever our spirit couldn't protect," she said. "A few trees have started growing back since, but..."

Emry could easily imagine what had happened. A wall of white spirit energy barreling through the forest, past the barn, the shed... then through the trees, shriveling their branches and stripping away their life...

The wave had struck almost the entire province, mangling whatever hadn't been protected by spirits or stone walls. Emry himself had barely managed to shield his family when the disaster struck— he had watched its approach with his own eyes, his loved ones mere steps behind him.

He gingerly reached for the closest tree, its dead, black trunk twisted like rope. Though no fire had touched its bark, his fingers came away smudged with gray soot. He grimaced; the streaks against his tawny skin made him immensely grateful he'd never see such a disaster again in his lifetime.

"So..." The farmhand cleared her throat. "Are you gonna fix all this with your music or what?" Her eyes fell on the lute on Emry's back.

"Oh. Well..." Emry wiped the soot off his fingers and shrugged the instrument off his shoulder. It had been a gift from his family—a much-needed one, now that Aspen maintained a permanent residence in his old lute. The feel of it in his hands still gave him a thrill. The wood as pale as morning, the carvings of aspen leaves along its face...

And most thrilling of all, the single gilded tuning peg—a shimmering calling card for the Auric Guild.

"No," he said gently. "This can't fix it." He nodded to the farmhouse on the hill behind them. "But they can."

They both turned to the three figures emerging from the stone house. The first was the owner of the farm—Owen, a short, potbellied man who strode down the hill with far more energy than the early hour warranted.

"I must thank you again for coming," Owen said to his companions. "I had hoped the Council would send a spirit researcher to help, but—to send a *spirit*? I can hardly believe it, truly, I can't..."

The spirit in question loped alongside Owen in their human form, making for a colorful silhouette against the gray sky. Bright purple waistcoat, green eyes glowing in the morning mist—and, as always, flowers sticking out of their pockets, buttonholes, lapels...

"Happy to help," Aspen said firmly. "I'll talk to the spirit here and see what I can do."

They gave a brief smile to Emry, and he caught a whiff of honeysuckle and mint—no doubt due to the plants growing in the spirit's dark curls—then Owen and Aspen bounded into the orchard, babbling in fast, hushed tones.

The farmhand quickly followed, forgetting all about Emry and his lute, but he didn't mind. He let them wander off and waited patiently for the last figure, who navigated the rough, hilly steps with practiced grace and a frustrated frown.

"You'd think that after twenty such visits," Cal said, arriving with a huff, "I'd have invested in a pair of boots for these sorts of outings."

Emry held out a hand and helped her down the last few steps. "Ah, but shopping for boots would require you to actually leave the Council building now and again."

She gave a reluctant hum and adjusted her heavy green skirts. It still struck him to see her decked in the forest-green hues of the Council, rather than the midnight blue of the Academy. Gone, too, were the Academy lace and puffs, replaced with a simple pelisse, stoic gold buttons...and a pair of muddy, pointed shoes.

Cal sighed at the mud splatters and took Emry's arm. After

checking to make sure no one was looking, Emry snuck a kiss on her forehead, drawing a small smile from her. He supposed forehead kisses during official Council trips were frowned upon, but it was his sacred duty as a boyfriend to provide them when frustration arose.

"So, what do we know of this farm?" he asked.

"There was a spirit here, to be sure," Cal said, watching Owen and Aspen approach the forest tree line. "It clearly answered Cedar's call to defend its home against the wave—"

"A big, white bubble, it was!" Owen boomed ahead of them, arms raised as he recounted the tale to Aspen. "A shield, fighting away the energy single-handed! You should have seen it—it was the biggest in all of Vornik, I know it."

Emry resisted the urge to roll his eyes. Nowadays, every farmer with a spirit on their land claimed similar feats. Their spirit had the largest shield, the strongest presence, the biggest grove... For people who had scoffed at the very notion of spirits half a year ago, they were certainly proud of their new neighbors now.

"We could hardly believe our luck," Owen continued, his eager words drawing in other curious farmhands. "But—well..." His arms dropped. "I'm afraid it hasn't done a thing since. You don't think it's that"—he leaned in here, his stage whisper doing nothing for the volume of his voice—"that Matlock city disease, do you?"

The farmhands looked at each other nervously. Cal let out a tired breath. "Oh, not these rumors again."

She quickened her pace, tugging Emry forward—but a twinging pain shot through his knee, and he stumbled rather than followed.

"Hara take me..." he muttered, shaking out his leg. Cal froze, her hand tightening on his arm.

"Em?"

"Sorry." He gave an unconvincing laugh. "I guess my knee doesn't like the reminders of the wave."

But the worry line on Cal's brow only deepened. "Perhaps you should wait back in the carriage," she said, assessing the distance between them and the tree line ahead. "You shouldn't rush your recovery—"

"Cal, please." He held up a hand. "It's just a short walk, and I've had months to rest as it is. Let me at least pretend to be useful here."

But the pain remained stubborn, and once they reached the forest, he quickly found a tree stump to sit on. Even half a year after being possessed by Aspen to protect his family, the pain in his limbs still came and went. *Give it another month or so*, the doctors had said time and again. *It'll disappear soon.*

As if they knew how to treat spirit possessions.

While Emry sat on the stump and rubbed his knee, Cal deftly wrangled Owen's fears.

"Sir, I can assure you, whatever drought Matlock might be experiencing is too far away to affect spirits in Vornik," she said firmly. "Now, if you'll allow Aspen to speak with the spirit and gauge its level of strength, I can take notes and compare it to other spirits in the area."

She slipped seamlessly into her usual presentation, the one she gave at every place she visited for her Council research. Like the other aides in her department, she was here to determine the state of the spirit, if one was present. The size of its grove, its estimated strength, what it had been able to protect during the wave, if anything...

Of course, no other aide had the assistance of a forest spirit and a bard to help gather such data, but the Council hadn't turned away their support yet.

As Cal talked Owen out of his hand-wringing and into her research plan, Aspen caught sight of Emry and bounded over, the worry on their face an exact reflection of Cal's.

"You all right?" they asked, their own lute slung behind them. The once-shattered instrument had been repaired with glue and vines, and a small waterfall of honeysuckle flowed out of its cracked sound hole. But it had received a more human upgrade recently: a gilded peg, matching the one on Emry's lute.

"Just fine." Emry waved away the spirit's concern. Aspen ignored his gesture and looked to the carriage.

"Maybe you should—"

Emry glared. "If someone tells me to wait in the carriage one more time, I'm going to give all of you up and live in a tree." He pointed into the grove. "Is the spirit still in there?"

Aspen gave him a look, then relented. "Yes," they said, their shoulders slumped. "But it's quiet. It doesn't want to talk to me."

Emry sighed. "When do they ever?"

Just like Cal's presentation, this was a staple of every research trip: the distinctly unwelcoming energy of Vornik spirits. It didn't matter what Aspen did—they tried asking questions, talking about their lute, inquiring as to how the spirit felt after the wave...and they would get little in response. A few terse answers, perhaps. A general sense of confusion, a vague irritation that they were awake, that someone was *talking* to them, of all things.

And with every trip, Aspen came back more defeated.

As the flowers in the spirit's hair began to shrivel, Emry reached back and tapped his own lute. "Want me to get its attention first?"

Aspen brightened immediately. "Yes, please."

They helped Emry to his feet, then backed away to let him shrug the lute off his shoulder once more.

"Ms. Breslin," Emry said, trying to adopt her professional tone. "Aspen believes a song might get the spirit out of its shell."

Owen's eyes almost bulged out of his head.

"A Guild musician, playing for our spirit?" he blurted out, fiddling with his hat in excitement. "Did Ella Sorman send you?"

His mention of the Guild leader's name sent awed whispers through the observing farmhands. Emry masked his delight with a polite laugh.

"No, I'm merely helping Ms. Breslin's research," he said. "But Aspen and I have our first meeting with the Guild later today. Perhaps Ms. Sorman will consider this performance part of my debut."

He tried to sound casual, but the farmhands behind Owen were far too curious for that.

"So, you've met her?" one asked eagerly, the trowel in his hand all but forgotten. "What's she like?"

"Is she really as lovely as she looks onstage?" another said. But the tallest of them, the burly farmhand who had stood with Emry earlier, narrowed her eyes. "Wait," she said. "Are *you* the one she wrote a song about—?"

Cal cleared her throat. "If you could give my associate some quiet, please."

The farmhands straightened and silenced themselves. Cal gave Emry a smile and stepped back, letting him and Aspen approach the central tree in the spirit's grove.

Standing taller than the rest, the pine tree sheltered a swath of broad ferns and the telltale sign of a spirit: delicate white rhythm blooms, nestled under the ferns' leaves. Aspen knelt to check the flowers, taking great care not to step on them with their bare feet. Though they typically imitated Emry's style of dress each morning—billowy shirt, waistcoat, occasionally a coat if they felt like it—they rarely went anywhere in shoes. Even after months in the company of humans, they claimed they didn't much see the point.

"Spirit's fairly strong," they murmured, then looked up and brightened. "Who built the fane?"

The burly farmhand gave a small cough and raised her hand. "That was me."

The fane, a little wooden cubby on a post, stood undecorated but sturdy: a simple and welcoming place for offerings to the spirit. Aspen plucked a yellow flower from their lute and placed it in the cubby, adding some color to the coins and pinecones that already cluttered the space.

"Hello," they whispered, then placed their hand on the pine tree. They didn't need to speak aloud in order to communicate with other spirits but had gotten into the habit of it for the humans' benefit. "I do hope you like this."

Then it was Emry's turn to coax the spirit into a more talkative mood. He slid a coin into the fane, gave the tree a nod, and began to play.

Today's human audience was warmer than others he had experienced at previous farms. Some of the other farmers had laughed at the idea of playing music to appease a spirit; others had scoffed or tried talking over him. Owen and his farmhands, however, listened in respectful silence, not murmuring or shuffling in boredom.

In thanks for their patience, Emry rifled through his memory for a piece they would appreciate—a bright, simple working song he had learned from a farmer back home in Senne. That farmer had enjoyed Emry's rendition of it then, and he hoped his new audience —and perhaps the pine spirit—would enjoy it now.

To his delight, they did. They caught onto the song quickly, their fingers tapping the rhythm against their farm tools. And when Aspen joined in, their soft, ethereal voice little more than a breeze, the group even hummed along.

After the final note faded into the morning mist, Emry gave one more hopeful nod to the tree and stepped back.

"Thank you," Aspen whispered, then closed their eyes, reaching back out to the pine spirit in the newly formed silence. For several minutes, Emry witnessed nothing but the birdsong and the breeze, and his mind began to wander. Aspen looked tall, standing before the tree—about as tall as him. How strange. The spirit's first human form, while roughly modeled after Emry, had been shorter than him, a thin, energetic bundle of limbs, freckles, and flowers.

Now they were...well, simply a taller version of that.

Before Emry could think further on how much the growth spurt unsettled him, Aspen opened their eyes with a furrowed brow.

"The spirit's still recovering," they said, their tone empty. "And it doesn't want to talk. I'm sorry." They gave an apologetic bow to Owen. "I don't think it can help regrow the rest of the orchard right now."

"Oh. I—I see." The excitement in Owen's eyes faded. "Well—thank you for trying, my dear spirit."

As Owen turned to dismiss his farmhands, Cal jotted something in her notebook, then approached Aspen and Emry.

"Thank you for trying, both of you." She lowered her voice. "Is that truly all it said?"

"Not quite." Aspen's face darkened. "It told me to go away and let it go back to sleep. Said it doesn't need any help regrowing the orchard."

"Absolutely no manners in the forest, are there?" Cal tucked her pencil behind her ear. "I'm sorry about that, but with such a response, there's no use trying further and wasting your energy. I'll request a few more measurements for my report, then meet you at the carriage." Her tone shifted into a thinly veiled command to Emry. "Do take care walking there."

He withheld a sigh and gave her a formal half-bow.

"Yes, Ms. Breslin," he said—but caught her hand as she passed and gave it a discreet squeeze. With a half smile, Cal followed Owen back into the rows of apple trees.

"If I may ask a few more questions about the size of the orchard..."

Once she disappeared, Emry shifted the lute strap crossing his chest.

"I wouldn't worry about this spirit, Aspen," he said, trying to keep his tone optimistic. "We'll find a friendly one soon. And you'll meet plenty of new friends at the Guild meeting today, won't you?"

Aspen gave a halfhearted nod, and Emry started toward the carriage, already thinking about how to prepare for the Guild event. He'd have to wash and change, of course. He didn't mind the smell of apples, but he certainly *did* mind the stink of mud—

But Aspen turned the opposite way, and the morning breeze whipped into a sharp chill.

"Aspen?" Emry called, wrapping his coat tighter around himself. The spirit stood at the tree again, their determined gaze looking not at the boughs but beyond them. Far above, the gray clouds darkened, and the ferns at their feet shifted and swayed. Emry stepped forward.

"What are you doing?"

"Helping the spirit with the orchard," Aspen said, placing their hand on the tree. Another breeze kicked up, and Emry looked over his shoulder—the closest dead trees stood many paces away.

"You can't. It's too far, even for you."

"But if I channel my magic through the rain..."

Aspen's hand flickered, betraying the illusion of their form as they poured their energy into the tree. Emry swallowed at the sight of it.

"Look, you don't owe this spirit anything," he said. "You don't have to do this."

They ignored Emry and leaned forward, their whole body now guttering. Rain sprinkled from the thin clouds above, and behind Emry, a series of rippling cracks sliced through the dead apple trees. Bark shifted against bark; twigs snapped and curled. His eyes widened.

"How are you—?"

Aspen faded and pitched backward. Emry leapt for their arm.

"*Aspen!*"

As soon as he touched their ghostly form, everything went black.

The nothingness sent him into a panic. His mind scrambled for purchase, trying to orient himself to anything he could feel or hear. He was no longer standing, that was for certain. He was on his knees, with soft pine needles cradling his palms. No, that wasn't right—he was holding on to the tree, its rough bark scratching his fingertips. Or perhaps he was doing both, thinking with two minds, smelling soil and leaves, fear and blood—

I'm sorry! Aspen's voice rang in his ears, both too loud and too high, as their presence darted around inside him. *I'm sorry, I was so focused, I didn't mean to—*

Get out! Emry's breaths came in fast and shallow. This couldn't be happening, not again—*Aspen, please!*

He spoke the last word aloud, and his voice pierced the grove around him, flitting around the trees like a strange, echoing bird. The sensation did nothing to help Emry ground himself.

I know, I know! Aspen said, their voice rattling Emry's ribcage. *On three. Push me out on three.*

Emry dug his fingers into the soil. *Okay.*

One...two...

It was like flexing a muscle Emry had forgotten—happily forgotten—he had. He used his energy to shove Aspen out of his body, out of his mind, while the spirit worked to yank themself out in turn. A flash of pain, a pull of energy—then all at once, everything returned. On his hands and knees, Emry gasped down at the grass, and Aspen collapsed next to their lute.

"What in Shiro's name—?" one of the farmhands shouted from far behind them. Emry looked up.

All across the orchard, the dead trees were now crowned in vibrant, dripping green. Black bark sloughed off to reveal healed bark underneath, like scabs revealing fresh skin. And on every branch, ripe apples gleamed, covered in fresh raindrops.

Emry looked at Aspen. Aspen looked at Emry.

"Was that you?" Emry breathed. Aspen shook their head.

"I, um..." Their form wavered. "I think that was us."

"Aspen? Emry?" Cal called, her voice urgent as it bounced between the trees. A different sort of fear latched onto Emry's throat, and he staggered to his unsteady, aching feet. Oh gods, she'd be so upset. He couldn't do that to her, couldn't make her worry all over again—

"We're fine!" he called back, helping Aspen up. This time, no darkness sprang from his touch—just the too-soft feeling of the spirit's wispy form underneath his fingers. In turn, Aspen grabbed Emry's arm.

"Are you all right?" Their green eyes nervously searched his face. "I'm so sorry, I just felt the energy and pulled without thinking—"

Emry shushed them. "I'm fine."

"But—"

"Aspen, was that you?" Cal came into sight, her muddy shoes splashing in newly formed puddles—but she hardly seemed to care. The bright grin on her face could have dried the rain soaking into her skirt. "That was incredible!"

Aspen stiffened. "I, um—"

"They just wanted to help the spirit out a little," Emry cut in with forced lightness. "And they used the rain to channel their magic. Did you see that?"

He turned his smile on Aspen, who kept their eyes narrowed.

"I did see that." Cal laughed in delight and took off her bonnet, rainwater spilling off its brim. "Though I would appreciate some warning in the future. The trees weren't exactly adequate shelter for a flash storm."

Emry offered his arm to her, trying not to betray the sudden pain in his motions. With this fresh possession, his old aches were devolving into sharper lances of pain. "Why don't we head home and get some tea, then? Aspen should rest before Owen can ask them more questions."

True to expectation, Owen was already hurrying forward, both beaming and utterly drenched from the rain. Behind him, the farmhands still stared in amazement at the trees.

"Oh, thank the gods!" Owen said, hailing Aspen with his soaked hat. "That was you? And it only took but a moment! How extraordinary. I'll need to tell the others about this—"

"I'm afraid I must accompany Aspen home to recover," Cal interjected, slipping out of Emry's hold to keep the farmer at bay. "But, of course, I'll cover this in my report to the Council and communicate to the other farms…"

As she spoke, Aspen tugged pointedly on Emry's sleeve. Emry didn't look; he already knew the spirit was glaring at him.

"There's no need to distress her," he mumbled to them, wiping smudges of dirt off his cuffs. "It's not like it'll happen again." He stepped forward and visibly winced at the pain throbbing in his knees. Aspen scrambled for their lute, pushing aside some vines to make space in the soil within.

"I'll grow you some moonflowers for the pain, then you should go to bed after tea," they whispered imperially, taking on Cal's tone. "Then nothing but sleep for you for the rest of the day. No, two days, at the *very* least—"

"Mr. Karic?" Cal turned back to them. "We should be on our way so you can prepare for your Guild meeting."

She gave Owen one last curtsy and hurried off to the carriage, leaving Emry and Aspen looking at each other in poorly restrained fear.

"How much time do we have until the Guild meeting?" Aspen asked weakly. Emry checked his pocket watch, and his throat went dry.

"About four hours."

CHAPTER TWO

EMRY

AFTER THE MIRACLE at Owen's farm, Cal didn't stop talking or taking notes throughout the carriage ride.

"I wish I had known you were going to do that, Aspen," she said, addressing the lute next to Emry. Aspen had retreated into the instrument to rest—though Emry could see pain-relieving moonflower buds slowly sprouting amidst the honeysuckle.

"Perhaps I could've timed the rainstorm or checked the amount of rainfall," Cal continued, tapping the end of her pencil against her chin. "Can you effectively summon rain on a sunny day? Or does it need to be cloudy?"

Aspen's response echoed through the lute. "It has to be cloudy, I think," they said. "I'm sorry. Maybe if I were stronger, I could—"

"What on earth are you apologizing for?" Cal instinctively reached out, as if to take the spirit's hand. "You were incredible. No one could have asked for more. Now, if we could try that on a few other afflicted farms..."

Emry stiffened, and Aspen's lute shifted on the seat. "Um, well, you see—"

"No, no." Cal waved the thought away. "You need to recover first, of course. After all, you both have a very important meeting with Ella Sorman today."

She smiled proudly at Emry, then ducked her head and continued writing, her words dissolving into soft mutterings about Council reports and rain magic. Emry gave a weak smile back and clasped his hands together to keep them from shaking.

He hadn't actually seen Ella since moving from Senne to Vornik. He had seen his manager Damir several times, who stopped by now and then to make sure he was settling in. But apart from that, there had been no word from the Guild—no mention of debuts or concerts or forming a troupe. And certainly no hint about the mysterious Guild origins Ella had mentioned months ago.

Not that the trio didn't have speculations on Ella's plans, of course.

"Maybe she's looking to refresh the Guild's style," Cal had mused last week. "So many of her musicians are older and settled in their ways. Perhaps she's looking for something new."

A flattering thought, one that Emry hoped was true—but there was another explanation that kept floating in the back of his mind.

"Hear me out." He had leaned forward. "What if the stories were real and she *was* a—"

"A spy?" Cal had finished for him. "Love, I wouldn't put any stock in gossip from the war. Let's just wait and see what she has to say."

But the meeting today wasn't just a friendly chat with Ella—it was a grand affair bringing together every major Guild performer in the city. It was where he would discuss his debut, the very beginning of his future as a Guild musician...

And now he could barely walk.

As he tried and failed to control his breathing, the carriage bore them out of the bumpy country roads and into Vornik proper, where heavy stone gates and buildings marked a city mostly spared from the wave. Upon first moving in, Emry had assumed Vornik would feel smaller once he got used to it—that he'd gradually explore the place, and all the nooks and crannies would shrink out of familiarity. But the city had only expanded further with time; the carriage trundled past fountains he didn't recognize, pillared buildings he couldn't quite place. It wasn't until the Academy campus gates rolled past that he could recognize they were nearing home.

Soon after passing the Academy, the carriage turned down a neat row of pale townhouses. Despite being made of stone, each one had a delicate air about them—swirling iron fences, artfully arranged shrubbery, haughty rose bushes lining their walkways. Emry was still convinced that he and Aspen needed nothing half so fancy to live in, but he had little say in the matter—the Guild had already secured him one such townhouse upon his arrival. The carriage slowed down at his appointed home, which boasted a dazzling array of white, pink, and yellow roses. Unlike their neighbors, these roses spilled eagerly over the fences, blooming with cheer even through frost and heat wave.

The Guild couldn't take credit for that detail, of course. Aspen tended to those roses every morning.

"Oh, are we here already?" Cal looked up from her notebook, blinking owlishly. "Do you need any help with—?"

"No, I've got them." Emry grabbed Aspen's lute; he needed to have a private word with the spirit, and quickly. "Best of luck with the report, my dear—"

He reached for the door, but Cal closed the window curtains and tugged him back, her eyes sparkling with pride. "Promise you'll tell me all about Ella and the debut tour she has planned for you?" she murmured.

It was an easy promise for him to make—but in the privacy of the carriage, he couldn't help but tease her a little.

"A tour, you say?" He let slip a grin. "So eager to get me back out of the city, are you?"

She bit back a giggle. "Ah, you've found me out."

He pretended to pull away, his free hand on his heart. "And here I thought you loved me—"

She cut him off with a kiss, warm and insistent, and Emry sank into it with a sigh. Gods, if kisses could heal, he'd be dancing his way to the Guild event in no time.

"I promise to tell you all about it," he mumbled against her lips, kissed her once more, then descended to the sidewalk with a string of pain-induced curses tucked under his tongue.

"Moonflowers aren't going to cut it this time, Aspen," he said through gritted teeth, trying to hide his limp on his way to the front door.

"Oh, dear." The flowers in Aspen's lute rustled. "What about your cane?"

"Not enough, either."

"Can you tell them you're sick?"

Emry became nauseous at the very idea. "Sick? For the most important meeting of my life—?"

"Wait!" Cal opened the carriage door. "I forgot my shawl from the last time I visited. Can I go get it?"

Emry stopped midstep and swallowed another curse. He couldn't let Cal see him like this—she'd panic, too. "I could go get it for you?"

But Cal had already shifted to the edge of the seat. "Aspen, do you have the energy to chaperone me to the door?"

Emry looked around at the empty sidewalk. "But there's no one around—"

"I can do it." Aspen appeared in their wispy human shape, then hopped up to the carriage and held out a gallant hand. "Ms. Breslin."

Cal gratefully took it. "Thank you, Aspen."

Emry tried not to roll his eyes at the ritual. Back home in Senne, no one cared if a single young lady made a brief visit to a bachelor's house to grab a shawl. Even at the Academy, most people had been willing to look the other way on certain...extracurricular activities, so long as scholarly knowledge was being acquired and degrees were being achieved.

But here in the upper echelons of Vornik, where Cal was no longer a student and he was no longer a tavern rat, people cared far too much. As Cal passed Emry, she nodded subtly to the townhouse next door, where a wrinkled old lady was peeking out through the curtains with a deep furrow in her brow.

"Don't mind her," Emry muttered and opened the front door. "I'm sure she's just jealous of the roses or something."

CAL STOOD in the sparse parlor, her hands on her hips. "I could've sworn I left it in here..."

Emry tried to lean casually against the console table in the foyer. The attempt made his spine scream. "It's not there?"

"No." After checking the last few moving crates still cluttering the corner, Cal ducked to look around a sofa. Emry stole a glance over at Aspen, who had their lute balanced on the narrow console. A new, unfamiliar flower within the lute bloomed at a leisurely pace, its orange petals creeping out from behind the other plants.

"This should work," Aspen whispered.

"What is it?"

"I don't know."

Emry stared. "What do you mean you don't know?"

"I'm trying something new! It's a"—Aspen gestured wildly—"I'm adding my energy to it so that I can give you some!"

"You are a brilliant and wonderful spirit, my friend." They both stared at the bloom for a moment. "Can it...grow any faster?"

"I'm trying!" Aspen leaned over the lute and focused hard—but they were still transparent from their earlier efforts in the orchard, and the flower continued to grow one petal at a time.

"Well, I'll need to check the drawing room." Cal turned to face them, and they both straightened. Cal stared quizzically at Aspen, then Emry. "Are you sure you're all right?"

Emry opened his mouth, words fighting in his throat. He should tell her, he should just tell her and risk her fear and distress and—

"We're fine," he said, the phrase flowing instinctually. "Just, uh, checking the mail, aren't we, Aspen?"

"Yes! We're, um..." Aspen scrambled for a pile of letters on the table. "Reading all these!" They picked up the stack, several inches thick and dotted with various ribbons and seals.

Cal raised her eyebrows as she passed by. "That's an impressive number of letters today."

Aspen shifted to hide the growing flower, then rifled through the mail. Cal wasn't wrong—it *was* a particularly large stack today. Some were for Emry, of course, from Marko, Stef, his parents... But most of them were for Aspen. As the only forest spirit who currently walked and talked in public, people all over the province were eager to ask them questions or beg them for advice or favors. Could Aspen really talk to spirits and make flowers grow? Could they grow poison ivy, perhaps? And could they do it in their ex-so-and-so's garden while they were at it?

At first, Emry had tried to toss the letters for the drivel they were —but Aspen insisted on reading every single one, just in case a spirit ever wrote to them.

"I don't get it," they said, ripping open a letter and waving around a paper that was covered front to back in cramped writing. "The farms I understand, but why does everyone else want me to visit their gardens and patios and talk to spirits for them? It's not like the spirits want to talk to me, anyway." They rubbed their face and tossed the letter back on the console. "Hara take me."

Fresh, stabbing pain wrapped around Emry's legs, and as he leaned more heavily on the table, Cal's footsteps grew louder in the empty hallway. Hara take him, indeed—he was on the verge of collapse. "Please, Aspen..."

"Right, right. Let me just..." The spirit turned back to the lute, closed their eyes, and stuck their fingers into the soil around the flower. The bloom's growth stuttered—then exploded, its petals growing to twice their former size and vibrance.

"Found the shawl!" Cal called from around the corner. Aspen ripped the petals from the stem and shoved them into Emry's hand.

"Here, eat it now—"

"Gods, thank you." Emry stuffed the petals into his mouth and choked. "Shiro's hairy *foot*, Aspen, this tastes awful."

"Well, sorry I'm not a *flower* chef—"

"Any decent mail today?" Cal approached them, wrapping her shawl around her shoulders.

Emry pulled himself together and gulped down the petals. For a brief moment, a strange shiver went through him, and a thick whiff of soil and sunlight passed his nose—

Then all was normal again, the taste gone from his tongue like it was never there. He steadied himself and sorted through the stack of mail.

"We did get something from..." He plucked a letter at random and surveyed the familiar handwriting: heavy and straight, blotted in its rush.

He couldn't help but stare at it. In the past, this particular type of letter would have made his heart stop and his throat close. Echoes of this old instinct rose up, curling around his windpipe...

He firmly pushed the echoes aside and held up the letter.

"From Georgie," he finished. Aspen gasped.

"Can I read it?" they begged. Emry handed them the envelope, which they promptly ripped open and began to read aloud.

Dearest Brother, Wonder of the Auric Guild scene—

Emry rolled his eyes. "Oh, gods."

By the time you get this, you'll probably have already met with Ella Sorman, so there's no point in me wishing you luck. I can only hope that you're setting your first concert here in Senne, or else Nana will write you out of her will.

Aspen turned the letter sideways to squint at the tiny writing in the margin.

Marley wants me to write that I'm kidding. I hate it when she reads over my shoulder.

Aspen turned the letter back around and resumed.

Once you tell us all about Ella, we'll need a more thorough report about how Cal's doing. Well, I don't need one. Mum does. She wants to know if there's a ring on her finger yet or not.

Cal froze. Emry yanked the letter from Aspen's hands.

"Actually, I think we'll read the rest later, thank you." He shoved the letter into his waistcoat pocket. "So sorry, Cal—"

"No, it's fine." She tried to sound light, but she was suddenly looking everywhere except for Emry. "I'd hardly expect anything less from Georgie." She smiled at Aspen. "What else did you get today?"

As she helped them look through the mail, Emry stood there, Georgie's letter heavy in his pocket, distracting him from his pain.

He would tell his family before proposing to Cal, of course. He wouldn't do anything so large without telling them first—not now, at least. He simply hadn't planned out when he was going to do it, was all. She was busy with the Council; he was about to be busy with the Guild...

"You really need to add some furniture to this space," Cal said to Aspen, peering thoughtfully at the blank wall above the console table. "A little cubby to sort your mail, I think."

Aspen frowned. "Like a fane?"

"Like a fane, yes." She took in the rest of the foyer, its walls still bare. "Then a mirror there, and a painting there..." She set her hands on her hips. "A painting of Senne, I think."

This dragged Emry out of his thoughts, and he tilted his head. "Senne?"

"Of course," Cal said brightly. "You don't have any reminders of home in here yet, and Marley showed me so many art galleries when I was there. Perhaps we could take a trip up there and..." She cut off her own words and smoothed her skirts. "I'm sorry. You can decide what to put on the walls, of course. It's your home, after all."

But Cal, who was rarely wrong on any count, was wrong on this one. It wasn't his home—not until it was hers as well.

"A painting of Senne would be lovely," he echoed softly. She met his gaze, and for a moment, he couldn't tell whether it was the flower or her that was driving his aches away.

"Well, I'm afraid I have to turn in these reports today." She cleared her throat and held up her notebook. "And I still require a report from you on your meeting with Ella today." She started for the door, then lingered. "I'm very proud of you both."

Warmth filled Emry's chest. "Thank you, Cal."

She left in a rush of skirts and shawls, the lingering scent of apples sweeping into an invisible spiral behind her. Emry closed the door, limped to a chair, then pulled out Georgie's letter in quiet determination. Council and Guild work be hanged—there was going to be a ring on her finger before the year was out, and that was that.

CHAPTER THREE

CAL

CAL STRODE TO WORK, clutching her silk-lined bonnet against the wind and trying very hard not to think about Georgie's letter—specifically, the parts of it that had given life to a flurry of butterflies in her stomach.

She was thrilled the Karics had asked after her, of course. When she had first met his family, part of her feared they would learn of her past breakup with Emry and harbor a familial sort of resentment. It was only fair, she reasoned, to hate the woman who had once broken Emry's heart and left him in Tazlo.

But after the events of Dawnstone, they had been more than kind to her. While Emry convalesced, they had let her stay with them, showed her around Senne, made her feel like part of the family...

But that, in its entirety, was the problem. She didn't want to feel like a member of the family. She wanted to *be* a member of the family, with such a force that made the butterflies in her stomach flap into an embarrassing whirlwind.

She sighed at herself and picked up her pace, trying to ignore the feeling. There was nothing she could do about it. Though every city had slightly different rules of courtship, her hometown of Etris was very clear on the matter: if one of the pair hailed from outside of Etris, the outsider must be the one to initiate the courting. To prove their grace and worth through social seasons, and promenades, and gifts, and dances—oh, she couldn't *wait* for the dances—

She let slip a giggle, then immediately cleared her throat. There was no room for excitement or impatience here, particularly not for two people so visible as a Guild member and Council worker. There were rules and processes to follow, and she would have to wait for Emry to follow them.

Up ahead, an older woman in multiple shawls trundled up the marble steps of the Council building. Cal straightened her posture and adjusted her bonnet. Enough thinking about a certain curly-haired bard.

She had a supervisor to impress.

"Ms. Novak!" she called, hurrying up the steps. "If I could have a moment of your time?"

Ms. Novak continued at her brisk pace, her round nose and wrinkled cheeks reddened against the wind. "Only a moment, Ms. Breslin," she huffed. Cal continued her pace undeterred. If her supervisor ever offered her more than a moment, she would have questioned the woman's health.

"I have this week's research ready," she said. "I covered the three groves reported on the western border of the city. Borchev Farm, the Chester garden, and the Hazelwood orchard. I'm very pleased to report that at Hazelwood, Aspen revitalized nearly a hectare of apple trees this morning."

She held out her notebook to punctuate the claim. To her delight, Ms. Novak paused and raised a gray eyebrow in surprise. "The spirit did this?"

"Aspen did it after communicating with the spirit on the premises," Cal said, her words quickening in excitement. "Through a rainstorm they summoned, ma'am. As far as I can tell, this is the first time we've ever documented an act of magic like this. And their range was extraordinary—if you observe the diagram I put together of the orchard and the distance to the spirit's grove..."

Ms. Novak licked a thumb and flipped through the notebook, navigating the vaulted interior of the Council building without so much as looking up. Cal, for her part, was not as used to the place, and had to exercise a little more grace as she waded through the morning crowd and into their wing of offices. Given the flurry of interest in spirits after the wave, the Council's newly established Spirit Research Division had been given one of the best wings in the building. It boasted windows facing the courtyard and back garden, where diplomats and officials often took tea and strolled. The dense foliage provided a welcome respite from the noisy central square and gave Cal's desk a lovely, warm patch of sunlight in the afternoons.

It couldn't hold a candle to her favorite Academy libraries, of course, but it would have to do.

"Well." Ms. Novak hummed through perpetually pinched lips and closed the notebook. "This work is quite promising. Thank you, Ms. Breslin."

Cal held back a smile—that was the highest compliment she had received from the withered woman thus far. "Thank you, I appreciate the—"

"But you'll forgive me if I take longer than usual to complete my full inspection of the report," Ms. Novak continued brusquely. "I have been given permission to expand our team with a research lead role, and I must focus on filling it."

A very different league of butterflies took residence in Cal's stomach.

"A research lead?" she repeated, trying to sound as calm as possible. "What would that entail?"

"It would entail keeping those blasted Council members off my back," Ms. Novak muttered, fumbling with the key to her office. Then, more loudly: "My lead would direct the aides, of course. Determine priorities, speak with the Council members on goals and research results. Report to me in all things, so on and so forth." She waved a hand and shuffled into her office, leaving Cal standing at the doorway, vibrating at the news.

She could do that, she thought. She could do *more* than that in such a role. As a lead, she could influence the direction of the department's studies, its projects, the entire future of the province's spirit research—

"Are you considering looking internally?" she blurted out, stepping into the sparse, drab office. Ms. Novak looked up from removing one of her five shawls.

"I realize I haven't been here long," Cal hurried to add, "but in addition to my research on the wave, this week's reports for the Council bring me up to over fifty groves confirmed or disproven on the eastern side of Vornik alone, and the establishment of over twenty working relationships with agriculturalists on behalf of the department. If you'd consider me for the lead role, I could leverage these into—"

"Ms. Novak!" another voice called out. The words slipped through the air like oil, yet still grated on Cal's ears. "Good morning to you!"

A blond head bobbed through the row of desks outside Ms. Novak's office, grinning and sliding his away around the morning gaggle of aides. It gave Cal the distinct impression of a snake swimming through water, and she wished she could recoil as such; instead, she gave him a bland, dismissive smile when he appeared at the doorway.

"Mr. Edwards," she said before the man could try to ignore her presence. "Good morning."

Mr. James Edwards, fellow Council aide with hair of gold and brain of wool, quickly smoothed over his flicker of surprise at her presence.

"Ms. Breslin!" he said. "Apologies. If I had known you'd be so punctual, I would have brought you a coffee as well."

Indeed, the man had two coffees in hand—one for himself and

one to bribe Ms. Novak. And unfortunately for Cal and her intensely immaculate notebooks, James' bribes absolutely succeeded at pleasing the curmudgeon.

"Why, thank you." Ms. Novak took one of the cups with something akin to delight. "I trust you have research for me as well?"

"Of course." He handed her a notebook—far thinner than Cal's, she noticed, and titled in handwriting that was far too neat to be his. She glanced behind him; a haggard-looking intern disappeared around the corner, coffee and ink stains on their sleeves.

But that hardly mattered—research wasn't what James specialized in, anyway.

"I spoke with my uncle Councilman Hasek this morning," he said loftily. "The budget vote was moved to next week. And I happened to pass by Councilwoman Kane on my way here. She's convinced she can add two more grants to the amendment once she talks to Hasek tomorrow."

He continued rattling off names ranging from well-placed aides to the most influential Council members. Half of them were extended family members or childhood friends, people James had openly bragged about knowing many times. Ms. Novak nodded along with each of his updates, humming in thought.

"Excellent," she finally said, settling into her leather chair. "Your information is invaluable, as always. We'll need such connections in the months to come." She shuffled through the papers on her desk. "Now, where is that morning post..."

James set his shoulders back proudly; Cal's jaw tensed. As much as she disliked it, Ms. Novak wasn't wrong. James' nepotistic networking did in fact work in his favor for the lead role.

And what's more, he knew it, too.

"I always endeavor to be invaluable," James said, his greasy smile widening. "And if I may be so bold, I do believe my dedication would be of greater service in...*higher* ranks. After all, an Edwards cannot languish at the desk of an aide for too long."

Cal briefly envisioned slapping the man's coffee cup into his face.

"And if I were to take on a larger role," James continued, "I could have far greater influence with my contacts in—"

A boy rushed into the office, cutting off James' self-aggrandizing speech and Cal's reverie about coffee stains.

"Morning post for you, ma'am," the boy said breathlessly, handing a stack of mail to Ms. Novak. She grunted and snatched the papers from his hand.

"Late. *Again.*"

"Sorry, ma'am," the boy said, already rushing back out the door. Ms. Novak gave a tsk, then pursed her lips at the unusually thin stack of envelopes.

"Should have expected this," she said, letting the envelopes fall onto the desk with a slap. "First hint of the social season in the papers, and everyone shirks their duties in favor of—of..." Her wrinkles deepened in frustration. "Visiting the tailors or some such."

James brightened like a polished wind-up toy.

"About the season," he jumped in. "Many of my associates are wondering if the office shall be closed for it? Over half the Council will be traveling down to Matlock in time for the opening ball—"

"And if half the Council decided to jump into a river, you'd still find me sitting here trying to get my work done," Ms. Novak snapped. "Attend if you must, but my department will *not* be closing so that half the city can gallavant across the border to dance a few sets."

"But—but—"

James was clearly not used to being declined, and Cal could almost see his thoughts scrabbling to change the situation.

"*But*"—his face brightened again—"there will be other researchers there as well! Like that Gray fellow, what's his name..." He snapped his fingers in thought.

Cal's look flattened. "Devrin Gray?"

"Yes, him!" James pointed at her. "You helped him with his wave research, didn't you?"

Cal's entire being seethed. Yes, she had assisted Dev with a key experiment in determining the wave's arrival, but *she* had been the one to present the research before the Council, to ensure that the country had enough warning before it struck. To ensure that people actually survived it.

But one would hardly guess that, given Dev's widespread perspective on the matter. Mere weeks after the wave had struck, the formerly secluded scientist had begun trotting out his years of spirit energy research, fascinating curious audiences at dinners and soirees. Before long, all of high society came to know him as a most charming expert on the subject—a startling turnabout from the ridicule his research had endured for years. Given his meteoric rise, Cal was not surprised to learn he was attending the Matlock social season. She only wondered if he would appear in his old tea-stained waistcoats, or if he now frequented the tailors Ms. Novak so despised.

"You see?" James stayed his noble course. "If I'm allowed to attend the season, I could introduce myself to such illustrious researchers as Mr. Gray. I hear he already has several investors lined up for further research projects. Who's to say we can't be one of them?"

"I suppose such a connection would be—" Ms. Novak started, then picked up one envelope from the pile. Though she angled it away from them, Cal thought she caught the name *Ella* on the front.

"I will finish reviewing your research later." Ms. Novak motioned to the door. "You both are dismissed. Now."

In a perplexed shuffle, they gave the requisite bows and curtsies and retreated to the outer offices. As soon as the door clicked shut, James immediately slouched into a desk chair, slurping his coffee.

"You," he said, pointing to a junior aide. "There's not nearly enough milk in this. Bring me some, and quickly."

Cal turned on her heel and slid behind her own desk. The problem with the well-appointed research office was that it was structured in a more modern style—rows of heavy desks facing each other, with a walkway down the middle where Ms. Novak occasionally paced when she was in a foul mood. Such an arrangement meant that her desk directly faced James', where he sat with his feet up, chuckling leisurely at the gossip column in *The Vornik Post*.

She gripped her quill so tightly, it bent. James surely didn't know the difference between a rhythm bloom and a weed, but Ms. Novak had a point. Her future lead must have influence outside the realm of reports and hypotheses, and James unfortunately had the ear of half the Council. All he needed was his networking skills and a letter of recommendation or two, and he would have the lead position in his pocket.

If she was to beat James to the role, she would have to do something beyond the farm reports languishing on her supervisor's desk.

CHAPTER
FOUR

EMRY

ONCE CAL LEFT FOR WORK, Emry began a careful walk up the stairs, his grip tight on the railing and his frustrated thoughts muddying from the pain. If Aspen's experimental flower didn't take effect soon, he'd have to scramble for a few last-minute moonflowers—or worse, some willow bark tea, deep and bitter. He shuddered at the thought of it. The first flower had tasted bad enough.

He tried to focus on getting ready—scrubbing off mud, sighing at the state of his hair, delving into his closet. But between his nerves and the simmering fog in his brain, his own attire had become an indecipherable mystery to him. He grabbed one coat, then another. Laid it next to a waistcoat, then three more, staring at the colors until his vision swam with the embroidered patterns. And he hadn't even dared look at the cravats yet—

"Emry?" Aspen piped through the door, then opened it without waiting for an answer. "How are you feeling?"

"I can't..." He rubbed his forehead, words eluding him. "I can't—"

"Sit," Aspen ordered, clearing space on the bed. "You're not letting the flower do its work. Just sit and breathe for a while."

Too muddled to argue, Emry did as he was told, sitting and breathing while Aspen sorted through the partially matched outfits scattered throughout the room. But his stumbling mind couldn't sit still for long, and it soon started pawing through his worries like a nervous dog. How many Guild members would be at the event? Twenty? Thirty? Should he arrive cautiously early to greet them, or fashionably late to blend in with them? No, Damir would murder him if he arrived late—but gods forbid he look too eager arriving early. He needed to be casually and precisely on time—

"Well?" Aspen touched his shoulder. "Is it working?"

Emry stopped mid-thought. In all his overthinking, he hadn't noticed that he was, well, *thinking* again.

"I..." He shifted, his movements oddly light and airy. The invisible weight of the pain had lifted not just from his mind, but his knees, his legs, his ankles...

He stood up and shook out his feet. Walked a loop around the room. Turned and blinked at Aspen.

The pain had disappeared.

"How did you do that?" he breathed.

"Do what?"

Emry gathered them up in an overly tight hug. Aspen frowned against his waistcoat, their voice muffled. "Are you...sure you're feeling all right?"

"Absolutely. I can't thank you enough." He let them go, tempted to take a run around the house simply because he could. "What on earth did you put in that flower?"

Aspen's shoulders rounded in relief. "I told you, it was just a bit of my energy." They handed Emry a waistcoat, then picked a cravat and looped it around his collar. "I took some of yours, didn't I? I thought it made sense to give it back. I'm just glad I didn't get my..." They stared into the air, searching for the right word. "My hyp..."

"Hypothesis."

"Hypothesis wrong."

After waiting for Emry to change, they deftly tied his cravat for him, then stepped back and hummed. "You're missing something."

Emry looked down. "What?"

Aspen bounded over to the dresser, pulled out a velvet bag, and shook two pins into their hand—gleaming gold circles engraved with vines and flowers. They pinned one to their own vest, then carefully pinned the second to Emry's. Emry angled it toward the window light, his heart catching in his throat. His Guild pin, gifted by Ella Sorman herself. If she hadn't bestowed it upon him, he might have convinced himself that her offer had been a dream. But the pin was there, shining in the light, the metal cool against his fingers. A silent promise of what was to come.

He looked up to find Aspen smiling at him.

"Ready?" they asked, their own pin half-hidden by a flower peeking out of their coat. Emry reached out, adjusted the flower, and nodded.

"Ready."

∼

"Emry?"

"Yes, my dear spirit?"

In a thoroughly breezy, pain-free mood, Emry glanced over at Aspen, who was sprawled across the carriage seat opposite him, their lute on their lap. They plucked the silent strings aimlessly as they watched the city pass by. "What exactly will I do onstage?" Their hand slowed. "When Ella sets up our first concert, I mean."

Emry gave a thoughtful hum. It was a fair question—Aspen had been progressing well in their lute lessons, but not well enough to perform onstage. They had taken a passing interest in other instruments, too, once Cal had begun attending concerts with them, but hadn't yet started to learn anything else.

"Maybe Ella won't actually let me onstage," Aspen mumbled. "She brought you on to play, not me—"

"Nonsense," Emry said firmly. "You're wearing a Guild pin. You'll perform with the Guild. How about you sing with me?"

"Sing?"

"You sing along all the time when we're at the spirit groves. Would you like that?"

Aspen twirled a loose peg on their lute. "Will that be enough?"

Emry smiled. "Aspen, you're always enough."

The carriage rolled to a stop. Emry jumped out with confidence, then extended a hand to Aspen and helped them down. "Let's go secure our first performance, shall we?"

The Guild was set to meet in the Vornik Grand Park—a wide emerald expanse beloved by the city's high society. For years, its well-trimmed paths had set the stage for many an influential person wanting to see and be seen. Diplomats and delegates took walks here; rich sweethearts promenaded in the dappled sunlight. If Emry had possessed any of Cal's society-oriented mind, he would've recognized most of the gentry parading by the entrance as he walked through the park gates.

As it was, he only recognized the two figures approaching him.

Ella Sorman and her manager Damir Nedrov visually clashed, as they always did. Damir slouched down the path in his customary black, with only a silver watch chain to break the monotony. In both wardrobe and mood, he was a shadow next to the leader of the Auric Guild, who was busy putting peacocks to shame with her ensemble. She floated forth in a shimmering blue dress that betrayed a palette of greens in the right light, pearlescent gloves gleaming alongside actual pearls tucked into her steely braids.

"Welcome to the Guild," Ella said, giving her new charges a curtsy that gently shook the pearls. Her deep voice melted against the light patter of birdsong in the park. "Everyone here is quite eager to meet you."

"Thank you." Emry bowed back, trying to maintain his air of

confidence—a difficult task in the face of someone so single-handedly responsible for his entire career. "I've been looking forward to meeting them. And," he ventured, "to discussing my debut."

"Of course." Ella smiled, and for a moment, he held his breath for the truth, for a morsel of what she had planned for him—

Then she turned and led him to the first cluster of musicians, all gathered in the dappled shade of a willow. "But first, please allow me to introduce you to your fellow Guild members."

To Emry's brief dismay, she deposited him with the musicians and swept off with Damir as quickly as she had arrived, continuing their graceful rounds between guests.

Then he turned to his new associates, and his disappointment dissolved.

Within minutes, he was shaking hands with people he had only seen up onstage—or merely envisioned seeing up onstage, not having the money to actually shell out for one of their concerts. And now they were right next to him, congratulating him on his new position, asking him how he liked Vornik. They spoke casually of upcoming concerts as if performing at places like the Waldman and the Trellis were normal, everyday occurrences. Like this group—this park—didn't currently host the best musical talent the province had to offer.

"So, Stella." One singer named Lou turned to the violinist at his side, his smooth words betraying the depth of his legendary singing voice. "Will you be performing here or in Tazlo next?"

Stella scoffed as she fanned herself with an array of scarlet feathers. Her Guild performances had been compared to a dozen things—to songbirds, to a lover's heartbeat, to the loveliness of a dawn. Emry believed all of them.

"Here in the city," she said. "Ella wants me to write something new for it, but I can't tell you how many sheets of music I've scrapped in the attempt. If I spend one more coin on ink or paper, Damir will have my head." She nodded to Emry. "No idea how Ella wrote *your* song so fast. I'll forever be jealous."

"Ah, the 'Dawnstone Reel,'" Lou said with a grin. "One of her better melodies, in my opinion, but the lyrics are too..." He wrinkled his nose and waved his empty wineglass in a circle. "Tame. Everyone up north talks of gods and such. Surely you and Aspen can tell us what actually happened there?"

Both musicians' eyes sparked at the idea of a tale. Emry's face warmed, and he searched for Aspen—but the spirit stood off under an oak tree, growing daffodils from their lute and handing them out to the members of the Forsgren Quartet. Emry would be on his own here.

"Well, you see..." he started. He shouldn't have been surprised that someone had asked about the song—it was his own fault. After the wave, rumors of Emry and Aspen's valor had spiraled into ridiculousness—that he had fought the wave single-handed, that he was the son of Hara, that he *was* Hara in some way. Less than eager to live under such a moniker, Emry had reached out to Ella for assistance, for a way to temper the narrative. To throw attention not to him, but to Aspen and the other spirits.

But her resulting song was a melodious double-edged sword. On one hand, it sufficiently disappointed people like Lou, who wanted to believe that Emry had indeed commanded the wave away with a single word.

On the other hand, everyone now knew who Emry was. The fact the song didn't mention him by name didn't matter.

"I'm afraid Ella stuck too true to the real tale for your liking," Emry finally said in apology, then hailed a wandering server and handed a fresh glass of wine to Lou in recompense. "Though if you express your disappointment to Aspen, I'm sure they'd be happy to grow you a flower or two to make up for the loss."

Lou gave a hum of feigned disappointment. "Toss in a front-row seat to your debut, and I'll consider myself satisfied."

"One for me, too." Stella closed her feathery fan, eyes alight once more. "A word of advice on your debut, Mr. Karic. The social events are far more tiring than the concerts themselves."

"Hear, hear." Lou raised his glass in agreement. "I had not only three concerts but ten soirees, fifteen dinners—"

"Five balls, all requiring different dresses," Stella piled on. "Not to mention, each concert should be as grand as the last, no matter how tired you are by the end." She raised an eyebrow. "Has Ella told you where it will be yet? Matlock, perhaps, for the season?"

Emry's heart leapt at the thought. He almost didn't want to imagine it, as if simply thinking about it would doom the idea. A debut performance in such a packed city, perhaps at the famed Trellis, on a beautiful, balmy evening...

"You honor me with the thought," he said, trying to discreetly look around for Ella. "But I'm afraid we haven't discussed my debut yet."

"It won't be Matlock," Lou said. "Karlson's always the favored performer for the season. Society down there is far too picky."

Lou and Stella devolved into bickering about which other city was best for a debut—Vornik the frontrunner, with Tazlo hotly contested—then finally passed Emry along to other musicians, other heroes on the stage. He could hardly believe he wore the same Guild pin as them.

After an hour of conversation, he finally managed to regroup with Aspen by a moss-covered fountain, while servers prepared an array of sunlit tables for high tea. All things considered, the gathering was simple—little more than small talk, so far—but Emry found himself grateful once more for the flower Aspen had grown for him. If he had tried to manage all these introductions when in pain, he would've succumbed right at the park gate.

He vocalized as much to Aspen, then gestured to the clusters of musicians. "And I haven't even *met* everyone yet," he said, trying not to spill his champagne as he gestured excitedly. "Like the Forsgren Quartet, or Lady Serrano, or—"

Aspen pointed to a tall man near the neighboring flowerbeds. "Who's that?"

Emry nearly dropped his glass.

"That's Karlson."

He had seen the man perform once, back in Tazlo during the Sada festival. The memories immediately came rushing back—the relentless energy of his songs, his voice both effortless and otherworldly, the crowd packed close to the stage to drink it all in. It had been one of the best nights of his life.

If a single one of Emry's concerts could be an echo of Karlson's, he would be more than happy.

Then Karlson turned around and met his gaze.

"Oh no." Emry whirled back to Aspen. "I'm not ready—"

"Ready for what?" Aspen said, then turned and waved happily to the man. "Hello, Karlson!"

A soft chuckle forced Emry to turn back around. "Hello, indeed."

Karlson was taller than he appeared onstage, with long brown curls tied back in a halfhearted plait. Despite his immaculately embroidered coat, his loping gait and relaxed posture made him appear far too informal for the event, too aloof. A true musician amongst musicians.

When he looked down his long nose at both of them with an amused smile, Emry stopped breathing.

"You must be Aspen and Mr. Karic," Karlson said with a graceful bow. "Your flowers precede you."

Aspen reached for their lute. "Oh, would you like one, too?"

Emry surveyed the park; half the musicians were now holding daffodils. Hara take him, he should have been keeping a closer eye on the spirit. "Aspen, I don't think that's necessary—"

"Oh, must I be left out?" Karlson took the daffodil from Aspen and tucked it behind his ear. "The highest honor. Thank you." He bowed and held out a hand to Emry. "Mr. Karic, I've been looking forward to meeting you. Mr. Nedrov has been speaking highly of your skills." He leaned down and lowered his voice to a conspiratorial tone. "Do you know how difficult that is to manage? The man hardly puts three words together on a good day, and they're mostly curses."

Emry desperately hoped his hand wasn't shaking in Karlson's grip. "Thank you so much. That's very kind of you."

"On the contrary, I should be thanking you. Damir's sourness gets so very tiresome after a while." Karlson straightened and appraised him with a narrowed gaze—gentle, but thoughtful. Emry prepared himself for the usual questions. About Ella's song, his debut, whether he was prepared to take on a dozen dinners and a hundred receptions with one hand tied behind his back—

"Pick one," Karlson finally said. "'Old Bridge Road' or 'Harvest Day'?"

The question mentally knocked Emry off balance. Those were two old songs, ones he hadn't heard in a long time. When he was a performer in Tazlo, his audience had loved the latter, but the former was an old classic in the Senne region.

He latched onto Karlson's accent—northern, like his.

"'Old Bridge Road,'" he said confidently. Karlson continued without a flicker of a reaction.

"Which would you open with, 'Boys of Foxhill' or 'Koda's Farewell'?"

"Koda, no question."

Karlson raised one eyebrow. "And who here is your favorite musician?"

Ah—a sticky question no matter how he answered. Emry looped an arm over Aspen's shoulder.

"Aspen."

The spirit beamed. Karlson maintained a stoic look—then his lips twitched into a smile.

"I knew Senne only raised good men." He clapped a hand on Emry's shoulder. "Good to have another northerner in the Guild. We need to balance out all that poor southern taste, you and I."

A bell tinkled somewhere behind Karlson. He glanced behind him, then gestured to a gazebo on the other side of the fountain. "I believe Ella is calling us for tea. Shall we?"

At this point, Emry would've followed Karlson into the ocean if asked.

∽

Karlson led them into the shade of a flower-laden gazebo that had been prepared for tea—one of many tables that the musicians were now sitting down to all across the green. Aspen immediately ran up to the structure, first admiring the tumbling flowers and crawling ivy, then the dainty little sandwiches and cakes laid out on a three-tiered tray. Standing within the gazebo, Ella Sorman watched Aspen's excited inspection with satisfaction.

"I did hope you would like it," she said as the spirit rushed from one delicate detail to the next. "Have a seat, if you please."

Emry did so, fully aware of the honor it was to sit with the head of the Guild. A perfect opportunity, too—to discuss his debut, to finally ask what Ella wanted from him and Aspen...

But as soon as they all sat down, the atmosphere in the gazebo tightened, and Emry's questions froze in place. Even Aspen pulled their hand back from the canapés, glancing around warily.

Whatever Ella had to discuss here, it was not merely about soirees and songs.

"Do you recall our conversation back in Senne?" she began, keeping her tone as light as the teacakes before them. But her words fell flat in the chilly air, and she angled her fan to hide her mouth from the other tables. Next to her, Damir sat stone-faced, and Karlson's relaxed pose didn't hide the fact that he kept a close eye on each person passing by.

"Of course." Emry lowered his voice and set out each word carefully. "You mentioned the Guild needed to return to its roots. To what it used to do during wartime."

"Very good." Ella gave a slight nod. "We are still musicians, to be sure, but in the past, music afforded us a certain...mobility in times of crisis." She took a cucumber sandwich but didn't eat it. "We had access to the salons and parlors of every general without being seen as warriors or infiltrators."

Emry nodded along. Wartime was, thankfully, an abstract concept for him. It had ended before he was born, and not many in his northern hometown had personal stories of border strife.

But Ella's eyes clouded as she spoke, memories playing back that he chose not to imagine.

"During that time, we did what we could," she said, pouring tea that no one dared drink. "We made music, certainly, but we also cemented alliances. Passed messages."

"Loitered in clubs where men were happy to spill secrets to innocent, empty-headed singers," Karlson murmured lightly, giving a ghost of a smile while keeping his eyes focused on the park. Ella set a teacup before Emry, but he just stared at it in disbelief. He knew it. He had known it all along, the stories had been *true*—

"So, you were—you were spies?" he whispered, making sure his words didn't escape the gazebo.

Aspen stared at him. "You mean Cal was actually wrong?"

Ella set down the teapot with barely a clink.

"We spied on occasion," she corrected. "Other times we were propaganda artists, ambassadors..."

"Whatever the Council called for," Damir finished. "And sometimes whatever they didn't." He grimaced. "The Council back then was about as competent as the one now, I'm afraid. Save for your Ms. Breslin, of course."

"Please, Ms. Breslin would agree with you, but"—Emry glanced to the other tables—"is everyone here...like this?"

Karlson coughed to hide a laugh. "I'd like to see Lou or Stella try to keep a secret."

Ella shot Karlson a chiding look. "Not everyone," she said. "Not for a long time. Today, it is just this table that knows our old ways."

Just this table—which now included Emry and Aspen.

Honor and dread fought in Emry's chest. To be let in on this secret, to be *trusted* by these people—it was far more than he ever expected or deserved.

But they hadn't lifted the veil on their past as a casual teatime story. They had only mentioned the old ways because they had to be resurrected.

Emry swallowed and lowered his voice further. "Are we headed for another war?"

A couple arm in arm passed by the gazebo, giggling at a whispered joke between them. The table let the pair pass, then waited a heavy, silent moment before resuming their talk.

"No," Ella said with quiet reassurance. "I do not foresee a war, Hara be thanked. But..." She leaned forward, locking her gaze with his. "I do fear for our new civilians."

"New..." Aspen frowned. "You mean the spirits?"

Damir cut in here, ignoring the lower tea trays in favor of a tiny chocolate cake on the top tier. "Turns out our province is filled with invisible, immortal beings that control our very farmland." He took a grumpy bite out of the icing. "Forgive us if we now have a vested interest in your peace and welfare."

Aspen gave them a flat look. "I feel so special."

"And who better to help us look after our new neighbors than such bards as yourselves?" Karlson interjected sunnily, giving Damir a pointed look as he took a canapé from the lowest tray. "Think of yourselves as musical...ambassadors, of sorts. You can talk to the spirits, keep an eye on their happiness, ensure they continue to recover after the wave..."

Aspen brightened at this. "Like what I'm doing with Cal on her trips."

"Precisely." Karlson placed a canapé on their plate. "Now, who's Cal, again?"

Despite Karlson's attempts to chip at the ice that had formed around the gazebo, there was one word from Ella that hung heavy and cold around Emry's ears.

"You said you feared for them," Emry said, looking at her. "You think the spirits are in danger?"

Karlson fell silent at this, and Ella's lips pressed into a line.

"I know the spirits are in danger," she said. "I have it on good authority that every spirit in Matlock is dying."

CHAPTER
FIVE

EMRY

The flowers around the gazebo immediately began to wither.

"How?" Aspen asked, the blooms in their hair also shriveling. Emry set a reassuring hand on the spirit's wrist, hoping it conveyed more comfort than he felt.

"But Cal—Ms. Breslin said that it was just a drought across the border," he said. "How is this not all over the papers?"

Damir shrugged. "Matlock doesn't want to have a panic on their hands," he said, sipping his tea. "The city's been passing it off as a temporary drought, but their researchers have been tracking the decline for months. Every grove of theirs is suffering, and none of their attempts at a fix are working."

Aspen leaned forward. "Are the spirits in Matlock actually talking to the researchers?"

Damir frowned in a wordless question not at Ella, but at Karlson, who shifted in his seat. "My contact there didn't specify," he said. "She's a Matlock spirit researcher who knew I had the ear of someone actually influential in the Council." He raised his teacup to

Ella. "Her team is small and inexperienced. Not unusual for a new department, but she needs support. She's hoping we can send aid—discreetly—before it becomes a larger issue."

He grimaced and took a sip of his tea. Emry picked up his teacup, trying to follow his lead, but found he didn't have the stomach for it; Owen's concerns at the farm kept echoing in his memory. "Has the problem spread across the border yet?"

Karlson shook his head. "It's limited to Matlock's gardens for now," he said. "But if it spreads north to our farms before the harvest—"

"They will ensure it does not," Ella cut in, looking to Emry. "Both of you and Ms. Breslin, if she is able. I would attend the season myself, but I fear my presence will attract more attention than is necessary for this investigation."

Aspen sat up straight, their gaze as intense as Ella's. "We'll do it," they said. "We'll go and save the spirits before it gets any worse. Right?"

They looked to Emry, who tried to untangle the disappointed knot in his stomach. He wanted to help the spirits, naturally...but not once at this event had Ella mentioned actually starting his Guild career.

"Of course," he said to Aspen, then dropped a sugar cube into his tea, buying time to formulate his thoughts. "Yes, of course, we'll save them."

Ella wasn't fooled—her gaze remained locked on him. "Is there something else?"

"No, no. It's just..." Emry watched the sugar cube dissolve. There was no gentle way to say it. "I admit I did think we would be discussing our debut, not a secret spirit crisis."

"Under normal circumstances, we most certainly would be." Karlson turned to Damir. "Surely there's a way he can still debut this season?"

Damir folded his arms in response. "We don't debut people in

Matlock," he said. "Perform badly there, and the season eats you alive. It's not worth the risk."

Emry could feel his hopes slipping away like notes too high for his voice to reach.

"But that used to be the whole Guild front, right?" he said, scrambling for an argument. "If Karlson's contact doesn't want to make people panic through an open investigation, we could attend the season as musicians."

Karlson bobbed his head along with him. "The man's right."

Emry was tempted to have Aspen grow Karlson twenty more daffodils—but Damir scoffed at the idea.

"I don't have a troupe for you," he said, grabbing another cake from the tray. "Matlock is calling for aid now, not in six months. There's no time to audition anyone."

Karlson shrugged. "What about my troupe?"

Emry's heart stuttered. "I'm sorry?"

"Have him perform with me in Matlock," Karlson said. "The season won't think twice about it, and he still gets his debut."

Damir snorted. "You think Sage and Riley will be all right with it?"

"Those two are never all right with anything. Let them suffer." Karlson waved a hand. "Well, Mr. Karic? How does that sound?"

He took the cake off Damir's plate and popped it into his mouth as if he hadn't just changed Emry's life in a few sentences.

"I'd love to." The words burst out of Emry as his hands shook under the table. "If—if Ella will accept it, that is."

Too afraid to even glance at Ella, he looked at Damir first. Damir's perpetual frown bored a hole into him, then reluctantly swiveled to Ella.

Ella nodded.

"You'll leave for Matlock this week." She stood up, and everyone else immediately stood with her. "Make the Guild proud, Mr. Karic."

CHAPTER SIX

CAL

WHILE CAL KEPT her head down and focused on her work, James made it his mission of the day to do the exact opposite. Once he was done with the newspaper, he gossiped about it with another aide for an hour. Then he went in search of more coffee. Then he walked the gardens with a junior Council member, hunted down a third cup of coffee, scrounged up another paper to read...

Normally, Cal would keep one bitter eye on him, waiting for the day when Ms. Novak would catch him in his leisurely act and send him packing. But today, she could hardly spare the effort; the back of her mind kept flitting around, just like James. To the lead role, to the letter from Georgie, to Emry and his Guild meeting...

Her mind settled on the latter as she packed up for the day. Surely, Emry's limp from the morning was gone by now, and if it wasn't, she'd insist that he rest tomorrow. Seeing his lingering pain always sent her down irrational paths. That he would relapse into the near-death state he had been in six months ago, that she would lose him again somehow—

She took a breath and twisted the pendant on her necklace, forcing her thoughts in a more positive direction. Emry was fine. He was healthy and planning a grand debut at this very moment. Would he perform in Vornik first? She certainly hoped so. The Sumac Hall was still under repair, but there was a beautiful venue near the Academy that would do—

"Ms. Breslin?" Ms. Novak called sharply from her office. Both Cal and James looked up—there was a biting note to their supervisor's voice that made James smirk behind his third newspaper. Cal gathered herself and strode into the woman's office.

"Yes?" she said. Ms. Novak hunched over her desk, her face a storm cloud of wrinkles and frowns. Cal waited, trying not to recall similar experiences with haughty professors back at the Academy.

Her supervisor finally reached for the envelope that Cal had seen that morning—the one from Ella Sorman. "Here," she grumbled. "Close the door and read this."

"All of them are dying?" Cal said quietly, looking up from the letter. "And she wants me to investigate?"

Her throat went dry. According to the letter, Matlock held an estimated two hundred spirits, all residing in the city's famed gardens. To learn that something was hurting them all at once, and so soon after the wave... She folded up the letter, cold fear curling in her stomach at the very idea of it.

But Ms. Novak didn't seem quite as concerned.

"Oh, Ms. Sorman wants you to investigate, certainly," she snapped, taking back the letter with a fierce hand. "With no regard for *my* priorities or plans. As if I established this division just to be bandied about by—by an old *singer*." Her words devolved into mumbling. "I ought to deny her. Stand my ground, send someone else to take care of this..."

"You can't," Cal started, then caught herself. The mystery in

Matlock horrified her, to be sure—but if she could solve it, if *she* could be the one to demonstrate her skills in saving the spirits...

"I must go," she said, steeling her resolve before Ms. Novak's irritated gaze. "Not only do they need help urgently, but this investigation can only strengthen our department, not hinder it. If we use it to establish a cross-border network of shared research, we could expand our knowledge of spirits a hundredfold in a matter of months. Weeks, even."

And if she could leverage such a feat to a lead role, all the better—but she kept that particular thought silent.

Ms. Novak sighed heavily.

"Fine," she said, handing the letter back to Cal. "Go and speak with Phyllis. She'll assist in organizing your lodgings for your journey. But"—she held up an arthritic finger—"I shall *not* hear of you becoming distracted with all the fripperies of the social season. You are a representative of the Council and must uphold decorum as such."

Cal curtsied graciously. "Of course, ma'am. Absolute decorum."

It took everything in her not to sprint to Phyllis as soon as she left Ms. Novak's office. She had to reach her before she left for the day, she thought, keeping her pace on the marble floor brisk and businesslike. All the best lodgings would be taken by now, but if she could manage to secure something close to Matlock's research quarters...

She caught sight of the woman's desk and deflated. On the bright side, Phyllis hadn't left for the day.

On the dark side, she hadn't left because she was gossiping with one James Edwards.

"Of course, I'll be down there for the season," James scoffed, leaning casually against a nearby cabinet. "I'm afraid it won't be all fun and games, though. Need to secure a few letters of recommendation for Ms. Novak, then I can come back and—" He turned and faltered. "Ah. Ms. Breslin."

"Mr. Edwards." She turned pointedly to Phyllis. "If I could...?"

James rolled his eyes and wandered a few steps away, allowing her to approach the desk.

"I'll be traveling down to Matlock for Council business," Cal said. "Ms. Novak said you could assist with lodgings?"

"Certainly." Phyllis scribbled notes with a quill, its rasp on the paper as scratchy as her voice. "When will you be leaving?"

"As soon as possible."

Phyllis nodded sagely. "For the opening ball, of course. I'll get you sorted."

The mention of the opening ball drew James back in like a horribly foppish moth to a chandelier.

"You know, I hear Mr. Gray might be there," he said to Phyllis, then turned to Cal with greasy politeness. "Perhaps you could be so generous as to introduce me?"

Cal stiffened. A letter of recommendation from Devrin Gray would be more than enough to secure James the lead role—and she'd sooner eat her bonnet than see anything of the sort happen.

"Of course." She pasted a fake smile on her face. "He'll be pleased to find someone with a mind so refreshingly blank and receptive to his ideas."

Before he could process what she had said, she took her satchel and strode out of the office.

CHAPTER SEVEN

EMRY

The Matlock Post presents

THE PEEK OF THE SEASON

Mrs. Highbury's Guide to Every Dance, Sighting, and Proposal in Matlock

My gentle readers, we are only days away from the opening ball of the Matlock season, and the city has filled to its brim with society from both sides of the border. A simple stroll by the Oakvale Grand Hotel informed me that a certain Mrs. Albingdale has already had tea with one Mr. Kolva. Mr. Kolva's daughter failed to make a match last season—shall we see sparks fly between the miss and Albingdale's son, Thomas? This writer finds it highly unusual to secure a match so early in the season, but a fast ship beats the waves, as they say.

If one is disappointed at the news of Mr. Thomas, be heartened that the Trellis has answered our most fervent prayers for the season—Mr. Karlson himself will be performing at the Trellis in just over a week's time, accompanied by the Guild's new debut, Mr. Emry Karic of Dawnstone fame. I dare say that by the time I finish writing this column, tickets will have already sold out.

"How many plants can I bring with me?"

"No plants, Aspen."

"What, none at *all*?"

Emry dragged out his luggage while Aspen stood agape by their cluster of plants in the corner. "But—but these orchids require daily care, and we don't know how long we'll be gone..."

Ella Sorman had decreed that Emry, Cal, and Aspen were to leave for Matlock that week, giving Emry mere days to pack and coach Aspen through their impending plant separation.

"All right, fine." Emry sighed. "You can bring one if you like."

Aspen gestured to the corner. "You mean I have to *pick* one?"

While the spirit fretted over their plant crisis, Emry focused on his other two tasks: shoving clothing into suitcases and writing letters to his family. They asked about his debut every month, after all—and now, he finally had the details needed to satiate them.

As expected, their enthusiastic response came days later, on the morning of his departure.

"Letters!" Aspen called from the foyer. Emry winced at their loud voice and trudged down the stairs. The sun had only just risen; it was far too early in the morning for shouting.

"Yes, you always have letters..."

"They're for you," they said, handing him a stack of envelopes. He yawned and read the names. They were from his family—all of them. Aspen peeked at them over his shoulder.

"Can I read them out loud?"

"No."

Aspen grumbled and dashed off to grab their plants for the trip, leaving Emry to tear through letters, keeping one eye out for the carriage and the other on his family's increasingly unhinged scribbles.

Your father and I dearly wish we could make the trip down to Matlock for your first concert. You must give us a detailed account right after, and Nana will want the full list of which songs you performed—

Emry smiled and flipped to Marley's message.

If I weren't about to start a research expedition in Foxhill, I'd be on my way to Matlock right now. I'm devastated to miss it—will you give Aspen a hug for me?

Then, in ink that contained traces of Marley's coy grin:

Will Cal be in Matlock as well?

Emry looked at Georgie's, sighed in advance, and ripped it open.

Matlock? Rotting MATLOCK? What do you have against performing in the north? Couldn't convince them to let you come up to Senne? Can't believe I have to sit here in this boathouse while you debut across the rotting border...

  PS – When you're there, could you tell those stupid tradesmen in Matlock that our tunnel construction north of the border isn't causing their stupid flooding? Because it's not.

  PPS – While you're at it, hit them with an oar for me.

Emry shook his head. He did feel bad about performing so far away—he would have loved to have his family in the audience. At least Cal would be there, cheering him on. She had been just as thrilled as his family upon hearing the news, even if it was shadowed by their dire mission in Matlock...

He began to fold up the papers, then pulled out Marley's letter once more. He knew precisely what she meant when she asked after Cal's presence in the city. Dire mission aside, the whole place was primed for a romantic social season, with plenty of balls and promenades and gardens at their fingertips...

A sudden rush of excited nerves made his thoughts tingle. He was a fool if he didn't propose there—but he was also a fool if he leapt into such a thing without a plan. Courtship was as much a social dance as it was a literal one, with rules and steps at every turn. The Matlockian customs, both unspoken and completely rigid—not to mention regional expectations from Etris, traditions from Senne, vastly differing views of what was considered modern or old-fashioned, sincere or trite...

He started to sweat. He was entirely out of his depth just thinking about all of it.

"This is impossible." Aspen tromped back down the stairs, arms wrapped around two flowerpots. "The carriage is coming up the street, and I still haven't decided which of these I'm going to—"

"I'll be right there," Emry said quickly, then wiped the sweat off his palm, leapt for a pencil, and dashed off a note to Marley on the first scrap of paper he could find.

Mar, I need your help with something.

UNLIKE EMRY'S hurried preparations for the trip, the multiday carriage ride down to Matlock began quietly and smoothly. After making a show of being escorted into the carriage by Aspen, Cal spent the morning poring over city maps, while her spirit chaperone focused on their embroidery hoop. Their scribble-like loops weren't much so far, but it was a handy tool for keeping them occupied. Today, they were deep into a tangle of green lines that looked vaguely like leaves.

"What do you think?" Aspen tilted the hoop toward Emry. "Blue or purple flowers along the edge?"

"Purple."

Aspen pulled out purple thread from their pocket and resumed working, humming half a melody to themself. Emry shifted in his seat, increasingly envious of the distractions both his companions had. The book he had brought for himself wasn't helping him ignore the growing stiffness in his knees. He tried to stretch his legs, tapping a rhythm with his foot to disguise his pained movement. Perhaps it was a silly thought, but he had hoped that Aspen's flower had rid him of the aches once and for all.

This carriage ride had made short work of that wish.

They continued bumping along, hitting cracks from wave damage and detouring where roads had broken entirely. Emry stared at his book, trying to look forward to his pending rehearsals with Karlson's troupe. But as Cal moved from map to map, the thought of two hundred dying spirits cast a long shadow over his thoughts. He kept checking the window for any sign of trouble: withered trees, dead grass, yellow skies…

To his relief, he saw nothing of concern—not even when the carriage let them out at a wayhouse for a rest. After helping Cal out of the carriage, he walked along the road a few paces to both stretch his aching legs and inspect the forest around him. But the air whistling through the trees felt as fresh as ever, bearing a hint of pine and rain. Thick, healthy foliage coated the ground as far as the eye could see, making him feel like he had disembarked into a green ocean.

Next to him, Aspen took a deep breath and swung their arms.

"It feels different here," they said, craning their neck to look up at the luxurious canopy.

"Yeah," Emry murmured, following their gaze. "Really does."

"Does it?" Cal squinted around. "I don't see what's different."

Emry opened his mouth, then closed it. She was right—nothing looked particularly different than the forests around Vornik. But it felt different all the same. He rubbed the back of his neck. "It's cooler, I suppose," he said, but the comment went unheard. Aspen and Cal were already walking to the wayhouse, Aspen eagerly describing the forest's subtle variation in foliage. Emry inhaled, savored the fresh air and relief in his knees, then followed them inside.

The wayhouse did little to impress—it was a mostly empty wooden building nestled in the trees by the road. Several laymen huddled in a corner, spattered with dirt and wolfing down a quick lunch. Upon seeing the trio enter, they ate faster and left, making the place even quieter than before. Not that Emry minded—the vacancy allowed Cal to take up a whole table with her maps.

"It's difficult to sort out where to start," she admitted, pointing to the gardens she had circled—her markings eclipsed every other landmark on the map. "Judging by the number of gardens in the city, two hundred spirits might be a low estimate for the area. We'll want to visit a decent sample of them, of course, but to try to cover all of them…"

Emry winced. The mere idea of that much walking made his knee hurt.

"Did any of these spirits help during the wave?" Aspen tugged the map closer to them.

"Any of them?" Cal said. "According to Matlock's reports, nearly all of them did. For being so close to the start of the wave, the city hardly sustained any damage."

"So, they're all awake?" Aspen brightened. "You think some of them are friendly?"

Cal exchanged a glance with Emry, who forced out an optimistic smile. For Aspen's sake, he could only hope that with more spirits came more civility.

"Absolutely," he said. "Want to help us pick which gardens to visit first?"

∼

DAYS LATER, with maps sorted and garden locations circled, they arrived in Matlock.

Given its reputation for being the city of gardens, Emry was surprised at how crowded and cluttered the place felt. The city originated in the center of a deep valley—docks and buildings first encroached on the Oakvale River, then rose in steep tiers up the valley's hills. Emry tried to peek up at the buildings on the highest tier, but since each structure was made of the same reddish stone, they all blurred together as they passed. The only element breaking up the warm, stately shapes was the city's famed greenery—tumbling fountains of green, ivy dripping from walls, flowers hanging heavily from trellises and planters. Just as Cal had warned, there were hundreds of these patches of vibrant color, far too many for Emry to accurately count.

But before he could take a closer look at them, the carriage turned, wading into a packed ramp that led up through the western tiers of the city. Here, they slowed to a snail's pace, fighting for space between crowds, food carts, and other carriages. Emry huffed; he could have walked to the hotel on his aching knees and still beat the carriage there by at least a half hour.

To entertain himself, he searched for more gardens out the window but found a different pattern instead. The park they rolled past was Halleson Park; the street Halleson Ave. Then a fountain, a library, a theater, all bearing the same name...

When he brought it up to Cal, she shrugged from behind her book.

"An old Matlock family funding the city," she said. "They've been doing business here for generations. Don't worry, you'll get to see more of their wealth soon." She gave a sardonic smile. "They're hosting the opening ball of the season at their estate."

When the carriage finally creaked to a stop in front of the Oakvale Grand Hotel—finally, a place not named after the Halleson family—Emry reached for the door, eager for a bit of fresh air and leg room.

But his manager had other plans.

"Finally." Damir yanked open the carriage door with a scowl, beating a poor footman to the task. "Get your things and unpack quickly. You've got a tour in an hour."

Emry supposed he should have expected this sort of welcome. Damir had left for Matlock shortly after the Guild gathering, charging ahead to prepare the way for the unexpected debut. According to him, a month in the city wouldn't have been enough to properly prepare—but he was clearly making do with the days he had.

"A tour?" Emry repeated, reaching for his lute case. Damir snatched it up first.

"Yes, with Karlson's contact," he said. "Then it's on to your publicity events. Come along."

Despite Damir's sense of urgency, Emry couldn't help but slow down to admire the hotel as they entered. Hotels of this sort were thin on the ground in Senne—one preferred a cozy inn in such cold places—and in a busy place like Vornik, they were more functional than fashionable.

But the Oakvale Grand prided itself in being a hub of the social season in Matlock, and it was certainly built to accommodate. Between the gold chandelier, the curving twin staircases, and the hallways veering off into grand ballrooms and plush card rooms, the place dripped with the promise of romance and gossip for the season.

Gossip, Emry didn't exactly need, but the romance would do.

"I've booked Karlson and you at the Trellis in two weeks," Damir rattled off at Emry's side, not even glancing at the chandelier as his heels clicked across the marble floor. "You'll have open practice time before then, of course, but your calendar will fill up once all society realizes there's a Guild debut in town. Which they *will*, once you attend the opening ball tonight."

Damir checked his pocket watch, gave a tired sigh, and began rummaging around for his pipe.

"Are you going to have any fun while you're here?" Emry asked.

Damir snorted. "I work for Ella. I don't have fun."

Emry nodded to the front doors. "Well, since Ella isn't here, I humbly suggest that at some point during this trip, you forget I exist and go have fun somewhere."

Damir's eyes narrowed. "What if that involves sleeping all morning and getting wine-drunk at lunch?"

"Then by all means, do that."

A pause.

"I'll take it into consideration." Damir waved with his pipe. "Now, off with you, and make sure tree-kid doesn't wander too far."

But Aspen was too intrigued by the hotel to wander off. As soon as Emry opened the door to their room—another opulent gesture of ivory, gold, and polished wood—they tore around the place, first in terrier form to explore each bend of the furniture, then flapping up as a hawk to inspect the papered walls. "Is every room like this?" they asked eagerly. "If I grew flowers in here, do you think they'd mind? It's just that they don't have any, and this corner looks a little empty—"

"As long as you don't get soil anywhere, I'm sure they wouldn't mind some flowers." Emry pulled back the velvet curtains and wandered out to the balcony. The space could hardly fit a chair or two, but the view more than made up for it. "Look, they've got some flowers out here for you."

Indeed, the railing of the balcony overflowed with bright bursts of vines and magenta flowers. It lent a whimsical vignette to Emry's view of the city—tiers of buildings sloping down to a glittering river, then back up in sumptuous layers of red stone, tiled roofs, and bursting gardens.

No evidence of spirit trouble so far.

"Fancy seeing you here," a voice called from his left. He turned; Cal was leaning against the railing of the neighboring balcony, smiling at him.

He waved, grateful that Ella had pulled some strings to let her stay so close by. His view of the city couldn't possibly match his view of her.

"Cal, can I see your room?" Aspen swooped over Emry's head toward her. "Is it just as big as ours? Do you want any flowers to decorate it?"

They banked into her room without waiting for an answer. Cal laughed and watched them go by. Emry continued to admire her, warm light from the stone balcony reflecting onto her cheeks, and thought back to the letter he had written to Marley.

"Em?" Cal brought him back from his thoughts. "What are you smiling about?"

His smile widened. "Nothing."

THEIR TOUR GUIDE was set to meet them at a garden near the hotel—garden 52A, according to the map Cal had folded into her pocket.

"It's just down the street," she said, making sure to stand closer to Aspen than Emry in the hotel lobby. With so many people whirling around them, she held herself more stiffly than she usually did, and had to keep stopping herself from leaning into Emry's arm out of habit.

Her stiffness only grew worse when her gaze landed on a man on the other side of the lobby.

"Is Wesley already in town?" James said, surrounded by several other men in polished boots and puffy cravats. "I must reach out to him, then. He owes me a card game, you know, and I've already got Samuel and Francis on board..."

Emry's eyes narrowed. He had met James once or twice—a regrettable encounter each time—and thanks to Cal, was more than aware of his efforts toward promotion. "So, he's here already. How lovely."

"He's wasting no time, to be sure," Cal muttered. Emry led her into the street, hoping she would relax once she was farther away from both the crowd and James.

"Karlson said our contact's name is Lydia Pietri," he said, side-stepping carriages and tired gentry urging their servants to unload the luggage faster. "Has she ever written your department?"

As he hoped, Cal's shoulders rounded, now distracted by the more relevant problem at hand.

"Several times. She used to be a botanist, but she's now Matlock's lead spirit researcher," Cal said, then tugged on Aspen's cloak. "Aspen, dearest, your lute."

"Oh." Aspen shifted until folds of fabric hid their lute. "How do I look? Normal?"

She tapped a flower peeking out from behind their ear. "The flowers, too."

Aspen grumbled and hid those away as well, shrinking the blooms into their curls until they disappeared. Emry tilted his head. He understood the need for discretion, but the spirit had been wearing flowers in their hair for so long now, it felt odd to see them without the decorations. Like they were too human, somehow.

"What do you know of Ms. Pietri?" Emry turned back to Cal, instinctively reaching for her hand and pulling himself away just in time. Cal hid a smile at the half gesture.

"Her data is impeccable," she said. "Well laid out, her methods thoroughly described. She structures her reports using Hart's method, which I find to be—" She stopped herself. "That wasn't what you were asking about, was it?"

Emry desperately wished he could hold her hand. "What of Hart's method? Good or bad?"

Cal brightened. "Good. I believe we can trust her."

"Excellent."

As they moved away from the hotel and down a less glamorous

avenue, the glitter and gold of society faded into earthen tones and outdated ruffles. And to Emry's pleasant surprise, Matlock's demeanor changed as well. Haughty frowns and judging looks transitioned into, well, loudness—loud haggling, loud hailing of a friend across the street, loud jokes and laughter from the iron balconies above them. Emry found himself able to relax here, but from Cal's description, he imagined that their tour guide Lydia would be rather uneasy in such a place. He envisioned her standing stiff and librarian-like amidst the shuffle of the city, an uncomfortable and stoic sentinel by the garden gate.

He did not imagine Lydia Pietri to be as loud as half the street.

"Ms. Breslin?" A middle-aged woman in trousers and wide glasses waved gaily at them from the stone garden wall. "Is that you?"

Emry could immediately see why Karlson had befriended this woman. She smiled openly and easily, not caring at all about the dirt on her trousers or that she was wearing trousers in a city riddled with glittering skirts. There was a sureness in her bones that fueled her every move—her eager handshakes, her rapid speech, her sweeping gesture to the garden gate.

"Welcome to Matlock!" she said, naturally loud even up close. "I hope I'm the first one to tell you that, and if not, let's pretend. And are you Aspen?"

"I am!" Aspen couldn't help it—a purple flower grew out from behind their ear. Lydia shook their hand again.

"Amazing, just amazing. Thank you for coming." She flipped her graying auburn hair over her shoulder. "Well, you came to see the gardens, not me. Shall we?"

They walked through the iron gate and into the shade of their first Matlock garden.

Unlike the sprawling parks and rolling hills of Vornik, this little garden was cozy and small, nestled between two buildings and ending abruptly at a balcony overlooking the city. But in its own stubborn way, the garden made do with the space it had. Trees stretched possessively over clusters of stone benches, while paved stone paths fought their way through all manner of bushes and flowerbeds. Even the buildings flanking the garden hadn't been spared—each had a staircase leading down to the greenery, and their railings dripped with tiny empires of vines and flowers.

Emry wandered over to the balcony overlooking the city. These city spirits had to be stubborn to survive amidst so much stone.

And, he thought as he looked around him, so many *people*.

Compared to those in the street beyond, the people in the garden were a quiet crowd—praying in front of the trees, huddled together on the benches, making donations at the fane in the corner. But their collective presence formed an unusually pleasant, reverent buzz, one that Emry had never witnessed in Vornik or even Senne.

"Is it always this crowded?" he asked Lydia, who gave a proud smile.

"'Course it is," she said. "We've got a lot to thank these gardens for, after all. You should've seen 'em, all lit up during the wave. Bet you some of these people took shelter under these very trees that day."

Emry imagined all these people learning that their beloved spirit was dying, and instinctively rested an arm over Aspen's shoulders.

With such a dense crowd, it took him a moment of searching to see evidence of the danger the spirits were in. Though gardeners had worked to hide the issue from visitors, the grass still yellowed in patches and lay bare in others. The trees obscured brown, limp branches behind green ones. The flowers lining the circular path were no different—the blooms drooped and wilted faster than the gardeners could prune and replant. Even as a gentle spring breeze sent motes spinning through sunlight, dry and brown husks of life rattled against each other all through the garden.

The entire sight unsettled him, like a drop of blood on a white handkerchief.

"Are there any Altas here?" he asked, looking around for anyone bearing Hara's emblem or acting vaguely managerial.

"There are too many groves to have an Alta each." Lydia shrugged. "Each Alta here manages at least twenty groves."

Emry thought of Brinna back in Vornik, trying to wrangle twenty Cedars with nothing but her dusty broom, and tried not to laugh.

"Lydia," Cal said, pulling out her notebook, "you mentioned in your letters that you've been studying soil samples here. This, ah"—she looked around at the garden patrons—"*anomaly* you and your team discovered. Was it in the soil samples?"

"You'd think so, but..." Lydia lowered her voice, and her welcoming cheer dimmed. "There doesn't appear to be a difference in the samples between the gardens with spirits and those without. But the ones that have, uh, *friends* in it"—she paused to let a woman walk by them—"are all in various stages of a previously undocumented blight."

"Who else knows about your findings?" Cal asked.

"My research team and a few others in the government," Lydia said. "The rest all think it's a minor drought. And for the peace of the city, we'd like to keep it that way until we know more." She nodded ahead of her. "Come on, let me show you some of the other gardens."

She led them through several other gardens on the street, all of them smaller but just as crowded as the first. To Emry's dismay, they all gave off the same unsettling aura, a dryness that didn't belong there.

"Can I try talking to the spirit?" Aspen asked when they reached the third such garden, this one crammed between a grocer and a tailor's shop. As the lunch rush died down, so did the crowd in the garden, affording them a reasonable space in the shade of the largest tree.

"Be my guest." Lydia gestured to the tree and plopped down on the bench, eyes wide and eager. Aspen stepped up to the tree, closed their eyes, and touched the bark. One silent moment passed, then another—

They quickly pulled their hand away.

"Didn't like that," they mumbled. "They weren't expecting me."

Emry frowned. "Could they tell you weren't from the city?"

Aspen shook out their hand, their face clouded. "Maybe."

Lydia encouraged them to try again at each garden they visited—but it was the same with each one. Confusion, annoyance, willful silence.

Much like the spirits back in Vornik.

"Maybe they just need a few days," Emry said, keeping his arm around Aspen's shoulders as they returned to the first garden. "To get used to you and all."

"Maybe," Aspen said with a shrug. But they hung at the fringes of the garden, aimlessly kicking a rock while Lydia and Cal traded hushed specifics about data. Once Cal finished, she invited Emry and Aspen over.

"I believe this will be our last garden for the day," she said. "I know the spirits haven't been the most...welcoming, but would you like to try talking to this one before we go?"

Aspen settled down in front of the tree, started to reach out—then sighed and pulled their hand back. "I don't see the point. They never want to talk to me."

Lydia crouched beside Aspen with an encouraging smile, her dusty glasses slipping on her nose.

"This garden's always been a good one to me. Always shady in the summer and never too icy in the winter." She patted the tree. "If this spirit is mean to you, I'll yell at them myself. Go on, try it."

Aspen relented and closed their eyes. While they worked on the connection, Emry checked the garden's fane. It stood right by the gate, overflowing with coins, fruit, and dried flowers—both an impressive display and a loving boon.

He put a coin in the fane to join the others. For good luck, he told himself—though whether it was for the garden spirit or for Aspen, he wasn't sure.

"Emry!" Aspen hissed from their seat in the grass. Emry hurried back.

"What, what is it?" he whispered back. "Does it not like coins?"

To his surprise, Aspen was grinning. "It's there," they whispered, digging their hands into the grass. "The spirit's talking to me."

Emry tentatively set a hand on the ground as well, as if the rumblings of a spirit would bubble up through the dirt. But he felt nothing—only grass and soil.

"What's it saying?" Cal urged. Aspen waggled their head.

"It's more like...feelings," they said. "It's hard to translate into your language."

"What are they feeling, then?" Emry looked up at the tree, where dead branches swayed like ghosts. Aspen's words quickened, trying to match the other spirit's pace.

"Weak. Frustrated. Surprised."

"Surprised?"

"About me. She's..." Aspen paused, still smiling. "She's happy."

"See?" Lydia pushed on Aspen's shoulder. "I told you this garden was a good one—"

Then Aspen's smile disappeared. "Scared."

Cal froze. "What?"

"She's scared." Aspen opened their eyes, the green of them nearly a light of their own in the shade. "Something's happening, something—"

Aspen suddenly flickered. Emry grabbed the lute on their back to keep it from falling over. "Aspen—?"

Aspen flickered again, then disappeared entirely. Emry gasped and reached for their nonexistent arm, his fingers finding nothing but air—

Then Aspen was there again, fully and solidly themself.

"Are you all right?" Cal asked, their shoulder in her terrified grip.

Aspen looked around. "Did anyone else feel that?"

His heart still pounding at the scare, Emry followed their gaze to the other visitors in the garden—none of them appeared out of sorts. They still prayed, spoke, and wandered as normal.

"Doesn't seem like it," he murmured. "You think that's what's doing the spirits in?"

Aspen set both palms back on the ground, frowning in concentration. "The spirit says she gets these nearly every three or four suns," they said.

"What, more than one a week?" Lydia stared. "For how long?"

"Not sure. A few moon cycles?"

Emry checked the grass around Aspen's hand. It appeared worse than before—drier, more brown. On the other side of the tree, the rosebushes had all drooped. Even the sunlight in the space felt weak and sparse.

After months of such energy-sapping blights, Emry was surprised that that was all that showed for it. This was a strong little spirit.

"We should go," Cal said, taking Aspen's elbow. "Before whatever that was strikes again—"

"Wait." Aspen leapt forward to touch the tree once more. In an instant, the garden breathed a little life into itself. The grass patched itself up; the rosebushes perked back to life. Even the tree shed some of its brown leaves and grew fresh ones in its place.

Aspen drew back, sunlight now streaming through their transparent form.

"We'll come back later," they said firmly. "I promised her."

As they spoke, a tiny scarlet rhythm bloom appeared at Emry and Aspen's feet: a quiet, lovely thank-you.

Emry decided he liked this spirit very much.

"Of course, we will," he said, helping Aspen to their feet and out of the garden. Lydia followed, talking to Cal in rushed tones.

"I'll send you all the research I've compiled so far, and I'll have my team send you any updates," she said. "I don't have information from every garden, but maybe with your help—"

"If there are hundreds of gardens, my help alone won't be enough. Not if the blight is truly worsening every week." Cal paused in thought. "Have you seen Mr. Devrin Gray in town for the season?"

Lydia blinked. "Of course, I have. I hardly know anyone who hasn't."

"Good." Cal nodded. "I'll talk to him straightaway and bring him aboard to help. You can trust him, I assure you."

Emry relaxed—it was an excellent idea, as always. If anyone other than Cal could get to the bottom of this, it was Dev. And if both

THE SPIRIT WELL

of them were in Matlock together, they'd have this blight problem sorted before the season was half over.

They finally left Lydia and turned back toward the hotel. Between the carriage ride and the long city walk, Emry found himself daydreaming of a brief moment of respite before Damir swept him off to the next event. A chair would be nice to take the weight off his knees. Then some coffee, to rid himself of his drowsiness. He wondered how the hotel would bring it up to him—on a golden tray, perhaps? Lined with roses and lilies? Given what he had seen of both the hotel's ostentation and the demands of its guests, he wouldn't exactly put it past them...

But as they reached the corner, his daydream fizzled in distraction. A shiny new presence had arrived on the street, something he hadn't noticed on his way into the garden—a wagon acting as a merchant's stall, glittering with an array of unusually bright jewelry.

"Spirit talismans!" the merchant called. He was a sunken sort of man—hollow cheeks, shadowed eyes—with a bright, encouraging voice. "Protection from bad luck, illness, and accidents. Bring it to your favorite garden and ask the spirit to bless it!"

Emry frowned at it—but Aspen was, quite literally, several steps ahead of him. Before Emry could reach for them, they had approached the wagon to inspect its wares, solidifying their form so as not to scare off the merchant.

"What are these?" they asked.

"Only the most potent talismans you'll find in all the land," the merchant said, eyes glittering as soon as he saw Cal and Emry approach. Now he had not one but three curious customers. "Each one is unique. You can't find them anywhere else."

He wasn't wrong at the last assertion. Emry had never seen jewelry like this: necklaces, earrings, bracelets, all simple gold chains adorned with clear gypsum. But it wasn't the style or quantity that surprised him—it was the twinkling light floating within the gypsum itself.

He picked up a piece and his fingertips prickled. The lights were familiar—reminiscent of Dev's lab samples, of surge energy whiffing past in the breeze.

There was spirit energy trapped in the gypsum. Every single piece.

"Where'd you get this?" Emry asked, but the merchant was already talking to another prospective customer, an old lady eagerly pointing to one of the necklaces. Cal turned to Aspen.

"Is it dangerous, do you think?" she murmured. Aspen bit their lip, placing a ring back on the velvet display.

"I don't think so," they whispered. Cal leaned in close to look at the pieces, then glanced up at Emry with concern. He grabbed a bracelet with a line of stones on it and held it up.

"Excuse me? We'll take this."

That afternoon as Emry rested his legs, he received far more than just a cup of coffee. With the cup came a letter and several bouquets, all delivered by a dour man in white gloves who looked like he had been working at the hotel for twenty years too long. Emry was sorely tempted to know what the man had seen over his tenure—but the man had a full cart of other goods to deliver, so instead he gave a polite thank-you and took everything off the golden tray.

"Who's it all from?" Aspen called from the balcony. Emry shut the door and inspected the flowers. He didn't recognize the names, but Damir surely would. He had warned them that people would begin sending gifts—a standard part of charming someone new and potentially influential on the scene.

"No idea, but..." He set aside the flowers and moved on to the letter's curly handwriting. "The letter's from Marley. Gods, she writes fast."

Aspen set down their embroidery as Emry slid open the letter's seal, a flower pressed into purple wax—no doubt done to please Aspen, who was very pleased indeed.

"Do you *have* to break the seal?" they asked.

"Afraid so." Emry unfolded the letter as deftly as he could, handed the flowery seal to Aspen to distract them, and read the letter's contents. The message was in a jittery hand, as if Marley had been too excited to properly get the words on the page:

Thank all the gods you asked me for help—please see the itemized list below for everything you must do during the season. In this order. Without deviating. Please read the footnotes—they're important. Read them, read them again, take notes.

Introduce yourself, dance the last set with her, send flowers to her room the next day, do NOT send letters, promenade at least once, then dance with her no more than twice in one event...

Emry frantically dug out a small pocket notebook from his pack and began taking notes.

CHAPTER EIGHT

CAL

Cal had every intention of checking on Emry and Aspen's health after they'd had a chance to rest in their room—but when she stepped out into the hall, she found Damir already dragging the pair out for their next obligation.

"We have an hour at the teahouse, then it's down the street to the tailors," he said, his tone and pace brisk. "Whatever you brought, it won't be good enough for the ball tonight, so I took the liberty of putting something together for you..."

Emry limped upon following Damir—but when he spotted Cal, he straightened and waved to her. "See you at the ball?"

Cal stepped forward. "Yes, but—"

"Bye, Cal!" Aspen waved alongside him, and then they were off down the marble stairs. Once they disappeared into the bustle of the lobby, Cal bit her lip and retreated to prepare for the ball herself.

She *was* looking forward to the opening ball, of course. It was meant to be one of the finest events of the season, and Ella had been extremely gracious in securing her an invitation at such short notice.

But instead of opening her wardrobe, she found herself pacing around the room instead.

How could she not have considered that whatever was impacting the city spirits would impact Aspen, too? Should she try to send them away while she sorted out this mess? She couldn't—they would never let themself be sent away. Not when they had just discovered a friendly spirit in the city, and certainly not while Emry was here.

And Emry—his lingering pain was another matter entirely. Cal twisted the pendant on her necklace, old fears from the wave creeping up her throat. Gods, why was it so hard to keep him out of harm's way? He was a bard. Music wasn't dangerous.

As her wrist moved, the glittering of her new bracelet caught her eye. She slipped it off her wrist, holding it closer to the window light. Emry had bought it in the hopes she could sort out what it was, but she hardly knew what to make of it. She hardly knew what to make of Lydia's research, either—soil samples normal, weather patterns normal, all while hundreds of gardens withered around her.

She had to find Dev at the ball tonight, she determined. The quicker he was on board, the faster she could solve the problem—and the faster she could get them all out of danger.

That evening, she approached Halleson's sprawling estate with nothing but efficiency and haste in mind—but she should have known that was never going to be the order of the day.

As she gazed at the long mansion, its stone stretched both wide and tall, she wondered how she was going to find anyone within its candlelit rooms, much less Dev. There must have been a dozen rooms already filled within, and the main entrance overflowed with even more attendees, all condensed into one horde to greet one another and begin their gossip circles. They rolled like fog up the carved staircases and past the towering bouquets, leaving Cal to begrudgingly slow down and follow their lead. She was accustomed to the protocol for events like this—it wouldn't help her or her cause to stand out now.

But as much as she understood the etiquette for such a ball, she found she knew very little about the man hosting it. She occasionally saw Halleson's name bandied about in the Vornik newspapers, but when it came to details, she only knew he was a businessman of significant repute and had hired an excellent calligrapher for his invitations; the paper in her purse shimmered with gold ink and wafted with the smell of roses.

Cal smoothed a wrinkle in her dress and waited for the crowd to shuffle through the gilded front doors. Unlike the invitation, she had opted for modesty befitting someone present on Council business—a simple ivory dress with few embellishments, while still adhering to the straight, column-like style that half the ladies in her department obsessed over. The only true adornment she had allowed herself was her tiara, a small crescent of gold and seed pearls that she carefully placed atop her curls. It had been a gift from her mother for her very first ball back in Etris, and she hoped it wasn't too showy.

When she finally reached the vaulted entrance hall, she realized she needn't have worried.

She had to squint to take in the absurd amount of sparkling. Gold-embroidered dresses, bright jewels tucked into hair, all reflected and magnified by the gilded mirrors hanging about the room. Everything and everyone here was a statement piece, a bold announcement of their presence at the opening event of the season.

And James, of course, blended right in. He loitered farther down the hall, carefully positioned to see everyone arrive and carefully dressed to appear like he was already a full-fledged Councilman. Only the finest silk for his coat, the shiniest buttons for his sleeves, and the most decadent embroidery crawling up through the entire ensemble.

Cal scoffed inwardly. It was a shame that defenestration was frowned upon in high society—Mr. Halleson's tall windows were perfect for it.

Upon seeing her arrive, James gave her a polite nod, then resumed his conversation with the woman to his left. Cal slipped into the crowd, angling her path to pass by him for a few discreet moments—just long enough to eavesdrop.

"Yes, I was thinking of hosting a garden party," he said, his voice as bombastic as his coat. "My cousin has the most beautiful property on the west side of the city, you know. Perfect for a little gathering now that we're all in town. All the best minds and such." He leaned forward conspiratorially. "Speaking of the best minds, has Mr. Gray already arrived?"

His companion knew nothing on that front, and James eventually sidled off to the rooms on the left. Cal watched him go, then ducked into the rooms on the right. She had to find Dev before James assaulted him with his overeager handshake and garden party invitations.

To her brief dismay, the room she had chosen to explore didn't hold Dev—but it did hold Lydia Pietri, standing in the back and humming along to distant music. She had abandoned her work trousers for an outdated dress, its fabric dull, faded, and scratchy, judging by the way she kept fiddling with the skirt.

Cal silently resolved to take her to a modiste for the next ball—she would simply stun in a well-fitted suit.

"Ms. Breslin!" Lydia brightened once she saw her. "I knew you'd come soon. Always nice to see a familiar face at these...things..." She grimaced as a pair of ladies floated by, buffeted by their gauzy skirts and floating hairstyles. Cal looked around the room.

"Are your colleagues not here?"

"Oh, some of them are." Lydia gestured vaguely at the room. "Likely hanging off the arms of Mr. Gray. Are you sure that man will stoop to work with us? Way he talks about himself, he's puffier than half these room's cravats."

Cal tried not to laugh at the comparison. "Self-assured he may be, but he's not too proud to solve a mystery like this. Let me speak with him tonight and you'll see." She leaned to look around the next doorway. "Could you point me to where he might—"

"Ms. Breslin," a familiar yet overly formal voice said behind her. "How lovely to see you."

Cal turned around—Aspen stood before her, their posture perfectly straight, hands clasped behind their back. She tilted her head and smiled. Such a stance was unusual for them, but she could go along with it. Perhaps they wanted to fit with the tone of the ball. They had certainly dressed the part—a soft gray coat, a green waistcoat patterned with gold vines. They had even put special effort into the illusion of shoes and a cravat, knotted in the simple, stoic Senne style.

"My dear spirit." She gave him her best curtsy. "Enchanting to see you as well, though I saw you just a few hours ago."

She expected them to break at this point—to eagerly tell her all about the carriage horses they saw or the quality of the bouquets at the entrance. But they didn't. They simply stepped aside and gestured to the man standing behind them.

"If I could introduce you to my good friend, Mr. Karic?" they said in perfect sincerity.

Cal immediately saw where Aspen had pulled the inspiration for their clothing. Emry wore almost the same thing, just in a darker, more charcoal shade—typical of a Senne man, in love with his grayscale wardrobe. The only hint of color was his deep emerald waistcoat, which sparkled when its embroidery turned in the candlelight. For a brief, intense moment, she longed to touch the silky fabric, to feel how cool it was under the soft coat.

She was so taken by the thought that she hardly had time to question why she was being introduced to her own boyfriend.

"Ms. Breslin," Emry said smoothly, stepping up to her as if this was not at all unusual. "It's an honor."

He gave her a bow, then took her gloved hand and kissed it. She couldn't count how many times he had done this in the past, but this time, the brief touch gave her an embarrassing thrill.

"The honor is mine, Mr. Karic," she managed. Something bright and nervous flickered across Emry's face.

"Are you at all engaged for the last dance of the evening?" he asked.

Cal nearly laughed—of course, she wasn't. She had only just arrived—then she stopped, the realization dropping on her like a chandelier.

"The last dance?" she repeated breathlessly.

Back in Etris, the last dance of any event was a special one. It was typically reserved for friends and family members, a chance to dance with someone who may have otherwise been occupied for the evening. But to specifically request the dance—to indicate they'd gladly wait all night just for a moment with this one person—was a traditional sign of particular interest.

A traditional beginning to an official courtship.

"Yes," she blurted out, her face flushing with heat, giddiness rising in her throat. "I mean—no, I'm not engaged. Engaged for the dance, I mean. I..." She took a steadying breath. "I would be happy to dance the last set with you, Mr. Karic."

Emry grinned, his face shining brighter than the gold embroidery at his collar.

"Excellent." He straightened. "Now, if you'll excuse me, I believe my colleague Aspen wanted me to inform them of what Matlock champagne tastes like."

"Yes!" Aspen brightened. "I'd like to know about the bubbles, please—I mean." They cleared their throat. "Yes, that would be nice. Thank you."

"Ms. Breslin. Ms. Pietri." Emry bowed his head to them one more time, then escorted Aspen out. The farther Aspen got, the more bounce filled their step, until they were back to their normal self, babbling eagerly about flowers and candles and dresses.

Over by the wall, several ladies smiled and raised fans to their faces, whispering to their companions behind fluttering paper. Cal's heart fluttered right along with them, and she had to fight down a burst of giggles.

"I didn't bring the right dresses!" She set her hands on her face. "If he's going to—to—I've got to write my parents, I need to visit a tailor, I need to—"

Lydia stared down at her. "Right dresses for what?"

Cal gathered herself and smoothed her skirts, cheeks burning fiercely.

"Apologies," she said. "Um—where did you say you last saw Mr. Gray?"

Lydia hummed and took her arm back, firmly looping it around her elbow. "Drinks first, then Mr. Gray. That man's gotta talk out all his hot air first. Why don't you tell me why you need new dresses?"

"Oh." Lydia blinked at her. "*Oh*. Well, in that case, I can point you to a tailor close to the Oakvale—"

Cal finished her champagne in one gulp. "No, no, no need. I shouldn't get ahead of myself."

"Ahead of yourself?" Lydia gave a barking laugh that rang across the high painted ceiling. "Look, I may be a spinster, but I know this sort of thing only comes 'round once, gods willing. Get ahead of yourself, young lady. Order the new dress." She adjusted the tiara in Cal's hair. "And find a bigger tiara while you're at it. Society's going to be watching you for the rest of the season." Then she set down her glass. "Now, let's go find that silly Mr. Gray, shall we?"

They wandered from room to room, sidestepping dancers, servants, and clusters of fierce gossipers in their element, but they didn't worry for too long about finding Dev—he made his presence known before Cal could even see him.

"In my years of studying spirit energy, I can definitively say..." A pause for dramatic effect. "It has always surprised me."

A smattering of chuckles followed. Cal turned the corner to find Dev standing in the middle of the room, partially hidden by fascinated listeners. But even amongst the shimmering dresses and coats, Dev stood out—not just because his shock of black hair stood a head higher than most, but because his eager gestures and the passionate glint in his gaze captured the eye immediately.

"We know far less about spirit energy than we do the stars or the ocean," he continued. "But if we dedicate ourselves to it, what we know today will seem elementary in a year's time. Common knowledge a year after. The opportunities that lie in the spirits, the underground chambers, the very trees, even—it is nothing but pure potential."

Cal shifted ahead of Lydia to watch him speak. He was both professor and showman, and she caught a glimpse of what he must have been like as an Academy student. Standing before the department heads, proposing his harebrained thesis ideas...

Back then, of course, he had been summarily rejected. Spirit energy was hardly a legitimate field of study, let alone a valid topic for a thesis. The Academy had chased him out, isolating him to a dilapidated house and his own wild experiments.

Now, he stood before a rapt audience at society's latest event. People—rich, influential people—murmured and nodded along with his words, pretending they had always believed in spirits and spirit energy.

What a difference six months made.

"Will you ever put on an exhibition of the research you've gathered?" one lady asked, and the man beside him cut in.

"Oh, but he must," he said in a deep baritone. "Once he finishes his current project, I'll see to it myself. A permanent exhibit, I think, in one of my own buildings."

Cal shifted to observe the generous man. They couldn't have been more different—he was broad where Dev was skinny, pale where Dev was bronze. And while Dev had fully embraced the ostentatious style of the season with his blue suit and silver embroidery, this man was strangely...understated. Brusque, businesslike.

But he didn't need to stoop to such trends to be given attention—the audience gave as much deference to him as they did to Dev. They didn't dare speak over him nor look away when he addressed them. In fact, their attention was so locked, it was difficult for Cal to find a way into the exclusive circle.

And she wasn't the only one who vied for space—James was making a similar round on the other side of the room, eyeing both Dev and Lydia in the other corner. Cal stiffened—reach Dev first, or save Lydia from a terrible, James-filled fate?

Then one of Dev's admirers excused herself from the buzzing conversation, and she made a silent apology to Lydia.

"Mr. Gray," Cal said, quickly taking up the blank space in his circle. "How lovely to see you here."

Dev gave her a surprised smile. Across the room, James huffed and pivoted toward Lydia.

"Ms. Breslin!" Dev bowed. "I didn't know you would be attending the season. You should have told me."

"I'm afraid I only just arrived," she said smoothly, "but how delightful to hear that you've found a project to work on here."

"Yes, yes," he said, his tone dripping with false humility. "Though I'm not alone in the endeavor, certainly. Wouldn't have my head on straight if it wasn't for Mr. Whitlock here." He gestured to a lanky man standing beside him, his dark skin reflecting gold in the chandelier light. "Ms. Breslin, this is Ezekiel Whitlock, or Zeke. My assistant—and the most organized man I know."

"High praise." Cal gave him a curtsy, recalling Dev's chaotic, ramshackle home. Zeke must be very organized indeed.

"I should say the same for you, Ms. Breslin," Zeke said politely, his voice shockingly quiet compared to Dev's. He also wasn't nearly as confident under the scrutiny of so many people—his hands couldn't quite stay still at his sides. "Mr. Gray has told me all about your collaboration on the wave research before it struck."

"Ah, so this is *the* Ms. Breslin you've mentioned?" The understated man on Dev's other side held out his hand to her. "Halleson. It's lovely to meet you. I'm a great supporter of the sciences, you know."

Ah—no wonder the man didn't need to peacock about the mansion to receive attention. This was his own house.

"A pleasure." Cal shook his hand. His smile was warm enough, but the rings on his fingers were cold, and his eyes appraised her as much as she appraised him—assessing value and potential out of business instinct.

"Are you continuing your scientific studies, Ms. Breslin?" he asked.

"As part of the Council's new division, yes," she said. "We're hoping to make great strides in spirit research, like Mr. Gray." She glanced at Dev. "We might even call upon his expertise, if he's so willing."

"Of course, of course," Dev said vaguely, then turned to his other admirers. Cal stiffened. She couldn't ask him any specific questions, not while so thoroughly surrounded by these people. She had to get him away from the circle, if only for a few minutes.

Then music tinkled from the other room.

"Would you care to dance, Mr. Gray?" she asked. He blinked at her. Of course, he didn't—dancing with her would take him away from his audience. There had to be a carrot, some sort of reward...

"I'm sure Aspen would love to chat with you after a set," she added.

Dev lit up again. "Oh, yes, are they here as well? Always happy to chat with our dear spirit. A dance would be lovely."

Once he made his excuses to the others, they headed toward the music. Cal passed two familiar faces—first, Aspen themself, hemmed in by people begging them to grow flowers.

"Another rose?" Aspen sighed. "Yes, of course. But I wanted to ask if any of you have tried talking to the spirits—oh, you want a camellia? Well, all right..."

The second face was just as tired—Emry, debating with some round man about construction.

"No, sir, the Karic sub-river service isn't causing any flooding in Matlock," he said. "Georgie knows what she's doing, I can promise you that."

As Cal passed, Emry's fingers surreptitiously reached out and brushed her gloved arm. His touch sent another thrill through her; she tamped it down. Professional, she had to be *professional*.

She flashed another smile at Dev and entered the dance line with him. On the other end of the line, James and Lydia joined as well. Lydia had her lips pressed into an unamused line, and across from Cal, Dev was already looking back toward Aspen.

Cal squared her shoulders. It seemed both Council attendees had their work cut out for them.

The music spun up, and she gave the requisite curtsy to start the dance.

"How long have you been in Matlock?" she asked, carefully balancing her voice to be heard just above the music.

"Several months," Dev said. "I am exceedingly lucky that people appreciate my work here. Matlock is far more open to the potential of spirits."

Judging by his tone, he didn't believe luck had anything to do with it. Cal played along and continued.

"Have you had much time to tour the city?"

"Hardly." Dev snorted, moving around her right side. "My research is highly intensive. I can't afford to dally."

She expected as much—Dev was never one for dallying, anyway.

As she focused on her next question, the dance made her switch partners, and she caught scraps of James' conversation nearby.

"Yes, I visit groves all the time in my line of work," he boasted to Lydia. "Leading the research efforts, one might say—"

Cal rolled her eyes and whirled back to Dev, remembering to

keep her questions casual. "So, you haven't had the pleasure of visiting the spirit gardens yet?"

To her surprise, he stiffened at the question.

"Of course, I have," he said. "For research purposes."

The dance led them closer to each other, giving her an opportunity to lower her voice. There wasn't much time left in the set—she had to make her point known. "Have you noticed anything off with the gardens in the city?"

He kept his gaze fixed beyond her shoulder. "I hear of a drought," he said, his tone forcibly light, "but I'm sure it'll clear up with the summer rains. Don't you agree?"

Then they switched partners again, sending Cal off with a confused frown. He'd observed the problem, surely—he must not want to say it in front of others.

As she spun, James' voice tugged on her ear again.

"I'd so *love* to meet more associates like yourself. How do you feel about a garden party?"

Annoyance surged through Cal, and if she had been any closer to him, she would have tried to step on his toes. Instead, she rounded back to Dev, her words coming out fast and impatient.

"You and I both know the summer rains won't clear it up," she said. "Are you not already looking into the issue?"

"I—" Dev started—then his gaze landed on her new bracelet, its spirit energy winking up at him. Anger and fear flashed briefly across his face.

"It's nothing," he snapped. "There is no issue to look into, Ms. Breslin."

She stumbled and missed the last few steps of the dance. "*What?*"

Then James veered close once more and made his final bow.

"It's settled, then," he crowed to Lydia. "I shall reach out regarding the event post-haste. It was so lovely to meet you, Ms. Pietri—"

Cal forcibly blocked his prattling out of her ears. She couldn't hear it, not now. "Dev, what on earth are you talking about?" she whispered furiously. "Do you know something about the—?"

The music for the next set picked up, and Dev hurried away from her with a curt bow.

"Have a good evening, Ms. Breslin," he said. "Tell that spirit of yours I'll talk to them some other time."

CHAPTER NINE

CAL

THE PEEK OF THE SEASON

My dearest readers, we have been waiting a full year for this moment, and our honorable Mr. Halleson did not disappoint. The opening ball of the season positively sparkled with the city's brightest and most beautiful, the height of the day's fashion on full display...

This writer is proud to reveal that she was among the first to greet Mr. Karlson at the ball and meet the very first spirit out in society, Aspen Karic. They are as darling as one can imagine, and even in the grand City of Spirits, their company is a treasure. Such lovely flowers they can grow.

And let's not forget the other half of the Guild's debuting pair, Mr. Emry Karic. He is indeed charming and handsome, but mothers, do not worry about your daughters falling for a bard just yet—in the final set of the evening, he appeared to only have eyes for Ms. Calliope Breslin of the Etris Breslins. A Guild musician may be an unusual choice for such a family, but the pair have been reported to be nigh inseparable since the events of Dawnstone. Shall we see an engagement before the season is out? Only time will tell.

THE NEXT MORNING, Cal woke to a flurry of memories both sweet and bitter.

She pulled the covers over her head and chose to dwell on the sweet memories first: her dance with Emry, the official beginning of his courtship. His coat had been as soft as she expected, his waistcoat cool to the touch, while his hand burned a trail on her waist. She recalled how he had smiled and whispered jokes in her ear as they spun, making her laugh and almost miss her next step. Then he had bowed, kissed the back of her hand, and asked—

And asked how her conversation with Dev had gone.

All the happy little bubbles in her stomach popped like last night's champagne. In her attempt to not sully the evening, she had deferred that conversation to the morning. And now the morning had arrived.

She reluctantly sat up and rubbed her eyes, her sleep-clouded mind still baffled by Dev's rejection. She had assumed he would say yes immediately. Part of her even hoped he had already started an investigation of his own, setting up samples and data points with the same chaotic fervor as his pre-wave research.

Instead, he had lied and dismissed her out of hand.

She removed her silk evening bonnet and shuffled toward the balcony, halfheartedly grabbing a dressing gown to pull over her nightgown. Bothering with full dress and hair for a sulk on the balcony felt unnecessary. If anyone deemed her unfit for public consumption this early in the morning, they needed to go back to bed.

A knock sounded at the door, and she hurriedly threw on the dressing gown.

"One moment!" Shoving a stray curl out of her face, she padded up to the door and opened it a crack. "Yes?"

"Flowers for you, Ms. Breslin."

On the other side of the door, an exhausted delivery boy held out a vase with a yawn. But the flowers themselves held the very opposite energy—little bursts of scarlet and yellow, hemmed in by perfectly trimmed greenery. Cal took the vase and looked closer to assess the flowers. Red tulips, yellow roses, a spray of calla lilies...

The delivery had no card, but it didn't need one. She knew exactly who this was from.

"Thank you," she tried, but the delivery boy had already trundled off with another vase to another room. Cal closed the door and took a delighted whiff of the bouquet. Early flower deliveries were common during the season, but she had never predicted she might be the recipient of one—and particularly not one so ardent. Whoever had ordered it was fully aware of the season's particular language of flowers. Red tulips for love, yellow roses for affection, calla lilies for beauty...

She wandered out to the balcony, looking for a sunny spot to show off her gift, only to find her suitor already out in the morning sun.

"Good morning, my dear." Emry leaned against the railing of his own balcony. He was also half-dressed, his hair tousled, his shirt billowing around him. Cal's face flushed as she set the vase on the corner of the balcony. The man had no right to look so good at sunrise, particularly when they were separated by both a railing and several social mores.

"Hello," she said, angling the flowers toward him. "I was pleasantly surprised to receive such a bouquet this morning."

Emry maintained his grin. "Oh, really?"

"Yes. And without a card, too." She kept her tone airy. "A secret admirer, but a most insightful sender, I believe. Their message was quite clear."

"How lovely to hear." Emry toyed with the ivy on the railing. "And said secret admirer could, um..." He hesitated. "Could continue? Sending you flowers, I mean?"

Her eyes fell on the bouquet once more, giddiness bubbling up inside her at the question behind the question. Flowers led to promenades, led to dancing, led to getting on one knee and—

"Of course." She beamed at him. "Please continue with the—the flowers."

"Excellent." Emry broke into a wide grin, then tried to compose himself. "The admirer can't send you too many, though. Aspen might get jealous—"

"Jealous of what?"

A hawk swooped down and landed on the railing next to Emry's hand. Emry leapt into the air, his hand on his chest.

"Shiro's hairy *foot*, Aspen—"

"Sorry! Better?"

Aspen sat on the railing in human form, their bare feet swinging carelessly in the open air. Cal withheld an instinctual shriek.

"Feet on the ground, please—"

Aspen groaned and swung their legs onto the balcony. "What's with you two today?"

"Nothing!" they both said. Aspen gave them both a look, and Cal clambered for a distraction.

"Did you have a nice flight?"

Aspen nodded eagerly and picked up their embroidery hoop from the railing. "I flew as close to the garden spirit as I could," they said, poking at the fabric with renewed energy. "Can't fly too far from my lute, but I was able to get close enough to talk." They pointed to their lute, which basked in a sunlit corner of the balcony.

"Did she say anything new about the blight?" Emry asked.

"Not really. But she did grow this for me!" They pulled a small scarlet flower out of their pocket. "I think I'll try to add this color to my embroidery..."

Cal watched Aspen fiddle with their hoop, the ivy on the balcony peeking through their ghostly arms—too ghostly for her liking.

"Were you out all night?" she ventured.

"No. Just the past few hours, waiting for you to wake up," Aspen said cheerily. Cal and Emry exchanged a glance. Aspen didn't sleep, of course, but they were normally more...well-rested come dawn.

"So." Emry cleared his throat. "Cal, what did Dev say to you last night?"

Cal bit her lip—this wasn't going to make the situation any better. "He declined."

Emry gaped.

"Dev *declined*?" he echoed. "Why?"

Cal ducked inside and retrieved her crystal bracelet. The spirit energy within the stones had faded overnight, revealing the jewelry to be as cheap and oversold as she suspected—but the light hadn't gone entirely. A few of the sparkles remained, as if taunting her.

"It was odd," she said, tossing the bracelet over to Emry. "He recognized the crystals, then told me there was no problem with the spirits. Said it was just a drought."

"If only he were right," Emry muttered, then held the bracelet up to the light. "I can't believe he dismissed you like that."

"You think I can convince him to help?" Aspen asked. Emry handed them the bracelet.

"You could certainly try."

While Aspen inspected the jewelry, Cal plucked a flower from the railing and twirled it in her fingers, staring hard at the blurred petals. She couldn't decide what was more puzzling: Dev's willful ignorance or his reaction to the crystals.

At least one was easier to investigate than the other.

"I'd like to visit Lydia today," she decided aloud, setting down the flower. "Perhaps there's something more to those stones I'm not aware of."

Aspen tossed the bracelet back to her, the jewelry flashing in the light. After some time in the spirit's hands, the energy within the gypsum had come back to life, sparkling against her palm like tiny stars.

"I'd say I could go with you," Emry said, "but Damir's got our day filled through the evening."

Cal pocketed the bracelet. "How about tomorrow?"

"Tomorrow's our first rehearsal. Got to show everyone how well Aspen can sing, yeah?" Emry clapped Aspen on the shoulder, then straightened with a wince. Cal glanced down at his legs—even through the railing, she could see him leaning against the balcony for support.

"Em?" she said. He caught her worried gaze and played it off with an exaggerated grimace.

"Oh, I'm fine," he croaked. "You see, I danced with someone last night, and she kept stepping on my feet—"

Aspen snorted. Cal couldn't help but roll her eyes. "I did not."

"Almost took off my toes, she did."

"Lies and slander, and I won't stand for it."

He laughed at that, then softened. "I'm all right, Cal. I'll take some moonflowers before Damir drags me off to tea."

She fidgeted with the bracelet. It wasn't a perfect solution, but it would suffice. "Thank you."

That afternoon, Cal set out for Lydia's office. The government buildings weren't far from the hotel, making for a pleasant walk past the city's fragrant gardens.

Or, at least, it would have been pleasant if she wasn't fully aware of what was happening to them. As it was, she hurried forward and tried not to look at them too hard.

To her surprise, the Matlock offices organized themselves quite differently from the Council's grand, stately square. These buildings were decentralized, splayed across several different blocks in a haphazard array. Lydia and her new division had been gifted a building on a quiet corner, within a...more well-loved structure—one of the few that was still made of brick, while its neighbors slowly transitioned to lighter, more fashionable stone.

But Cal found she preferred this building. She liked the ivy trailing the walls and the worn, mossy benches outside. Its facade alone held more charm than all the surrounding buildings combined.

And Lydia's energy only made it more charming.

"Come in, come in!" She ushered Cal through a wood-paneled hallway. The researcher was back to her comfortable self in her comfortable trousers, and her words bounced rapidly off the walls. "Glad you caught me here—I'll be out in garden 72B later today. You recovered yet from the ball? Saw you dancing with Mr. Karic for the last set." She grinned back at Cal, the sparkle in her eyes discordant with the streaks of gray in her hair. "Read it in the papers, too. How do you think they write so fast? Must be on the same sort of coffee that James Edwards is on. Already got a note about his garden party—as if I need another event." She finally paused at a set of double doors, old and scuffed. "Speaking of silly men, did Mr. Gray say he could help us?"

Cal stiffened. "I'm...still working on it," she said. "He's busy with his own research."

Lydia snorted. "Did he ever say what his research actually is? Gods know I've asked, and he's always waved it off. For all I know, he's working very hard at studying Matlock's varieties of wine." She pushed the double doors open. "Tea? Coffee? Cookies? I always keep some stashed away. Learned that trick back in university..."

Lydia puttered around her office, a little wood-paneled square tucked away in the back of the building. The room was nothing at all like her orderly notes and data. Pillars of books and papers littered every surface, some stacked so high that Cal thought they might be responsible for holding up the creaking ceiling. But as sunlight warmed the dark wood accents all around her, Cal found an endearing coziness about the place—as if the columns of books and notes were a comfortable fortress and not an organizational nightmare.

"I was actually wondering if I might ask a few more questions for the investigation," she said, then checked the hallway for any potential listeners. But apart from Lydia, the place lay silent—everyone else was still sleeping away the champagne from last night's ball, it seemed.

"Well, I don't have much beyond the reports I sent you yesterday." Lydia assembled a pile of cookies on a tray. "Unless you already came across something new?"

Cal unclasped her bracelet and held it out to the woman. "Do you know anything about these stones?"

The energy in the jewelry was already fading again, dim in the office's warm light. Lydia took the bracelet and gave an unimpressed hum. "Sure hope you didn't pay much for it."

Cal deflated—so the crystals weren't unusual after all. "Call it a professional curiosity," she said. "Are these stones common here?"

"Not exactly." Lydia inspected the settings. "This gypsum can only be found deep underground, far deeper than the river routes. But when we do find some of it, it's usually not enough to turn into jewelry like this. And generally not worth it, either—I'm surprised the energy inside has lasted this long."

"All credit for that must go to Aspen, I'm afraid," Cal said. "When they touched the bracelet this morning, it seemed to revitalize the stones."

"Wish I could've seen that." Lydia gave the piece one more thoughtful turn, then set the bracelet down. "Look, I can't blame you for buying the thing. The energy in the stones is intriguing enough. If I had the funds or time to organize a dig toward the well, I'd probably be able to gather more samples for you."

Lydia handed a cookie to Cal, then took one for herself. Cal held the cookie, frowning in thought at the woman's last sentence.

"The well?" she repeated.

"Oh, it's what my division's started calling the deep chamber." Lydia waved her cookie. "The theoretical one, of course."

Cal took a distracted nibble. "I see."

She had heard of this theory a few times before. It was new, but then again, every theory about spirit energy was new.

But it *was* one of the more intriguing ideas out there.

Some theorized that there existed a deep chamber, or a well, acting as a repository of spirit energy—the original source of every surge and every wave, and by extension, every spirit. Some of the more lyrical scientists out there characterized it as a chaotic pit of volatile plasma, fathoms wide and fathoms deep. Others insisted it was a shallower, more disparate network, spread out under the provinces like a root system.

Cal tried not to get excited about the theory without further proof—but if Lydia's team had more information…

"You said you wanted to dig to it," she said. "Do you have an idea of where it might be?"

"Oh, it's an untested idea. Hardly put down on paper yet. Barely an inkling of a thing." The sparkle in Lydia's eye sharpened. "Want to hear it?"

Cal grinned. "Absolutely."

Lydia swept a stack of books off her desk and spread out a map of the country, cookie crumbs falling across the paper as she pointed to various circled areas.

"I'm remapping all the areas impacted by the wave and at what times," she said, her words speeding up—not unlike Dev when he spoke, but less bombastic and more straightforward. "We all know the wave moved north…" She pointed to the provincial border near Matlock, then dragged her finger up to Dawnstone. "But as far as we can tell, the wave didn't travel farther south than Hawthorne Bend." Her finger rested on a small dot below Matlock. "If Matlock really was the epicenter of the wave, the well must be here, too. Under our feet." She straightened. "Hopefully *very* far under our feet."

Cal swallowed and set aside her cookie. Lydia's theory made sense—but it presented problems of its own.

"If we...entertain this idea," she began. Lydia folded her arms and nodded along.

"Yes."

"That the well is underneath Matlock."

"Mm-hmm."

"It would be underneath Matlock's spirits, too." Cal's chest tightened. "Do you think the blight could be coming from the well? That there's something wrong with it?"

Lydia let out a long, slow breath. "It's a possibility..." She reviewed her map again. "But it's hard to say with my paltry research. For all we know, there isn't a well down there at all."

Something bubbled up in Cal's stomach—not excitement, exactly, but an urgency. A notion that she was onto something, and it wouldn't do to let it go.

"And there's no existing cave system that goes deep enough?" she pressed. "No mine or construction area?"

"Not as far as I know. Nothing of much value to dig for around here." Lydia picked up the bracelet and handed it back to Cal. "Except for wherever these came from, maybe."

Cal slipped the bracelet back onto her wrist. Perhaps it was time to make another visit to the jewelry cart.

"I'll look into it. Thank you." She checked the clasp, then stood and looked at the map one more time, growing wistful. Hardly any of her colleagues were so excited about spirit energy theories—and that was even after taking James out of the equation.

"Are you sure you don't want to come work in Vornik?" she asked hopefully. Lydia laughed.

"Appreciate it, but I've got my own problems to sort out here." She reached behind a stack of books and pulled out a note, its calligraphy posh and immaculate. "Besides, that would mean attending more of your colleague's garden parties. Did he invite you, too?"

Cal grimaced. "I haven't been so lucky yet."

"Come with me, then." Lydia brightened. "I'll have a few associates of my own in attendance, and I'd love for you to meet them. If you're not too busy, that is."

Cal tried not to recoil. A garden party hosted by James sounded as thrilling as a library without books—but if Lydia's associates were anything like her, it would be worth the mild torture to meet them.

"Not too busy at all," she said. "I look forward to it."

CHAPTER TEN

EMRY

The morning of his first rehearsal, Emry found himself working up a headache over two lists: one with his plans to court Cal, and one with a set of potential songs for the upcoming concert.

Thanks to Marley's advice, his courtship plans were fairly straightforward. Promenading, more flowers, attending another ball and dancing with her twice (no more, no less, of course)...

The set list, though, proved to be more difficult. He wasn't sure if Karlson would even let him pick any of the songs, much less approve of the ones he had written down. There was so much to consider: Karlson's style, his own preferences, what their opener would perform. Even the atmosphere of the venue itself, the luxurious Trellis, had to play a part...

As he rubbed a growing ache in his temple, a curious shadow fell over the paper.

"Will I know any of these songs?" Aspen asked, looking over his shoulder.

"Some," Emry said. "But even if you don't, I'll teach them to you so you can sing along."

"All right." Aspen wandered off and began fiddling with a teapot in the corner, obscured behind Emry's near-daily shipment of bouquets and gifts. He leaned back in his chair and frowned.

"You do still want to sing, right?"

"Of course." Aspen paused. "I just..."

"Yes?"

"Well, you have your lute, and the other folks have all their instruments." Aspen glanced into the teapot, then set the lid back on. "I wish I had something to do onstage, too. You don't need me to sing, not really."

"'Course we need you to sing." Emry gestured to the paper. "By rehearsal, I'll have a set list you're going to love. I promise."

But as the day wore on and the rehearsal approached, all Emry had to show for his effort was a paper riddled with crossed-out song titles and splotches of ink—an accurate representation of his nervous, unprepared self.

His growing anxiety traveled down to his joints, and he rubbed his knee. He was joking to Cal earlier, but perhaps he shouldn't have danced with her so late in the evening. Pain was the last thing he needed before rehearsal.

"Okay, I think I've got it," Aspen called from their corner. "Want to try it?"

They brought over a teacup filled with gray water. Emry tried very hard not to recoil. "Try what, exactly?"

"Moonflower tea," they said cheerfully. "If willow bark tea helps with the pain, why not moonflowers? Here, have some."

Emry stared at the cup. Dumped two teaspoons of sugar in it. A dollop of honey. One more teaspoon of sugar for safety.

Then took a sip and immediately spewed it out. "Hara drag me to *dust*—"

"Sorry, sorry!" Aspen grabbed the cup before more of the gray, sugar-sludged water could spill on the rug. "That recipe will, uh, need some tweaking."

An impatient knock sounded from the door. "Karic? You ready for rehearsal?"

"Aspen tried to kill me, Damir!" Emry called between coughs.

"I did *not*—"

Behind the door, Damir sighed.

ALAS, atrocious tea did not get Emry out of the rehearsal, and he half limped behind Damir to a private corner of the hotel's gardens. Walled off with hedges and tidy stone walls, the little patch of green afforded them an oasis in the middle of the city, complete with a flower-laden trellis, several chairs, and a table topped with pastries. They were the first ones to arrive; apart from the pastries, the garden was empty.

Aspen immediately went to inspect the trellis. Damir held up a hand. "Please don't anger the gardeners—"

"I'm only looking at it!" Aspen retorted, then added under their breath, "Angering the gardeners, indeed..."

Damir shook his head and turned to Emry. "Any progress on the spirit situation?"

"Some," Emry started. Cal had made progress in her conversation with Lydia, but he didn't exactly know how to phrase that a suspicious jewelry seller was their only lead so far. "I'll find you once we have something more concrete."

"So, it's not just a drought after all?"

"Afraid not."

Damir scowled at nothing—a habit of his as common as his pipe—then checked behind him to ensure the path was still empty.

"Tell me as soon as you have more," he said, "and be careful. All three of you."

Emry set his hand on his heart. "Is that a hint of care I detect?"

Damir rolled his eyes and strode off. "All right, I'm leaving you to the wolves now."

"Wolves?" Aspen looked up, but Damir had already escaped behind the hedge. Emry surveyed the empty garden. At least this place hadn't been struck by the blight. Since it had no spirit in residence, it looked and felt perfectly normal. Flowers in full bloom, verdant grass, bright sunshine. Not a bad place to make a good first impression, he supposed.

Just as he had grown somewhat comfortable in the space, the troupe began to arrive.

"Mr. Karic?" A vaguely familiar woman popped up at the garden arch and gasped. "So, it *is* you!"

She rushed in, a flurry of pastel skirts with matching ribbons trailing in her wavy blonde hair. Emry might have mistaken her for another young season attendee on her way to tea if it weren't for the hurdy-gurdy tucked under her arm.

"Please, call me Emry." He stepped forward and held out his hand. The woman shook it with a ferocity that nearly snapped his arm in two.

"Goodness, it's an honor!" she said, her freckled smile brightening her blue eyes. "I've heard all about you. I was thrilled to hear you'd be joining us for our Trellis concert—we haven't had any fresh faces in so long. And Aspen, of course!" She leapt over to the spirit, shook their hand, then set her hurdy-gurdy aside to properly take in the garden. "Oh, isn't this beautiful?"

Her skirts swirled about her as she spun to absorb all of it, paying special attention to the improved trellis, its flowers blooming tenfold. Aspen didn't bother hiding how pleased they were about the admiration—a trail of proud little buttercups grew in her wake.

"I'm sorry, um"—Emry cleared his throat—"what did you say your name was, again?"

"Oh!" The woman poked her head out from around the trellis. "Sage, if you please."

His memory clicked into place—he had seen her onstage with

Karlson years ago. She had sung right alongside him, her energy as vibrant and infectious as it was now. But before he could voice any such compliment, Sage plopped down on a chair and pulled a sky-blue notebook out of her pocket, her words whipping into a blur.

"I thought a lot about the concert on the way down here," she said. "I already have a rough idea of what sort of set list you might like."

Emry blinked. "You do?"

"Yes, of course." She didn't look up from her notebook. "I had plenty of time to ask around, and I'm familiar with Senne's traditional style."

Emry still hadn't quite caught up. "That's—that's impressive—"

"But I must know one thing." Sage snapped the notebook shut, and her eyes went wide once more. "Was Ella's song true? Did you really get possessed by a spirit in Dawnstone?"

"Oh." Emry glanced at Aspen, who now sat on top of the trellis. He should have guessed the questions wouldn't stop once he left Vornik. "Well, yes, but it's more complicated than—"

"So, I'm thinking fireworks," another voice interrupted.

All three of them turned to the figure slouching under the archway: a short woman, holding a drum and rubbing her tired, eyeshadow-smudged eyes.

"Fireworks?" Aspen repeated. The newcomer sauntered into the garden, pushing her mussed, choppy hair out of her face. Eschewing Matlock's colorful fashions, she wore a waistcoat in a deep black that Damir would have been proud of, with no coat to hide her rolled-up sleeves.

Emry was glad she held her instrument to identify her. When he had last seen Karlson perform, the drummer had been so hidden behind such an odd stack of drums that he never got a good look at her.

"Fireworks for our concert," the drummer explained, her voice heavy with morning crackle. "Go big or go to the bar, am I right?" She set her drum down with a thump.

"Is that how the phrase goes?" Aspen asked. Emry shook his head.

The woman flopped into the chair next to the pastries, and Sage's expression set into a shadowy glare.

"I don't need fireworks to impress, Riley," she said primly, taking the opposite chair and dragging it away from her.

Riley scoffed and poured herself a cup of tea. "Could've fooled me," she muttered, then held out her hand to Emry and Aspen. "Welcome to your debut. How many events has Damir thrown you into so far?"

Emry shook her callused hand. "Only a hundred."

"He's been slacking, then. Just wait until he starts dragging you to the theater." She shook Aspen's hand, then squinted at them for a thoughtful second. "Wait. You're the one Ella sang about, right?"

Before Aspen could respond, four other musicians filed in, most of them half as sleepy as Riley but half as talkative as Sage. They greeted Emry in a more normal fashion—polite nods, handshakes, no questions of spirit possession—then began to take their seats. Off to the side, two people built Riley's unusual set of drums while she sat in the middle, directing and adjusting the instruments until she was half-concealed behind the display. She twirled her drumsticks, rolled through each drum in turn, and grinned.

Off to the other side, Sage needed no such preparation. She remained by the pastries, chatting rapidly with the other two musicians. Each troupe member had quietly selected one side to sit on—Sage's or Riley's. As the chatter fell into a lull, both women looked at Emry expectantly.

He remained next to Aspen and hoped he wasn't already ruining his standing with the two of them.

"Good morning, good morning." Karlson finally swung in, his informal, loping nature an immediate relief for Emry. Every musician, no matter what side they sat on, immediately locked their focus on him.

"Everyone ready?" he continued, pouring himself some tea. Tired cheers and whoops rose from his troupe, and he chuckled. "Good gods. We go onstage like this, and the audience is going to fall asleep with us." He caught sight of Emry and gestured to him. "You've all met our guests for the season, yes? Mr. Karic and Aspen…"

"Karic," Aspen added.

"The Karics." Karlson nodded. "Quite pleased to have you. We're sure you'll fit right in."

The words were encouraging, but Emry took in the staunchly divided group and doubted that very much.

After tea and pastries were passed around, Karlson lounged on a seat by the trellis, his voice filling the garden with ease. "All right. We all know the nobility of the season won't let us get away with something so ghastly as reusing a set list." Light laughter from the troupe. "Who has thoughts on the first song?"

"'Crow's Roost.'" Riley rubbed her hands together, dark eyes glittering. "We all agree on that, yeah?"

Emry brightened—that song had been on his own list—but Sage recoiled instantly. "Absolutely not."

Riley gave her a flat look. "Why not?"

"Because the Forsgren Quartet started their first set with that song last week," Sage said. "We can't just copy them. In my opinion"—her eyes sparked here—"we start with 'The Sunlight Reel.'"

Riley slouched. "What, and bore everyone to tears?"

They continued bickering, tossing out song titles and trampling on the other's choices. Emry glanced at Karlson, but the troupe leader leaned back and smiled, letting them go on for a moment.

Then he turned to Emry. "Mr. Karic, what do you think?"

Everyone looked at him. Emry straightened.

"I'm sorry, sir?"

"Our first song. What do you think it should be?"

Internally, Emry screamed in excitement. It was real, it was happening, he was actually picking songs for a concert with Karlson—

Externally, he took a breath and responded casually.

"'Before I Leave,'" he said. "Its energy is similar to 'Crow's Roost,' but stylistically, it's closer to your signature. And as far as I know, the only troupe that regularly plays it is Stella's—and they usually perform the Vornik season, not the Matlock one."

A heavy pause. Then Karlson gave a hum and turned to the rest of the troupe.

"'Before I Leave'? How about it?" he asked, eliciting murmurs of agreement in response. Sage lit up.

"Oh, I do like that one."

Next to her, Riley gave a slow, approving nod. "Would go well with fireworks."

"You don't set off fireworks at the beginning of a show, Riley."

The conversation moved on, and as Emry's heart burst with happiness, a light breeze ruffled his hair. He looked up at the trellis; Aspen grinned and gave him a thumbs-up.

Rehearsal continued with no further quizzes and only mild bickering once Sage pulled out her hurdy-gurdy—

"What?" Sage glared at Riley.

"Nothing." Riley snort-laughed into her tea. "It's just—it's a *hurdy-gurdy*—"

"I'd like to see you sing and play one of these at the same time."

"Please, like I need to overcompensate for anything."

"You mean your six drums aren't compensating for anything?"

—And eventually, they got around to playing actual music.

Rehearsing here was a refreshing twist on seeing Karlson's troupe onstage. Their energy softened and relaxed, taking a cue from their leader's mood. The fact that Emry was playing alongside *Karlson* still baffled him, of course, but once he grew accustomed to that, he found Sage and Riley to be just as impressive. It was little wonder they had garnered the backing of the others in the troupe. Sage's voice aligned perfectly with Karlson's in a familiar sort of roughness that sank into his bones. And Riley—well, he had never seen anyone with such mastery over so many drums before. Her instruments may have well been extensions of herself for how gracefully she moved between them.

Such expertise should have intimidated Emry, but instead, he found it easier to play along with them like this. It felt more like rehearsing with friends than with stuffy musicians, particularly once the sun warmed the garden. And once Aspen picked up on the songs, they began to sing along, happily adding to the sound like a soft breeze. After one such song, Emry looked down by his chair and gave a small laugh—several tiny buttercups had sprouted in the grass around him. Aspen must be enjoying themselves, indeed.

At the end of the set, Karlson gave a pleased hum and jotted something down on a scrap of paper by his teacup. He seemed to hum often, whether in approval, thought, or simply humming half a melody here and there.

"I'd like to switch 'Sunset Jig' and the 'Maiden and the Tree,'" he said. "Can't have such a drop in energy close to the end of the concert, can we?" He looked up to the troupe for approval—another thing he did frequently. "Any nays?"

Riley chomped into a pastry. "No nays."

"All right, then." Karlson waved at the troupe. "Off with you all to a short break. And no wandering to the pub—if you must, day-drink the hotel's wine like a responsible socialite."

The troupe didn't spread far, mostly gathering to squabble around the last of the snacks. But to Emry's delight, they were as easy to talk to as they were to play with. Soon, he found himself in a small circle with Sage and a fiddler by the trellis, chatting over half a strawberry pastry they had wrested away from the cellist.

"So," the fiddler said to Emry, "are you actually from Dawnstone?"

"Senne, actually."

"Did you play there often?" Sage asked eagerly. "When we were last there, we played at the Boat and Oar, that lovely little tavern off..." She snapped her fingers. "Oh, what was that street..."

"High Vine, and yes." Emry grinned. "Loved playing there. When were you last in the city? My sisters might've seen you, if—"

"Emry?" Aspen's voice warbled above him. Emry looked up; Aspen gripped the trellis with both hands, their form soft and hazy. "I don't feel well."

Emry's hands went cold, and he set down his lute. "How can I help?"

But Aspen ignored the question. "The other spirit doesn't feel well, either."

Then Emry saw it—a trail of scarlet flowers growing within the trellis vines, their petals already furling. "How did she find you all the way over here—?"

Aspen fell backward through the trellis, their form slipping straight through the wood beams. Emry leapt to catch them, but they fell right through his arms, too, leaving only their lute in his hands. "Aspen!"

He set the lute on the grass beside the spirit's flickering form and knelt down, trying his question again. "What can I do?"

"I—I don't know—"

All around him, Sage and the others gathered in confusion.

"Are they all right?"

"What's happening?"

Emry ignored them as Aspen's form briefly disappeared and the flowers in the lute began to curl. "Your lute isn't enough right now, is it? Why don't you...?" He looked around him for a solution. Would the trellis provide them with enough energy? The hedges? No, they needed more than that—

"Stick with me until it's over." He held out his hand. Aspen shook their head furiously.

"It'll hurt you."

"I'm not the one winking out of existence right now!" Emry fearfully gestured again with his hand. "Just for a few seconds!"

Aspen flickered, gasped, and grabbed Emry's hand.

This time, the darkness that preceded the possession was

short-lived—a long blink, and then his senses were back, Aspen far too weak to control them. He staggered to his feet, clutching Aspen's lute with both hands. Through the spirit, he could feel the deadly pull of the blight, trying to claw at their energy in its last throes.

"Hold on," he said, his voice echoing like a bell as he worked to push the feeling away. Whatever that rotting thing was wasn't going to hurt Aspen, not today—

Then the blight crumpled. It tugged once more, then disappeared in defeat, leaving him light and weightless in its absence.

Aspen—?

He didn't even need to ask. The spirit tumbled back into their lute, which fell out of Emry's hands and onto the ground in a discordant jangle. Emry leaned against the trellis in both relief and dread, one hand on his heart. The possession pain would come soon—it was only a matter of time...

A familiar orange flower grew at his feet.

"Thank you," he murmured and yanked the healing flower out of the grass. As he straightened and lifted it to his lips, he looked ahead of him and froze.

Karlson and his entire troupe were staring at him, slack-jawed.

"Um." He quickly lowered the flower. "Bit of a, uh—a brief spirit illness, you see. But...Aspen's fine now. Aren't you, Aspen?"

He gestured to the lute on the ground, which rocked in agreement. "Oh yes, just fine!"

"Your eyes glowed." Sage hadn't blinked in a full minute. "Your eyes glowed, and your...your *voice*—"

"Ah." Emry had forgotten about the rather unsettling side effects. "Apologies."

"Apologies?" Riley repeated in disbelief. "Are you *kidding* me? That was incredible!" She threw her arms in the air. "They just—jumped in and out of you! I *knew* the Dawnstone stories were true!"

The entire troupe began to gossip at that, loud rumblings filling the garden. As their talk grew, so did a panicked fear in Emry's chest.

What had he done? If they spread the word of the spirit illness, if anyone connected it back to the groves in the city—

Then Karlson held up a hand, and the garden went silent.

"No one will breathe a word to anyone of this," he said, his serious tone a shock of cold water in the warm sun. "Do you understand?"

"But—!" Riley gestured to Emry. Karlson glared at her until she relented. "Understood."

Then Karlson turned on his heel and placed a hand on Emry's shoulder, his tone softening instantly. "I apologize," he murmured. "Damir and I should have anticipated that whatever's affecting the spirits here would impact Aspen as well. You both should go rest, and I'll contact Ms. Breslin—"

"No," Emry cut him off, his panic rising at the mention of Cal. Karlson's eyebrows rose.

"I mean," he fumbled, "I don't want her to worry. I'll—I'll tell her myself once Aspen has rested."

He swallowed. He never thought he would find himself lying to someone like Karlson, but then again, he never thought he would be possessed by a spirit during rehearsal, either.

"All right," Karlson said, dropping his hand, "but I still insist you both take some time. You did well today. I have no doubt you'll do wonderfully onstage."

Between his lingering anxiety and melting fear, Emry was going to need at least three days to properly process that compliment.

CHAPTER ELEVEN

CAL

THE PEEK OF THE SEASON

Many of you have inquired as to the best gardens in the city for picnics and promenades. Of course, every citizen of Matlock has their own favorite, and I am no different—but for those of you traveling in from Vornik and beyond, I will endeavor to be objective in my guidance...

And no list would be complete without mentioning the Melibea garden near the Oakvale Grand Hotel. While not the largest garden, it provides some of the best views the city has to offer, and is particularly lush year-round. As such, its spirit is quite beloved, and I will always recommend that visitors leave a coin in its fane in thanks.

"We have to get them out of the city."

"Cal, that's impossible."

"Well, I'm not going to let them stay and *die* here."

Emry and Cal walked together to the spirit garden, whispering their argument and keeping a careful distance from Aspen up ahead. Cal watched their movements carefully. They looked the same as yesterday—solid enough, if somewhat transparent—but Emry's report of what had happened during rehearsal yesterday made her hold his arm a little tighter.

"You said they disappeared," she said. "How long did it last?"

"The disappearance? Only a second. Then after a few minutes, they were all right."

Cal frowned. "And that was all? They just needed to wait it out?"

"That was all." Emry nodded, his gait stiff. Rehearsal had been more tiring than expected, he had said. It was nothing to worry about.

So, Cal tried to focus her worries on Aspen instead.

"I know they won't like it, but I can't let them stay here while the blight continues," she said. "Perhaps they could stay outside the city and travel in?"

"And abandon the one spirit who's talking to them?" Emry gestured ahead; Aspen was now running into the garden, the ivy brightening as they passed it. "That isn't going to happen. I don't like it any more than you do, but there's no getting Aspen out of here. Not now."

Given the green grass around the garden's entrance, Cal had hoped against all odds that the spirit within was in better shape today—but the ensuing crunch of dryness under her feet told her otherwise. Indeed, the entrance seemed to be the only part that thrived. The rest made Cal's throat dry just to look at—dead grass, dusty soil, shriveled roses that should have been at their peak...

Ahead of her, Aspen sat under the largest tree and closed their eyes. As soon as they took their place, tiny red rhythm blooms grew all around them, and Aspen's fingers tapped excitedly on their knees.

"She's all right," they said, relief buoying their voice. "A bit weaker, but she's still there, and so are the others."

Cal sat on a bench close to Aspen. "The others?" she repeated, pulling out her notebook. "They're talking to each other?"

Aspen scrunched their nose. "Sort of. There's another spirit down the street, and one on the lower tier..."

As they pointed and spoke, Cal jotted down a rough sketch of the spirit's locations—a slowly growing network of beings all throughout the surrounding gardens. Not just existing now, but talking. She'd have to get these findings to Lydia before any of these poor spirits disappeared.

"We need to find the jewelry seller quickly," she murmured to Emry. "If Lydia's theory from the other day is right, we could sort out where they're getting the crystals, then check the health of the well ourselves. If there is one, of course," she added, professional embarrassment setting in. "I promise I don't normally pursue such untested theories. If Ms. Novak finds out I've been chasing something that doesn't exist..."

"You reckless scientist, you." Emry laughed softly, then squeezed her hand. "It'll be all right. We'll look for the jewelry cart today to start—"

Scraps of a melody interrupted them: Aspen, humming part of a song, then stopping and trying a different one.

"I'm trying to explain my lute to her," they finally said. Beside them, the flowers planted inside the lute had changed—they were now red, like so many of the blooms in the garden. Though Cal was tempted to drag them all out of the garden and hunt down the jewelry cart right away, she forced herself to stay on the bench for a moment longer. Aspen deserved this time with the spirit, after all.

"And how is it going?" she asked. Aspen paused, then looked up at her.

"How do you explain music?"

She blinked. "I—I don't think I'm qualified to answer that." She turned to Emry, who raised his hands.

"If *you* can't, then I certainly—"

"Emry, you're a bard."

"I am but a simple man with a lute."

Cal gave him a look. "Who is in a Guild. For *music*."

"All right, all right, um..." Emry stood up, ran a hand through his curls, and stepped up to the tree, looking around for inspiration. His gaze settled on a bird fountain, where several pigeons tottered and splashed. They bobbed their heads in the leaf-dappled water, getting droplets all over themselves and their friends.

"It's play," he said, then turned back to the tree. "Playing with sound."

Aspen fell silent as they translated. "What do you do with the sound?"

"Anything." Emry shrugged. "Everything."

Another pause. "She wants to see it."

"Oh. Well—it's not visible, exactly, and I don't have my lute on me, but..." He glanced at the garden's patrons. "I suppose I could sing a little. Aspen, can I hold your lute?"

Aspen handed it over with a frown. "But it doesn't work."

"That's fine," Emry said, slinging the strap over his shoulder. "Doesn't feel right to sing before a tree without holding one." He cleared his throat. "Any requests?"

Cal smiled; she hadn't expected to hear Emry sing today. As often as he hummed and sang to himself through the day, an actual performance like this was a treat. "What about one you'll be performing with Karlson?"

Emry grinned. "Someone wants a sneak peek. Very well." He rolled his shoulders and turned back to the tree. "This is a bit of 'Before I Leave.' Hope you like it."

Cal sat up straight. She had heard the song back in Tazlo and wasn't surprised to learn that Karlson was going to perform it. It was perfectly in sync with his style, and Emry's, too—upbeat, exciting, both alluring and down-to-earth. Emry's soloist version couldn't capture the energy of a full troupe, of course, but as he sang and tapped against the lute to accompany himself, his version still compelled her to tap along on the bench.

> *I know the road is calling me back home*
>   *It says I must be on my way*
>   *But before I leave, I want to believe*
>   *That your heart is begging me to stay*
>
> *So, tell me now*
>   *'Fore the road drags me down*
>   *That in your pulse you hear a vow*
>   *That you love this runaway*
>   *Say it out loud and I'll stay*
>   *Oh, please, 'fore the road drags me down*

The other gardens' visitors perked up at the song, and some of them wandered closer, a hum on their lips—but before Emry could draw too much of a crowd, he stopped, letting the song fade into the branches above. Aspen hopped to their feet, brushing dirt off their knees.

"She loved it," they said. "Thank you."

Emry gave a small bow in response, then held out a hand to Cal. "Now, if it's all the same to the spirit, I believe Ms. Breslin has a quest for us," he said. "Time to find the jeweler—?"

But then the song he had just sang echoed above them in a stuttering chirp. A few notes, then a stop and a start, as if a bird were trying to recall the melody. Cal looked up at the branches of the tree.

"Is that—?"

A pigeon swooped down and landed on Aspen's shoulder.

Seeing them side by side, Cal realized how much she took for granted Aspen's ability to shape-shift so perfectly. Next to Aspen, the city spirit looked strangely misshapen. Her wings were too large, her feet too long, her edges rising and falling like smoke. And in place of the typical green of a pigeon's neck, she bore a tiny sunset of iridescent orange and red.

But none of that bothered Aspen—they gazed at the bird in wonder, a smile spreading across their face. "My friend," they said softly.

Cal leaned forward to get a closer look. "A pigeon?"

The bird cooed at her.

"She says thank you for the music," Aspen said. "She's going to tell the others about it, too."

Emry nudged them. "She should come to our concert with Karlson, if she wants to see something a little more sophisticated."

"She'd like that," Aspen said. "She liked that name, too. Pigeon."

"Really?" Cal held out her hand. After a few clumsy flaps of her wings, Pigeon landed on it, her claws feeling more like feathers against Cal's skin. She watched the spirit in fascination. No one else in the garden knew that the spirit they were praying to, donating to, honoring, sat in her hand right now, cooing scraps of a drinking song.

"Pigeon," she said, then bowed her head. "It's an honor to meet you."

ONCE PIGEON RETREATED BACK into her tree, Aspen left the garden with renewed energy.

"I wish I could feel the spirit well," they said, their eyes scanning the road for any sign of the seller. "It must be very deep down. Do you think it's really as big as Lydia said it was?"

But they were off before Cal could respond, dashing around corners and running up ramps in search of the jewelry cart. Cal sighed and followed. How eager they were to dart about a city poised to kill them. Emry was right—there would be no getting them out of danger now. She'd just have to work faster.

To their brief frustration, the seller wasn't near Pigeon's garden that day, nor was he at the gardens a level above. Right when Cal was about to suggest they ascend to another street, they found him: a man in discreetly shabby clothing, with a discreetly shabby wagon, selling very sparkly wares. He had done his best to hide his scruffy nature with shiny new buttons, bolts of cloth over the display, and hasty repairs, but a ten-second analysis on Cal's part betrayed him. His hems were frayed, his suit several years out of date, the back of his wagon sun-worn and splintered. The shiny exterior was truly all the man had—but fortunately for him, it seemed to be working well.

"Spirit talismans!" he called. "Limited edition pieces! Bring them to the garden while you pray and fill them with the spirit's blessing!"

As they watched from a distance, a customer bought a necklace and hurried into the nearest garden. Aspen huffed.

"I'll go ask him where he got them," they said, but Cal set a hand on their shoulder.

"Let's not spook him yet," she said quietly. The seller had picked a good spot for business today. The cart buzzed with people, all rich enough to afford the jewelry but not snobby enough to be above buying it. And the plaza itself bore the weight of the lunch rush—families clustered around food wagons; couples strolled about; a man in a top hat loitered by a streetlamp...

Cal bit her lip. Given the highly public space, getting the right information from this seller would take a more subtle hand.

"I'll take a look at the jewelry," she said. "Aspen, you take a look at the wagon."

"And me?" Emry whispered.

"Well, I need someone to beg for pin money, don't I?" She looped her arm around his elbow. "Just look handsome and stay by my side."

Emry feigned a sigh. "You ask too much of me."

They approached at a strolling pace, Aspen making sure their cloak covered their lute. The man's eyes lit up as soon as he saw Emry—a wise man to not forget a customer's face.

"Back for more, are you?" he said eagerly, gesturing to the larger and more expensive pieces on display. "Is the lady enjoying the bracelet?"

"Oh, very much." Cal held out her wrist. "I've been boasting about it to all my friends at tea."

Thanks to Aspen's proximity, the bracelet sparkled just as strongly as it had the day she bought it. The seller quickly masked his look of surprise.

"You must be particularly blessed, for the energy to remain so strong," he said. Aspen snorted; Emry bit back a laugh.

"Now, now, my dear, I'm afraid I can't buy the whole cart for you," he said loftily. Cal bent to inspect the display.

"Oh, but if I could pick just one thing?" She plucked a brooch from the display, then an earring. It was as she expected—each piece had been hastily made, like the bracelet. Poor settings, cheap glue to hold the stone in place, the shapes only vaguely imitating the fashions of the day. The crystals themselves also seemed irregularly cut —as if they had been clumsily shaved off larger pieces.

As Cal placed the earring back on the faded velvet cushion, she wondered at the haste in which these pieces were being crafted.

"Where did you find these crystals?" she asked. "They must be so rare."

"Rare, indeed." The seller leaned forward. "They must be mined during a full moon, then placed at the precise center of the garden so the spirit can imbue it with its blessing. Each one's a treasure in its own right, and is sure to disappear soon."

Judging by the amount of traffic the cart was getting, Cal didn't doubt that last part—but she wasn't about to get an honest answer from him this way. When the seller went to attend to other customers, Aspen leaned closer to her and lowered their voice to an impatient whisper.

"I can get the answers from him," they said, their fingernails unconsciously sharpening into wolf claws. Cal set a firm hand on their wrist.

"Not with so many people around," she whispered back, then looked to Emry. "Could you be a distraction?"

Emry blinked. "How?"

Cal assessed the crowd; these customers weren't the high-society folks who had crowded Emry at the opening ball, but they *were* the enthusiastic target of Matlock's many gossip rags. It was more than likely they had at least heard of Emry. "Do you have your Guild pin?"

His look flattened. "Oh, come on—"

"Please?"

He rolled his eyes and fastened his Guild pin to his coat lapel, ensuring it was visible. Cal cleared her throat and angled herself toward the other customers. "Mr. Karic," she said loudly, "please tell me when your concert with Karlson is again?"

As she had hoped, this flagrant name-dropping turned a few heads.

"Next week," Emry responded just as loudly. "At the Trellis. And I know you want to hear what we'll be playing, but I simply cannot tell you."

"Pardon me." One older woman approached cautiously. "But are you...*the* Mr. Karic of the Auric Guild?"

And that was that. As Emry fielded a growing number of admirers and questions, he edged away from the cart, drawing everyone's eyes away from Cal, Aspen, and the seller. The seller didn't immediately realize what was happening; at the mention of a Guild member so near his cart, he had coins practically floating in his gaze.

"Is that really—?" he began, pointing at Emry. But Cal didn't have time to entertain him. She leaned forward, adding a darker edge to her voice.

"Yes, and he'll buy another of your foolish pieces if you tell me precisely where these crystals came from."

The seller's excitement evaporated into unease. "Miss, I'm not at liberty to say—"

Aspen set a clawed hand on the cart, sharp thorns curling around both their fingers and the jewelry. Cal's gaze narrowed.

"Then liberate yourself."

The seller stared at the thorns. "Follow me," he warbled. "I have some, ah, pieces to show you in the back."

Cal followed him to the back of the wagon, and Aspen shifted into a wolf, their fur pressing against her side in a silent promise of protection. Cal patted the top of their flickering head in gratitude.

But the seller wasn't used to such shape-shifting—once in the back, he turned and immediately shrieked at the sight of the wolf.

"What the—?"

Emry raised his voice to cover the shriek. "Yes, I *have* been rehearsing with Karlson. His talent absolutely astounds. I'm so very honored to perform alongside him—"

"We don't have time," Cal snapped at the jewelry seller. "Tell us where you found the crystals."

He held up his hands, his fear truncating his words and dissolving his bright customer-service accent. "Look, I don't know where exactly these things come from," he said. "This man approached me with a bag of 'em a few months ago, more than I've ever seen in my life. Said he smuggled 'em from a dig down south and could get more, so long as I gave him a cut."

"North," Aspen corrected, sniffing around the cart and pawing at pine needles around the wheels. "Not south. Something in here smells like the wayhouse we stopped at."

"That's a spirit." The seller's body went rigid. "Gods, where did you find a *spirit*—?"

"Doesn't matter," Aspen growled. "Now, who and where is this man you've been talking to?"

He swallowed. "I never got his name, and I don't know where he lives. They keep a tight leash on the dig workers, making 'em live close by and be all secretive-like."

"When will you meet him next?"

The seller looked at his supply in the back of the cart—a vanishingly small number of boxes and bags. He slumped. "See, that's the thing," he said. "I wasn't exactly lying when I said these were limited-edition pieces. I was supposed to meet him yesterday, but he never showed. If he doesn't show again, I'll have nothing to sell." He fidgeted. "You don't think they caught him, do you?"

Emry's voice floated in again from the plaza, edged with urgency. "Yes, thank you, I *so* look forward to seeing you at the concert..."

Cal checked around the cart. People were starting to wander back, searching for the jewelry seller.

"Thank you for the information," she said curtly, then set her hand on Aspen's ruff, her fingers sinking into several inches of fur. "Let's go, dearest."

The seller leaned forward hopefully. "So, will you be buying something now that I told you what I know, or—?"

"Absolutely not."

Aspen shifted into their human form and strode purposefully away from the cart with Cal, picking up a relieved Emry on their way out.

"Thank the gods," he said. "One of them almost wrangled me into dedicating a song to them. What did you find out?"

Cal opened her mouth, but the hairs on the back of her neck prickled, and as they turned down the road, she glanced over her shoulder. The man in the top hat was walking behind them—not too close, but not too far either, carefully angling his hat to shade his face.

They walked a little farther, Cal guiding them to the left. The man veered left. To Emry's confusion, Cal ducked right. The man followed right.

Then a carriage rumbled by, and he made the mistake of looking up at it, briefly exposing his face to the sun.

"Mr. Whitlock?" Cal said in bewilderment. Ezekiel Whitlock, Dev's assistant, caught her gaze in horror—then veered away, ducking into the closest side street.

"Mr. Whitlock! Why are you—?" she tried again, working to keep track of him through the crowd—but Emry caught her arm and jarred her attention.

"Who was that?" he asked.

Cal blinked, and Zeke was gone, vanished into the shadows. She gripped Emry's arm and turned back around. "Can we go elsewhere to talk, please?"

Emry immediately changed course, leading her down toward the river. "I've got an idea."

CHAPTER
TWELVE

EMRY

BY ALL ACCOUNTS, a river promenade was supposed to be a relaxing event.

The path Emry had chosen lay far away from both the docks and the wind bearing their fishy smell. It was clean, appropriately dotted with trees and benches, and—most importantly—highly visible to all who picnicked and lounged there. Visibility, according to Marley's notes, was of utmost importance in a promenade. If no one spotted them walking arm in arm, laughing at each other's jokes and leaning in close, what was the point?

At least, that had been Emry's hope as he had scoped out the path the other day. Now that they were using it as an escape route, the place bore no hint of romance.

"What do you mean Dev's assistant was trailing us?" Aspen asked.

"It could've been a coincidence," Cal murmured, her voice shaky, "but he followed our path on the way out, and he fled when he saw me—"

"Then let me bite his head off," Aspen said, cracking their knuckles. "I'm your chaperone. I'm supposed to protect you."

"That's not exactly what chaperoning means, Aspen."

For his part, Emry couldn't bring himself to admonish them.

"You know, we could do this the Karic way." He nudged the spirit. "You round up your siblings, you get some oars—not the good ones, or else your dad will kill you—"

Cal sighed. "No one is hitting anyone with an oar today."

Emry held up a finger. "You say that now, but swinging an oar is more fun than you think it is."

They continued walking, the path bringing them closer to the water's edge. Whether she realized it or not, Cal's pace had quickened, a consequence of her thoughts running faster, and Emry's knees could hardly keep up.

"Regardless of whatever Zeke may have been doing," she said, "I don't like this dig site the seller mentioned, either. Whatever it is, I can't imagine it's above board."

"Oh, not at all." Emry scoffed. "*Secretive-like* is not how I'd describe a fully legal operation."

"And if that's the case, getting access to it will be..."

"Fun?"

Cal looked at him. "*Fun* is not the word I'd use in this scenario."

She tried to maintain her brisk pace, but as Emry's gaze swept over the river, he slowed down. The water's muddy edges were particularly ragged today, strewn with leaves, sticks, and patches of brown water. And closer to their walkway, deep puddles soaked the grass.

Strange—it hadn't rained since they arrived in the city.

"Huh," he mumbled offhand. "Looks like the river flooded."

"Hm?"

He waved a hand. "A small one, I'd guess. Must have happened sometime yesterday." A humorless laugh escaped his lips. "Someone's probably going to blame Georgie for it again..."

Something in the mud flashed, and he ventured closer. Chips of sparkling rock lay embedded in the muck. He bent with a wince and carefully dug one out, expecting some sort of fool's gold or other common river rock—but the shard glittered from within, just like the crystals laid into Cal's bracelet.

He straightened and refocused his gaze on the mud. This wasn't an anomaly—similarly glittering pieces lay scattered up and down the water's edge, multiplying the more he searched for them. He checked the flow of the water, then looked north to the mountains. The silt deposits would have come from there, following the flow of the water...

He tensed and held the rock up to Cal.

"The flooding isn't from anything Georgie's doing," he said. "It's from the dig site."

Cal stopped in her tracks. "What do you mean?"

"It's likely not intentional." He rubbed dirt off the shard and turned it so she could see the light within. "But I've seen it before—improper tunneling around the river routes can lead to things like this. Damaged waterways, flooding, silt and rock deposits entering the rivers. Just like the seller said, someone's digging deep up north, sending these sorts of rocks into the water." He pointed to the mountains. "Georgie's letter was right—the flooding isn't her fault at all. She's just getting framed for whatever shoddy work they're doing at the illegal dig site."

Aspen folded their arms. "Georgie would let me bite someone's head off, you know."

"But if the dig site is causing damage like this..." Cal took the shard and turned it over in her hands. "What if it's causing damage to the spirit well, too?"

Aspen bristled. "Then we have to stop whoever's digging—"

"But we don't even know who it is." Cal rubbed the shard like a worry stone. "We don't even know *why* they're digging. Lydia said there's nothing of value to dig down to in this area."

"Except for the spirit well," Aspen said.

"If it exists," Cal corrected.

"If it exists."

Their eyes all fell on the crystal and the tiny white particles swirling elegantly within the stone.

"Cal," Emry said slowly, his thoughts going down a path he didn't like, "who do we know in the city who wants access to spirit energy? Who might also believe the well exists?" He met her gaze. "Who wants the energy badly enough to order a poorly run dig to the center of the earth?"

Cal's voice went taut. "Our dear friend Mr. Gray."

CHAPTER THIRTEEN

CAL

THE PEEK OF THE SEASON

Is there anything so satisfying as a riverside picnic? One can enjoy the spring air, reunite with family and friends, and—most importantly— observe the day's promenades.

Ms. Kolva and Mr. Thomas Albingdale have promenaded twice this month—an auspicious sight, to be sure. So have the Misses Golding and Wren. But this writer had the pleasure of observing several new couples out and about this week: Mr. Balmont and Mr. Sava, Mr. Karic and Ms. Breslin, Ms. Vichy and Mr. Fielding...

Cal hadn't exactly planned on bringing anyone else to suffer through James' garden party—but once Aspen learned that Dev might be there, they refused to stay behind.

"I'll be quick," they said from Emry's balcony, pacing along the stone railing in their bare feet, arms raised. "As soon as he gets there, I'll just turn into a wolf and tell him to stop the dig."

Cal tried not to have a heart attack at both their precarious pacing and their strategy. "We don't actually know if it's him," she reminded him. "We only need to find out if he's involved. If we openly accuse him and he's innocent, we'll get chased out of the city by all his admirers."

"If we get chased out of the city, does that mean I can skip a few of the luncheons Damir has planned for me?" Emry asked lightly from his corner of the balcony, lute in hand. Both Cal and Aspen shot him a look.

"I'm kidding, I'm kidding." He settled further into his chair, plucking out an aimless melody. "Just follow Cal's lead, and I'll bother Damir about my part at rehearsal today."

"How long do you think it might take him?" Cal asked.

"Knowing Damir?" Emry shrugged. "A few days."

Cal hummed and rested her elbows on the railing. Now that they were, well, digging into the dig site, she had discovered another wrinkle to all this, one that had kept her awake in thought last night after the promenade.

The money.

A dig, even a legal one, wasn't something one merely scrounged up a few coins for. The jewelry seller had mentioned workers, workers' lodgings, a dig lasting for months. Not to mention the implied equipment, travel, food...

No, if Dev were indeed the brains behind the expedition, someone else was fueling his work. Someone in Matlock with very deep pockets.

But it was the social season—such a description matched almost every person staying in their hotel.

"Damir knows everyone in the city," Emry continued, directing his reassurance to Aspen, who hadn't stopped pacing. "He'll be able to find out where the money's coming from."

He checked his pocket watch and stood.

"Now, both of you," he said, "please enjoy lightly accosting Dev in my absence while I'm at rehearsal. All I ask"—he held a finger up to Aspen—"is no biting."

Aspen's arms flopped at their sides. "Well, that just took all the fun out of it."

JAMES KNEW PRECISELY what he was doing when he had selected his cousin's estate for his garden party. While not as expansive as Halleson's mansion or as flashy as the Oakvale Grand Hotel, the estate's lawns communicated what they needed to. Long stretches of trimmed grass demonstrated just how much land his cousin owned, and delicately carved fountains and pristine hedges nodded to the bevy of artisans and gardeners they could afford. At first glance, the garden awed and captivated—ideal for a social season where attendees sought to associate themselves with luxury at all times.

But Cal stepped in with hesitation. The place radiated sterility. It had no benches to sit on, few trees to provide shade, hardly any space to relax or nap or read a book. It was all stiffness and distance—an object to be seen, admired, but never truly enjoyed.

Beside Cal, Aspen's fingers twitched.

"I could turn it all into moss," they whispered, eyeing the grass with disdain. "I could do it. Just give me a few minutes—"

"No." Cal firmly looped her arm around Aspen's. "Not right now, at least. I don't see Dev yet."

They wandered around in search of the scientist and found a bustle of activity instead. Ninepins on one lawn, croquet on the other. Tables of food and drink at every corner, their mouthwatering scents making up for the lack of flowers in the garden.

And all around, James' guests mingled, taking full advantage of the spread. So early in the season, most of them still had the energy to chat, play games, and socialize the afternoon away.

Cal grew weary just looking at them. She didn't need this—she needed a quiet day in an actual garden, not whatever hostile patch of grass this was. Ideally, with some wine, a book... Her imagination ran faster. Wine, a book, a box of chocolates—and Emry lounging beside her, of course, eyes closed in the sunlight—

James' voice shattered her peaceful reverie.

"Ah, Ms. Preston, how good to see you so soon after the luncheon!" He stood by the entrance, first clasping hands with a woman, then greeting the man behind her. "Mr. Lorne, I did promise you a rematch in ninepins, didn't I?"

He did this for all the guests who arrived—personalized greetings, as if he were dear friends with the whole city. Cal allowed herself a bit of silent fuming. While she had been studying spirit gardens and fruitlessly poring over Lydia's reports, James had been attending every tea, picnic, and ball the season had to offer—and, clearly, it was paying off.

"Come on." She tugged on Aspen's arm. "Let's go find Lydia, at the very least."

They dove deeper into the energetic mingling, pulled into conversations here and there as they went. Half of them were people who had met Aspen at the ball and now begged for another flower from them. The other half were eager to hear of Emry's impending concert, and if Cal had met Karlson yet. But beyond songs and bouquets, they had very little of value to say.

"So, do you grow flowers all day back in Vornik?" one woman asked, twirling a freshly grown lily between her fingers. Aspen frowned.

"Not really," they said. "Emry and I help Cal with her Council research. Mapping the spirits and getting them to talk to us."

The woman pinched her lips in disappointment. Beside her, her partner gave a light laugh.

"A bard assisting with Council research?" He sipped from his champagne. "Can't imagine he's very helpful. What, does he sing songs for them?"

Aspen's frown deepened into a glare. "As a matter of fact, he—"

"There you are, Ms. Breslin," a loud, positively angelic voice called behind Cal. "My colleagues and I have been looking all over for you."

"Hara be praised," Cal muttered, then turned a bright smile on her savior.

"Ms. Pietri." She gave a curtsy to Lydia, then nodded to the couple. "If you'll excuse us, please..."

She and Aspen hurried away with Lydia as quickly as was socially acceptable. "Thank you for that," she murmured, keeping a steady pace directly away from the insipid couple.

"Any time," Lydia said. "Though part of me wishes I hadn't jumped in so fast. Aspen looked like they were going to turn them inside out, and I would've liked to see it." She patted Cal on the arm. "Come on, I've got some more interesting people to introduce you to."

Lydia led her to the opposite corner of the lawn, where the more *interesting* people had formed their own isolated huddle, untouched by James or his ilk. The only visitors they had were the servants passing by with trays of canapés.

But when they saw Lydia approach with Cal and Aspen, their faces all brightened in welcome.

"Everyone," Lydia said, "this is Ms. Breslin and Aspen. The researchers from Vornik who've come to assist with our, ah, particularly pressing project." She gestured to the group. "Ms. Breslin, these fine folks are responsible for many of the garden reports I've been sending you."

The short, balding man in front hurried forth in delight. "Ms. Breslin, it is an absolute *honor*." He gave such a deep bow that Cal thought he might topple over.

"It's lovely to meet—" she tried, but he hadn't finished.

"I read the copies of your Council reports on the wave after it struck," he said. "Those patterns in the stories—and the spirit spreading the warning—" He looked to Aspen, his glasses magnifying his reverent gaze. "Was that you?"

Aspen beamed and held out their hand, tiny flowers growing along a vine around their cuff. "Technically, it was Cedar, but I did help a little."

This set the entire circle ablaze with chatter until Cal could hardly keep up with their questions and theories. Not that she minded—this sort of conversation was as refreshing as a spring breeze, and twice as special. They wanted to know everything about Cal and Aspen's research: their theories, their findings, if Pigeon or the other spirits had begun to speak...

And not once did any of them ask for Aspen to grow them a pretty flower.

"Oh, I'd love to talk to Pigeon one day," Ms. Preston said with a jealous sigh. She was a former astronomer turned spirit researcher, and her voice was as quiet as the stars. "Do you really have no spirits in Vornik proper? Are they all beyond the city limits?"

"There are a few in the outer gardens," Cal said, "but I've been visiting the nearby farms with Aspen to get a count of how many surround the city."

"And there's no such blight there?" Another associate lowered their voice and turned to Aspen. "*You* haven't been affected by it, have you?"

Aspen hesitated. "Well, sort of—"

The chatter rose into a concerned flurry.

"Well, that won't do." Ms. Preston nervously smoothed her skirts. "That won't do at all."

"Please allow us to help," Mr. Spencer urged. "If there's anything you need, any samples, any data, please let us know—"

Cal was both endeared and overwhelmed.

"I may...have a lead on the cause," she said carefully. "In the meantime, if you could continue tracking the state of the gardens, that would be immensely helpful. Aspen, Mr. Karic, and I will continue with our process."

A servant soon rounded the corner with more canapés, drawing a few members of the group away with bite-sized towers of tomato and goat cheese. While the others were distracted, Lydia nudged Cal with a wink. "Speaking of Mr. Karic—how is that *other* process going?"

Cal's cheeks warmed. That particular process, in her view, was going well. Emry had followed all the steps of courtship so far—wisely seeking advice from his sister Marley, if she had to guess—and they even had a date lined up.

Well, a hint of a date. As much as could be gotten away with during the season.

"I'm attending the theater with him this week," she said casually, trying to remain professional. Lydia grinned.

"A good step, a good step." She hummed. "Have you thought about what you'll be wearing?"

Cal paused. "Oh. Not exactly, no."

"Come on, even I know you're supposed to do that." Lydia stepped back and appraised her. "You're about the same size as my niece. Tell you what—I'll find you something so nice, he won't be able to speak when he looks at you."

The heat in Cal's cheeks spread to her ears. "That's very kind of you. I—"

"Cal?" Aspen tapped her on the shoulder, then pointedly shifted their gaze toward the entrance. Cal nodded to Lydia to excuse herself.

"One moment, please."

She let Aspen lead them over to a garden wall, partially shadowed by a large willow tree.

"What is it—?" she started, then stopped herself. A pair of voices were arguing beyond the wall, holding back from entering the garden party.

"We're almost there," Dev said, barely audible over the swishing of the willow branches. An unusual moment for him—his voice typically carried with little effort. "If we can just make it past this last hurdle and set up at the edge..."

"Should we talk to them?" Aspen mouthed. Cal shook her head and leaned closer to the wall.

"Of course, I can't solve these problems while I'm at these stupid events," Dev muttered, huffing and flipping through something that sounded like paper.

"The publicity will be important once you present your findings." This was Zeke's voice, maintaining a line of forced evenness.

"The publicity won't mean a rotting thing if I can't deliver," Dev snapped.

"You will deliver. I have full confidence." But Zeke's voice began to quaver. "Look, only a half hour here to make an appearance, then we'll be off. All right?"

A dramatic sigh. "All right."

They rounded the corner, Dev tucking a notebook into his pocket. But his suffering had only just begun—for James Edwards had caught sight of their arrival.

"Ah, Mr. Gray!" James hailed him, smiling wide. "Just the man I wanted to see."

He didn't bother hiding the opportunistic gleam in his eye, and Dev's posture immediately went rigid. Cal hurried out from under the willow, silently thanking James and his misplaced ambition.

He had set up the perfect opportunity for Dev to pick his poison.

"Mr. Gray." She approached the group, making sure her tone was far more smooth and unbothered than James'. "Good afternoon. How lovely to see you."

Dev regarded his two options—James' oily smile and Cal's not-quite-smiling eyes—and ducked toward Cal. Zeke immediately veered toward James as a consolation prize.

"Thank you so much for inviting us," he said to James, shaking his hand for longer than was necessary. "How efficient you were in planning all this before the season gets too busy..."

As Zeke bought them time, Cal and Aspen led Dev in the opposite direction.

"Aspen, it is a pleasure to see you again." Dev gave them a brusque nod. "I hear you'll be performing with Emry at the Trellis soon?"

A deft distraction, in theory—but Aspen kept their expression as tight as Cal's.

"Oh, yes," they said. "As long as I'm feeling well enough for it."

Dev swallowed, and so did Cal. She should have rehearsed a set of talking points with Aspen on the way here, if only to rein in their tongue.

"We are all looking forward to the concert, I can assure you." Cal shot Aspen a sharp look, then searched for something to occupy them—something to keep Dev there before he could escape to another social circle.

Her gaze landed on the ninepins laid out on the lawn.

"Mr. Gray, do join me in playing ninepins, will you?"

Judging by his flat gaze, there was nothing he'd rather do less.

"Oh, but—"

"Here, have a drink and come with me." She grabbed a glass from a passing server, shoved it into his hand, and tugged him toward the game.

Despite the diversion, she still didn't have long—Dev grew more fidgety as they lined up to play, his gaze hunting for someone else to talk to.

He was trapped and he knew it.

"How are you liking Matlock?" Aspen asked, stepping up to Dev's other side. Their nails and teeth were a normal human shape, but their humorless smile might as well have been as sharp as a wolf's.

"Very well, thank you," Dev said stiffly. "And you?"

Aspen's expression went taut. "A little dry for my taste."

Then it was their turn to play. Cal handed the ball to Dev first and let him step forward. Aspen threw her an impatient look.

"Let me think," she mouthed to the spirit, then tried to plan her next words carefully. She couldn't accuse Dev immediately, but she likely only had two, perhaps three questions before he found a polite way to escape. She had to time them right, phrase them perfectly—

Aspen cleared their throat. "So, how long have you been digging here?"

"Five months," Dev answered.

He froze as soon as the words escaped his lips, and his ball rolled to the far right of the pins. None of them made a move to retrieve it. Cal didn't even dare breathe.

Five months—only a little longer than Lydia's first reports of the blight.

"I—I mean..." Dev looked around wildly. "Mr. Edwards!" He hailed the man. "I believe you, ah, wanted to speak with me?"

Then he was off, burrowing straight into meaningless small talk to hide himself away. Cal turned to Aspen, her jaw slack. Aspen grinned and handed her the second ball.

"I believe it's your turn?"

∼

"So, he said it?" Emry leaned forward. "He actually said it?"

They sat in the garden Karlson used for rehearsals, huddled around an abandoned tea table with the crumbs of the day's pastries. The troupe had left no treats behind in their wake, which was a shame—the canapés at the garden party had been charming, but not very filling.

"He admitted to digging, thanks to Aspen," Cal said, silently willing the pastry flakes to regenerate into a tart. "But that was all."

"Isn't that all we need?" Aspen said from their spot on the trellis, ivy curling around them in victory.

Cal hesitated, gathering her thoughts as she watched the ivy grow. Aspen's straightforward method had worked in their favor once, but she couldn't depend on it again, not when it came to gathering irrefutable evidence.

"I need more precise proof before going to anyone else about this," she finally said. "Something that clearly shows his plans, something he can't just wave away as a misunderstanding."

Her thoughts wandered back to the notebook Dev had slipped into his pocket before entering the party. Surely that had something she could use. If she could get a small glimpse of a few of the pages—

"Ms. Breslin?"

A servant appeared in the garden, bearing a silver tray and a single envelope. "For you, ma'am," they said, lowering the tray. "An urgent missive."

"Thank you."

As the servant strode away, she took the envelope and flipped it over. There was no return address nor seal on the wax. Merely blank cream paper and an unmarked blob of crimson holding the message closed.

"Who's it from?" Aspen asked.

"I hardly know." Cal opened the letter, expecting paragraphs of text and only finding two simple lines in a thick, blotted hand:

Stop looking into this. Leave the city now.

CHAPTER FOURTEEN

EMRY

Rain doused the city overnight, refreshing a city already worn by the season's constant hustle and bustle. Even Emry could move easier that morning, his legs hardly bothering him as he watched the thick, gray clouds roll by. But he couldn't quite enjoy the pain-free morning nor the mist curling around the balcony—not when a threatening note sat on his girlfriend's dresser, burning a hole in his thoughts.

Once they had hurried back to her rooms, read the letter, and reread the letter, Cal had given a bitter laugh at the short missive. They were on the right track, at least. She had scared someone who deserved to be scared, and this was their sad attempt at chasing her off.

Emry found very little reassurance in the perspective.

So, in a churning mix of fear and grim satisfaction, he set off to meet the others in Pigeon's garden and discuss the latest threat to their party.

As expected, the garden lay empty, save for a layer of fog and Pigeon herself, who flew around Aspen's head the moment they walked in. Aspen smiled at them, but the gesture was weak, and the grass failed to turn green under their feet like it normally did.

Emry hoped it was only due to their mood and not their strength.

"How is Pigeon this morning?" Cal asked Aspen, taking a seat on the stone bench under the tree. Thanks to the branches above, it was the only dry space in the garden.

"The rain was nice." Aspen hopped over to the railing overlooking the rest of the city. All around their hands, little flowers in different colors burst forth on the ivy. Red for Pigeon, of course, but Emry also spotted yellow, purple, blue...

"Willow's feeling worse, though," Aspen said after a moment of silent communication. "Persimmon's wondering why no one's playing in the rain. Violet doesn't feel like talking because the city is quiet..."

Emry sat close beside Cal, instinctively checking every corner of the garden before turning back to Aspen. "So, they all have names now? That's impressive."

"Sort of." Aspen looked sheepish here. "I...may have picked them to keep them all straight."

"I love the names," Cal said, but like Aspen, her attempt at positivity broke upon execution. She kept folding and unfolding the corners of yesterday's letter in her hands, her eyes periodically darting to the garden gate. Emry took one of her hands and kissed it, trying to infuse the gesture with a semblance of comfort.

"It's all right. Damir will know what to do."

Cal huffed. "He's going to tell me to leave the city."

"And he'd be right, love."

"No." Her grip on the letter tightened. "I refuse to leave."

"Now who sounds like Aspen?"

"This is *different*."

Damir hunched through the garden gate, the mist settling over his unamused shoulders. In his customary black against the gray fog, Emry thought he caught a glimpse of the kind of wartime life Damir used to live, maneuvering between mystery and danger.

Not that their current lives had much less danger, these days.

"All right," he said, approaching them with an outstretched hand. "Let me see this letter of yours."

They all gathered under the tree, Pigeon hopping from branch to branch above them. Cal explained her encounter with Dev and handed Damir the letter to read. He paced as he read it, flipping the lid of his pocket watch open and closed at an increasing tempo.

"Damn." He flipped the paper over. "And no address? No seal on the wax?"

"None. But I'm almost certain it's from Dev."

Damir grunted and closed his pocket watch one more time. "You need to leave the city."

Emry raised his hands. Cal glared at both of them.

"I will *not*," she said. "I just need more proof of what he's doing."

"Can't we tell someone about Dev now?" Aspen tried. "We know he's digging somewhere—"

"But it's not just him," Damir cut in. "I've been asking around. Over a dozen people have met privately with Dev since he arrived, all of them with coffers deep enough to fund a dig. And whoever did end up throwing money at him"—he held up the letter—"is willing to condone threats, if not outright demand them. I will not have us throw around vague accusations, not when we don't yet know who we're up against."

"Have you looked into Halleson?" Cal asked. "He was the one talking with Dev at the ball."

Damir's gaze darkened. "Nearly everyone was talking with Dev at the ball, and *that* is not a name I can throw around lightly. We're lucky the very garden we stand in isn't named after him, and if he catches any of us looking into his affairs, it's more than likely our prison cell will be engraved with his family crest."

"Then what do you suggest?" Cal asked, her tone still simmering. Damir rubbed the spot between his eyebrows, then handed back the letter.

"Stop searching for a day or two," he said. "Whatever eyes are on you right now, let's get them away from you first. Go to the theater this week. Act like everything is normal. I'll inform Karlson so he can help look out for trouble, then I'll keep asking around."

Cal opened her mouth to argue, but Emry squeezed her hand. "Just for a day or two," he echoed pointedly.

Damir nodded. "Would you like for me to accompany you all to the theater?"

Aspen puffed their chest out. "I've got it."

"Good." Damir clapped a hand on their shoulder. "Not sure I can match up to an immortal wolf, anyway." He pointed at all of them. "Don't let each other go anywhere alone for a few days. Not until I have more information, all right?"

They huddled for a few more minutes, reviewing their schedules until Damir was satisfied that no one would be alone for a minute out of the day. Then Cal checked her own pocket watch and stood up.

"Thank you, Damir. It is rather silly, but I'm afraid I need to go and meet Lydia at the modiste—"

"Of course, of course." Damir gestured to Aspen. "Spirit guard, at the ready."

Aspen seamlessly shifted into wolf form and leaned against Cal's side. Emry squeezed her hand one last time.

"I'll see you later?"

Cal planted a quick kiss on his cheek. "Of course."

Then they were off into the mist, leaving Emry, Damir, and the occasional patter of rainwater dripping off the leaves.

"Modiste," Damir echoed Cal. "That's wise of her." A ghost of a smile crossed his face, and Emry frowned at him.

"What?"

He shrugged. "You already made the first few moves, didn't you?" He nodded out to the street. "Now it's her turn."

Several days later, Emry arrived at the theater early upon Damir's command, making his appearance for a private society event before the show. Given all he had to keep track of, he hardly knew who was hosting or what the gathering's purpose was—but at least he had the rest of Karlson's troupe with him, all chatting and glad-handing people to varying degrees of success. Karlson slipped through the crowded upper lobby with ease and grace, clearly an old friend to many here. Emry did his best, proud that he was finally beginning to recall names and faces from past functions. Mr. Merton, who loved to paint in his garden; Miss Boone, who was once a renowned pastry chef...

He was just waving goodbye to Mrs. Elton—who had seven daughters and a parrot—when he spotted troupemates Sage and Riley, standing several feet apart and shifting uncomfortably. This was no stage or rehearsal garden for them. They made no efforts to greet the gentry or even bicker with each other—they simply held their wineglasses and waited for the event to be over.

Taking pity on their state, Emry wandered over and slotted himself between the two of them.

"Surviving the evening?" he asked lightly.

Finally in the presence of a sympathetic face, Riley leaned against the wall and groaned. "Barely." She held her glass up to the light of the chandelier as if expecting to find bugs in it. "This wine tastes like mud."

"We're not here for the wine," Sage chided, though she herself fidgeted with the pleats of her blue dress. "We're here for the—you know." She nodded to the crowd. "The socializing."

"*Socializing.*" Riley snorted. "If I wanted to socialize, I'd get out of here and go down to the Dancing Rose. Have a good pint, listen to a troupe." She handed Emry her wineglass, already eyeing the exit. "And if the troupe's garbage, we can go up there and show 'em what's what ourselves, right, Emry? I'll borrow a drum, you can back me up with vocals—"

Sage shot her a look. "Don't drag him into this."

"He'll have fun!"

"He doesn't need to get in trouble, not before his debut."

Emry opened his mouth to comment on the fun and trouble being proposed—but both women ignored him.

"You *cannot* tell me you're having fun here," Riley said to Sage, who set her shoulders back in instinctual defiance.

"I'm having *so* much fun," she retorted. "See?" She beamed and waved to a passing couple, then took a large, pointed gulp of wine—

Her face scrunched up instantly in disgust, and she gulped with a shudder. Riley cackled.

"All right, fine," Sage snapped, handing her wineglass to Emry. Emry stared down at the two glasses in his hands. "I hate this as much as you do. But we can't get into any mischief—"

"We're not getting into mischief. We're getting into a good pub with a decent vintage, gods willing." Riley straightened her maroon waistcoat and grabbed Emry's arm. "Now, if we time this right, we can get out the door and down the street without anyone noticing."

Sage squinted at the lower lobby—then her eyes widened, and she grabbed his other arm. "He can't."

"Sage—"

"No, I really mean it." She whisked the glasses out of Emry's hands, shoved them at Riley, then began to fuss over Emry, fixing his collar and straightening his cravat. "Take a deep breath and prepare yourself."

Emry raised his hands, his nerves spiking. "What, what is it—?"

"Ms. Breslin." Karlson's smooth voice floated from the top of the stairs. "Enchanting, as always."

Before Emry could take a deep breath, Sage shoved him forward, and he found he was not at all prepared.

Cal floated with confidence on the elegant carpet, her feet hidden under the deep, velvety layers of her crimson dress. When she smiled and extended a gloved hand to Karlson, the pearlescent fabric on her arm flashed in the light. But that was not all that shimmered—gold and pearls sparkled at the base of her throat and in her hair, gracefully pulled up to expose a low, sweeping neckline. If Emry hadn't known better, he would have guessed she'd take the stage herself in such a display.

"Look," Riley whispered. "If Emry doesn't offer up a ring, *I'll happily—*"

"Oh, gods." Sage sighed and pulled her away just as Cal's gaze eagerly scanned the crowd, searching for Emry. He approached her with an unbridled grin and a buoyant gait of his own.

"You look stunning." He took her hand and kissed it, the glove cool under his lips. The feel of the fabric left him both thrilled and frustrated that he couldn't kiss the skin underneath.

"Thank you." She curtsied and stepped aside, revealing her guard Aspen, who proudly mimicked her appearance with a deep red waistcoat.

"Aspen." Emry gave them a bow as well. "I trust you kept my lady safe through the journey?"

Aspen fought a grin as they bowed back. "Very safe."

"Thank you."

Around them, people began filing into the theater, signaling the approach of the curtain call. Emry offered his arm to Cal, then held back, waiting for others to shuffle in first. Selfishly, he wanted more time to admire her in the light of the chandelier. She truly stunned—and what's more, she knew it, too.

"Looking forward to the play?" she asked, the twist in her smile teasing him as he stared at her. He set a hand over hers and leaned close in the growing quiet of the lobby.

"The play?" he murmured. "How can I possibly pay attention to the play when I have you sitting beside me?"

Though he said it half in jest, it turned out to be true. They settled into a box with Aspen, Karlson, and other troupe members, and as soon as the gas lights dimmed, Cal discreetly took his hand. After that, he could hardly follow the plot of the play, focusing only on their intertwined fingers and the warmth of her arm against his. Despite the touch, there was far too much space between them. How long had it been since he'd kissed her, truly kissed her? Or been alone with her at all? He dared one more glance at her dress, the off-the-shoulder sleeve slipping down slightly. It was a beautiful, light sort of torture, one that only grew worse when the couple onstage—some sort of doomed-lover situation—kissed passionately against a painted starry sky. Emry grumbled silently to himself. Oh, sure, *they* got to kiss in front of everyone, but gods forbid *he* do more than walk alongside his girlfriend in this wretched city—

Then the curtain dropped, signaling intermission, and a few words from Cal brought him back to reality.

"Oh, no," she muttered, looking at the box on the other side of the theater. "Don't let Aspen see."

Across the room, Dev, Halleson, Zeke, and several others slipped into a box, fashionably late and utterly uncaring of the play they were there to see. But it was too late to hide their presence from Aspen—a low growl came from behind Emry.

"We're laying low, remember?" he quietly reminded them. "Act like everything is normal. Now isn't the time."

"But—"

"How are you liking the play so far?" he asked them forcefully. The spirit gave them a look but relented and began talking about the play. Sage and Riley soon joined in with vastly divided opinions on the leads, and Emry nodded along until the curtain rose once more, and the enemies on the other side of the theater fell into darkness.

The rest of the play passed in a flurry of saccharine emotions onstage—or at least, that's what Emry guessed. Cal had set her head on his shoulder partway through the final act, and he hadn't really thought of much else. Then the lights came up, the cast appeared for their final bow, and the audience started to filter out of their seats. Emry peered over at the box opposite them—Dev and Halleson, thankfully, were already gone. All he had to do was get Cal and Aspen out of the building and back home.

But as Karlson, Aspen, and the others filed out, a foolish rush of determination filled him, and he took Cal's wrist to hold her back.

"Em?" she started. He held a finger to his lips, waited for the last person to leave...

Then he tugged the curtain closed, pulled Cal into the shadows, and kissed her.

Joy shot through his spine the moment his lips touched hers, the feeling set aflame when she leaned into him just as eagerly. He had intended to pull away quickly, make the interlude brief—but her stifled moan, her fingers sinking his hair, everything about her told him she had been thinking about this as much as he had. So, he pressed her deeper into the curtain, letting his hands wander over the velvet of her dress, as soft and lovely as he had hoped—

Cal suddenly broke off with a breathless gasp. "Tell me I didn't hear a wolf growling."

A snarl floated down through the hall. Emry froze.

"You...didn't hear a wolf growling?" he tried.

They both broke into a run down the hall.

As he feared, Aspen stood in the middle of the lobby, squared against Dev, while Sage and Riley lingered behind them in confusion. The spirit hadn't taken their wolf form—yet—but the claws on their fingers had started to grow in an obvious threat.

To Dev's credit, he stood against such a display with little more than a stoic glare.

"My good spirit," he said, his voice barely wavering. "I am sure I don't know what you're talking about."

"Oh, I think you do." Aspen bared their teeth. Sage reached tentatively for the spirit's arm.

"Aspen, perhaps we should—"

"Stand down," Emry cut in, reaching Aspen's other side. "Now."

He wasn't the only one jumping in to intervene—on Dev's side, Zeke stepped in with both hands raised.

"Look, I'm"—he stared at Aspen's extended claws in fear—"I'm sure it's just a misunderstanding."

"Sending threats and killing spirits?" Aspen spat. "A misunderstanding?"

Zeke's gaze snapped up to Aspen's face. "I beg your pardon?"

Riley stepped forward. "I'm sorry, *what?*"

But Dev wasn't done defending himself. He leaned forward and spoke in a voice low enough for only Emry and Aspen to hear. "I'm not *killing* them," he snapped, eyes flashing. "It's a brief injury of little consequence, once you see what I'm about to achieve. The scientific significance of the wave was nothing compared to this—"

Aspen's eyes went black. "Say that one more time."

"*Aspen,*" Cal hissed. Emry grabbed Aspen's arm, about to pull them away—

Then another voice boomed.

"What in Hara's name is going on?"

The astonished crowd parted to let the newcomer in, their eyes averted, murmuring silenced. The newcomer acted as if the observers weren't there at all, nor the broad-shouldered men flanking him on either side. His bristled gaze only had room for Aspen—and by extension, Emry.

"Halleson." Dev straightened his coat, his voice stiff. "I was merely catching up with my old associates."

Halleson's voice could have sliced the carpet under his feet. "And do your old associates typically greet you with threats and claws?"

Aspen's gaze locked on Halleson, and long, angry fangs grew out of their mouth. "Only when we get threatened first."

The words echoed loudly through the lobby. A brief flush took over Halleson's face—though whether out of anger or embarrassment, Emry wasn't sure—then he snapped his fingers, and his men stepped forward.

Emry threw himself in front of Aspen, blocking their snarl. In turn, Cal leapt for Emry, and behind her, Sage yanked on Riley's curled fist, trying uselessly to drag at least one person out of the fray.

But before anyone could land a blow, a final figure strode forward —Karlson, his footsteps hardly making a sound as he placed himself firmly in the middle of the advancing lines.

"Halleson, how lovely to see you." He gave a smooth bow, his voice even smoother. "Please forgive my troupe—it's been a very long day, and clearly there was a simple misunderstanding. Allow me to speak with them and clear it up, won't you?" He turned on his heel and lowered his voice, and only Emry was close enough to see the fear flashing in his eyes. "Time to go, dears. All of you. Right now."

Emry grabbed Cal's arm and pulled on Aspen, guiding them all to the door as shocked whispers bubbled in the crowd again.

"Are you quite well, Mr. Gray?" Halleson said, his voice carrying over the general murmur. Emry glanced behind him—Dev, Zeke, and Halleson now murmured in a huddle. Halleson's face darkened, and his gaze followed Emry and Aspen all the way out of the lobby.

"Into the carriages. *Go.*" Karlson threw open the carriage doors for them. Riley and Sage piled into one, Cal and Aspen into the other. Emry threw himself onto the seats with them and closed the door.

"Seems I should write to Georgie," he mumbled as the carriage rolled away from the theater. "We're going to need those oars after all."

CHAPTER FIFTEEN

EMRY

"You threatened him?"

Damir had cornered Emry and Aspen alone in the hotel's private garden before Karlson's next rehearsal. Emry thanked Hara that no one else was there to witness the man's stare—he was fairly certain it had melted the hedgerows behind him.

"We may have"—he cleared his throat—"exchanged some words—"

"I did it," Aspen cut in, their glare as strong as Damir's. "He had to know I won't let him near either of them."

"But you did it in front of *Halleson*." Damir gestured back to the hotel with a frantic hand. "Whether he's funding Dev or not, you just picked a fight in front of Matlock's most influential man. If you want to keep Ms. Breslin and yourselves safe, that is *not* how you go about it."

He pinched the bridge of his nose and walked in a circle around the garden table, his eyes closed in thought. Today, the table was laden not with pastries but wine bottles—Emry had preemptively brought down a few as an added apology for Karlson. Several of them were overpriced gifts from various admirers, and Emry had grabbed them at random, unsure of what Karlson actually liked.

Damir stopped, looked at the bottles longingly, then thought better of it.

"And Ms. Breslin hasn't changed her mind about leaving the city?" he asked.

"I've already asked her twice. If I ask her again, she'll order Aspen to bite me."

"I wouldn't do it," Aspen muttered.

Voices floated over the hedge, and Karlson, Sage, and Riley strolled through the archway in their typical moods—Karlson humming, Sage and Riley snipping.

"If I have to hear 'Farleigh's Reel' one more time in my life," Riley said, "I will throw my drum at someone. My biggest drum. I'll do it, I swear."

Sage began to belt out the first verse. *"O'er the hill and o'er the dale—"*

"That's it, I'm getting my drum—"

"Children, children..." Karlson lightly chided. His hum lifted into a delighted noise when he spotted the wine bottles. "Wine to go with the pastries? Would my manager approve of such a treat?"

Emry jumped in right away. "We're so sorry for causing you all trouble last night," he said. "We didn't think that Dev would be there—"

Karlson held up a hand. "Please, I'm sure Damir has already admonished you. Besides, I'm a terrible influence." He grinned. "A little bit of drama before a concert always makes the audience more intrigued."

He plucked one of the bottles from the table and examined the label. That particular bottle had come in this morning, an elegant red that looked far too dry for Emry's taste—but he had no idea who was to thank for it. When he'd asked after the accompanying card, the delivery boy had just shrugged and dashed off to make his next run.

"But not to worry," Karlson continued as he uncorked the bottle. "To ensure Damir doesn't suffer a heart attack, I already visited with a few witnesses this morning. Did my best to play off the event as a small squabble, nothing worth thinking about."

"Small squabble," Riley repeated. "I wanted a decent fight. What was all that about, anyway?"

"None of your concern," Damir countered. Sage's gaze narrowed.

"But Aspen said something about—"

"Please, ladies, I can't drink all this wine by myself," Karlson said. Riley relented to the distraction first; Sage pursed her lips, then followed her to the table. Once they had clustered around Karlson, Damir turned back to Emry, his voice lowered.

"I need to let Ella know about this," he said. "We won't be able to corner Mr. Gray for a full confession, not if he's under Halleson's control. But if we can find any more information about the site itself, what exactly he's up to…"

"We'll work on it," Emry said firmly. "I promise—"

Glass shattered behind them, and they all whipped around.

Riley's glass lay broken before her, wine soaking into the earth. But she hadn't dropped it—Karlson had shoved it out of her hand, his arm still outstretched before her. Riley stared in disbelief at him.

"Karlson, what the—?" she tried, but he ignored her, his gaze piercing Damir instead.

"Nedrov," he commanded, stiffly holding out his own glass to the man. Damir strode over, gave the liquid a whiff, and recoiled.

"Shiro's beard—"

Karlson doubled over in a burst of coughs. Emry froze in fear.

"Karlson?" He started forward, Aspen making similarly panicked strides—but Damir waved them all back, already kneeling at the man's side.

"Hold on," he ordered Karlson, twisting a small gold vial off his watch chain. "This is all I have."

"You—" Karlson managed through wracking coughs. "You unprepared bastard—"

"Sorry I don't carry five antidotes on me anymore!"

As Damir tilted the contents into Karlson's mouth, Riley stared at them, dumbfounded. "How do you just happen to *have* an antidote on you?"

Sage half hid behind Riley. "Why are you being *poisoned*?"

Emry's gaze fell on the bottle—the one that had arrived at his doorstep that morning, the one with no card. Horror dropped like a stone into his stomach.

"The poison wasn't for him," he breathed. "It was for me."

Karlson's coughing persisted in loud, concussive bursts. Damir staggered to his feet, his face drawn. "All of you, help me get him inside."

To maintain a semblance of discretion, they dragged him through the servant's hallways, where Sage opened doors, Riley distracted servants with nonsensical questions, and Aspen hurriedly grew witnesses flowers as bribes. After several wrong turns and staircases, they finally stumbled into Karlson's room—or, rather, rooms.

His appointments in the hotel encompassed both a bedroom and a sitting room, both spaces awash with light from wide, ornate windows. But they had no time to admire the windows or furnishings—they hurried through the sitting room and deposited Karlson on the bed, where he could hardly lie still for all his coughing.

"That's it, get it all out..." Damir mumbled and checked Karlson's pulse, while Aspen hovered nearby.

"If you know what sort of flower the antidote came from, I could—"

"Haven't the foggiest, tree-kid, but that's a nice thought."

As Damir worked, Emry stayed rooted by the door, his mind frantically running through a dozen thoughts. Where was the closest hotel clerk? How fast could a doctor arrive? If he was in danger, was Cal at risk, too? She was at tea with Lydia, in a public space—but what if the tea had been poisoned like the wine—?

Finally, Karlson's coughing subsided, and he settled back on the bed, closing his eyes through deep, exhausted breaths. Everyone else in the room let out a collective sigh of relief.

"Will he be all right?" Sage ventured, peeking out from behind Riley. The two of them huddled at the bedroom door in both fright and curiosity. Damir ushered them all out into the sitting room, then closed the bedroom doors behind him.

"Eventually," he said quietly. "It wasn't a strong poison, but it also wasn't my best antidote. It'll take him weeks to fully recover from this, if we're being completely safe."

Emry sank into an armchair, hands shaking, his horror churning into guilt. That could have been him—it *should* have been him.

For all his words about getting Aspen and Cal out of the city, he hadn't considered that he might be next.

"This is our fault," he said, staring at the poisoned bottle Sage had the forethought to bring with her. It now stood on the coffee table, silently taunting all of them. "This wine was sent to me this morning. Aspen and I will find out who sent it and we'll fix this—"

Damir held up a hand. "Let me handle that. Don't go sticking your neck out more than you have to. I don't want any more injured musicians on my hands."

Sage knelt by the table and examined the bottle, her voice trembling. "But why was someone trying to poison you?"

"And why do *you* have the antidote?" Riley pressed Damir.

"Force of habit," Damir said, then turned to Sage with a tone akin to gentleness. "I wouldn't worry about it for now. We have it handled—"

"*Handled?*" Sage glared and gestured to the others. "My troupemates are being threatened, and I have a right to know why!"

The demand only made Emry feel worse—he didn't deserve the title of *troupemate* at the moment.

"I promise"—Damir held up his hands—"once this is all resolved, I'll explain fully…"

As he tried to talk Sage down, Riley settled on the sofa, her mouth opening and closing in thought, eyes narrowed at nothing.

The bewildering sight added confusion to Emry's remorse—he had never seen her so hesitant before.

"Look," she finally said, running a nervous hand through her hair. "I don't want to ask, but someone might as well. What do we do about the concert?"

Sage whipped her hard gaze from Damir to Riley. "Karlson nearly died, and you're asking about the concert?"

"Karlson nearly died and we go onstage in four days," she shot right back. "We have to talk about it at some point!"

They all fell silent, their gazes flickering toward Emry. For any other event, the answer would have been simple. Cancel the concert, allow Karlson to rest, then resume weeks later, once the season was over.

But this wasn't a normal concert. This was the start of Emry's entire Guild career.

Damir didn't look anyone in the eye when he next spoke. "We'll have to cancel."

The words struck Emry like an anchor, pinning him to the depths of his own guilt. He opened his mouth, trying to argue, to say something that would save himself...but nothing came out. Karlson was in danger because of him. A botched Guild debut was the *least* he deserved—

Riley and Sage both jumped to their feet.

"Like rot we do," Riley snapped. "You think Karlson would want us all to run like this? To give whoever this maniac was"—she pointed to the wine bottle—"exactly what they wanted?"

Emry expected Sage to chide her, to take Damir's side—but she stood right beside Riley, her words firm.

"She's right," she said. "You can't do this. Not to us, and not to Emry's debut. If you cancel now, he won't have another opportunity like this until next year. People will have forgotten by then. It'll be a disaster—"

But Damir held fast. "I realize that, but with all due respect to your talents, I'm not throwing a troupe without Karlson to an audience expecting *Karlson*." He picked up the bottle and inspected the label. "If he's not there, they won't come, and I can't think of a bigger disaster for Mr. Karic's debut than an empty audience."

Sage and Riley looked at each other, no immediate comeback on their tongues. As Emry's brief flicker of hope fizzled, Aspen took his hand and squeezed it.

"It'll be all right," they said weakly. "We'll—we'll figure something out."

Sage stood straighter. "Aspen's right. We'll figure something out, and we'll figure it out now. What if we came up with something else to entice the audience in?"

Riley raised her eyebrows. "So..."

"Not fireworks," Sage said without looking at her. "They've seen fireworks already. It has to be something completely unique, something..." She pulled out her blue notebook and flipped to a blank page—but Riley's face had already lit up with an idea.

"Easy." She nodded to Aspen and grinned. "Matlock hasn't seen a spirit onstage before."

Aspen blinked at her. "Me? I'll just be singing."

"But you can do more than that, right?" Riley gestured to the spirit, who was still holding Emry's hand. "You possessed him at rehearsal that one time. You had the glowing eyes and everything!"

Aspen flickered in shock.

"You want me to *possess* him?" they repeated. "Onstage? He almost died the first time I did it—"

"Well, not the other times," Emry said, then caught himself. Riley pointed again to him, looking at Damir this time.

"See?"

Damir gave her a flat look, but Sage had caught on to the idea. "What does it sound like if you sing?" she asked, closing her notebook. "When you were possessed the other day, your voice did something strange when you spoke."

"Can you still play when possessed?" Riley pressed. Emry held up his hands.

"I—I have no idea."

He looked to Damir, who appeared as unconvinced as Aspen. "Whatever trick you're talking about, I'm not letting you do it onstage unless I see it for myself."

Emry swallowed, a nauseous mix of hope and fear. To say that Cal would hate it would be an understatement, and he didn't even want to consider the other factors: the pain, what his family would say. It was stupid, dangerous, absolutely foolish...

And his only shot at saving his debut.

He turned to Aspen. "Do you think we could try it once? Just to see?"

Aspen folded their arms and sat on the coffee table. "It'll hurt you."

"You didn't hurt me the last time." Emry leaned forward. "You've said before that you wanted to do more onstage. If this works, it—it could be something we do together."

"And if it doesn't work?"

"Then we won't perform." Emry held out a hand for a handshake. "I swear it."

Aspen stared at him for a long moment, then set their lute on the table, plucked a healing flower out of it, and placed it in Emry's outstretched hand.

"One song," they said. "I jump in, I jump out, you eat this flower right away. Understood?"

"Understood."

They all gathered on the far side of the sitting room, as far away from Karlson's bedroom as possible. Emry steeled himself and held out his hand, palm up.

To his surprise, the possession was even easier than last time. He remained standing, only swaying slightly when his senses flickered in the span of a blink. When his sight returned, his manager stood frozen, his normal scowl dropped in favor of unguarded awe.

"Weir's eyes," he said softly. "Is that really what you did in Dawnstone?"

"Oh, not you, too," Aspen said, their voice floating through Emry's throat. Sage gasped and ducked behind Riley once more.

It's all right, Emry tried to reassure her—but Aspen had full control now, and his voice went nowhere. *Aspen, you'll need to give me back my voice.*

Aspen's power jittered as they sorted out where to let go and where to hold on. Emry's head tingled, and he tried to speak once more. "Hello—?"

He jumped—his voice echoed around the parlor, filling the space in a way his natural projection couldn't possibly account for. Riley grabbed Emry's lute and held it out. "Here. Try playing this."

Emry tried to move his hand; nothing. *Aspen, my hands, if you would?*

More jittering—a shudder of stinging pain this time, which he winced through—then the spirit settled in his chest, still firmly there, but not controlling. Emry's shoulders immediately rounded in relaxation. *That's not bad, Aspen. How are you feeling?*

Feeling all right, Aspen said hesitantly. They wiggled around, and an odd sensation spread in his chest. *There's weird corners in here.*

Emry laughed; the other three stared at him.

"Sorry." He cleared his throat. "Aspen made a joke."

He took the lute, slung the strap over his shoulder, and played a few test chords. Half an aimless melody, more for the sensation of playing than anything else.

The improvised tune rang out in the parlor, turning the little space into a concert hall—reverberations of every color sank into the curtains and twirled around his listeners. Emry stopped in surprise, and internally, Aspen perked up in delight. It was just like his first performance at the Red Rat, when his lute had been possessed. The same warm echoes, the same hint of joy.

But the effect wasn't contained to only the lute this time. Riley gave a curse in awe—and her voice echoed, too. She clapped a hand over her mouth.

"What the—?"

It echoed again. She clapped her other hand over her first hand and looked at Sage.

"We have to sing something," Sage breathed. Then more insistently: "We have to sing something, all of us."

Riley glared at her. "I don't sing—"

"You do now!" Sage looked to Emry. "'Before I Leave'?"

Sharp pain jolted through his fingers, an echo of what he had felt during his first possession—he pushed it away. "'Before I Leave,' on three."

He counted them in, and they began to sing, amplifying the echoes tenfold. And as the sound surrounded them, buoying them, so did Aspen's delight, bubbling up into the notes themselves. Emry could feel them focusing on the lute strings vibrating under his fingertips, on how each note sounded on his tongue. They weren't listening to the music; they were living inside it, and their awe only made the music louder.

Emry never wanted it to end. If their audience felt a fraction of the fascination that Aspen did, a mere hint of the exhilaration...they wouldn't need Karlson onstage, not even for an audience as finicky as Matlock.

Then the song wound down, and the stab of pain at his fingers crept into his wrist—their time was up.

Okay, that's all, Aspen. He set down the lute as quickly as he could without dropping it, but his movements were becoming jerky again, more painful with every change in direction. *Time to go—*

With a brief push from both sides, Aspen dove back into their lute, letting it rock back and forth on the table. Emry grabbed the healing flower and stuffed it into his mouth.

"How are you feeling?" Aspen appeared cross-legged on the table, watching Emry's every move in concern. Emry rubbed his wrists, but the bitter taste of the petals had already stripped away the layers of sharp pain, leaving only his more familiar aches. Thank Hara for Aspen and their flowers.

"Fine. Good, actually." He grinned at Aspen. "Did you have fun?"

The spirit's concern melted, and they nodded, their smile wide and bright.

"Can we do it?" Sage asked. "Can we perform?"

Damir, still slack-jawed, stared at her, then Emry. "*Can* you?"

Emry paused, flexing one hand, then the other. "If Aspen and I practice...I think we could do a song like this. Maybe two." He looked to Aspen, who nodded once more. "Would that be enough?"

"Enough?" Damir repeated. "I don't know of a single person who will have even *dreamed* of a concert like that." He passed a hand over his face. "Gods, I can't believe I'm doing this..."

"So..." Riley leaned forward, eyes glittering. "It's still on?"

Damir let his arm drop in resignation. "What do we call you?"

Emry frowned. "I'm sorry?"

"Well, I can't advertise you as Karlson when Karlson isn't there," Damir said. "For this concert, you'll need to be known as something else."

Emry turned to Sage and Riley. Riley immediately raised both hands. "Don't look at me. I'm not fronting, I don't wanna talk to the crowd."

"Sage?" Emry said. As the one always beside Karlson onstage, she was the most natural choice to lead them, and he expected her to accept just as naturally.

But to his surprise, she shook her head.

"Not this time," she said. "I'm not the one risking my life so we can perform." Her expression softened. "Just for the night, I think it should be you up front."

Emry's heart stopped. "You mean like my own troupe?"

Damir waggled his head. "A borrowed one, but yes. And the name?"

Sage and Riley were still looking at him expectantly, and he knew why. Most Guild troupes took on the lead's name. Karlson, Sylvia Forsgren's Forsgren Quartet... Even Ella's troupe was simply known as Ella Sorman.

But that tradition had never sat quite right with him. The name had to be a reflection of all of them, what made them unique, what united them.

He turned to Aspen's lute.

"Spiritsong," he said, then let it rest in the air for assessment, his body tensing. He expected Sage to brush it off as not aligning with Guild tradition, or Riley to mumble something about cheesiness.

They didn't. Instead, they looked at each other—and when no argument came from either of them, turned their gazes to Aspen.

Aspen's hands clasped together in pride. "Spiritsong."

CHAPTER SIXTEEN

EMRY

THE PEEK OF THE SEASON

My dear readers, we have only just breached the start of the season and have already experienced a staggering shock. Karlson has fallen ill and bowed out of his concert. But before you tear apart your tickets in despair, steel yourself for yet another shock—in his place, he has bestowed the stage to his troupemates and the Karics, who are set to perform under the temporary moniker Spiritsong.

A highly unusual name for a highly unusual act, but one must wonder...what exactly is it like to see a forest spirit tread the boards? The dear spirit has been so busy chaperoning Mr. Karic and Ms. Breslin, they have not yet demonstrated the scope of their magic—nor has society yet experienced Mr. Karic's promised talents.

This writer confesses that the curiosity of the Karic mystery has gotten the better of her, and will be keeping her ticket intact.

WHEN EMRY next arrived in the hotel gardens for his own rehearsal, he showed up twenty minutes before start time and spent the remaining minutes stewing in his anxious thoughts.

"Um, Emry?" Aspen watched him move the chairs from one patch of grass to the other. "That's where you had the chairs five minutes ago."

Cal set a hand on the spirit's arm. "Hush. Let him have his chairs."

She wasn't wrong—focusing on chair positioning was distracting Emry from his darker thoughts. Damir had left it to each individual member of Karlson's troupe to choose whether they wanted to perform with Spiritsong for one night. Emry knew he had Sage and Riley on board, of course, but the troupe at large barely knew him. All through the night, he had nightmares of no one showing up for rehearsal. That the troupe had determined that no performance was better than a paltry Spiritsong performance, and his debut would sink faster than a rock in the river.

He stared at the new chair arrangement without really looking at it. "Cal, what if they—?"

"Darling." She smiled and took his hands. "What if they do all show up? Have you thought of that?"

Emry gave a weak laugh. He hadn't, out of fear he'd jinx the very idea.

"You will be fine." She squeezed his hands. "Just don't drink anything, please."

He caught sight of a new bauble on her necklace—not a charm or jewel, but a tiny antidote capsule. A quiet gift from Damir that morning, an attempt to appease a terrified Cal.

He grimaced. Her very presence reassured him, of course—but if he had known Matlock was going to be so dangerous, he wouldn't have ever let her set foot in the city.

"And you'll be safe?" he asked quietly.

"I'll meet with Mr. Spencer and Ms. Preston, then come right back." She shifted a curl off his forehead. "Don't worry about me. You have more than enough worries filling your head right now."

"I always have time to worry about you," he said, then paused. "That...sounded more romantic in my head."

Cal laughed and kissed him—a gesture that did more to ease his thoughts than the chairs ever could.

"I should really stick to flowers for romance," he mumbled. "Do you think the florists have a flower to symbolize worry?"

She rolled her eyes. "Em..."

He dared to kiss her again. "How about concern?" Another kiss. "Protection from danger? Anti-poison flowers would do the trick. Or daggers hidden inside the bouquet."

As Cal giggled between kisses, Aspen gave a long sigh behind them, and Emry pulled away with a grin.

"All right, all right." He stepped away from her. "Off with you. I need to rearrange the chairs again."

After wishing them luck one more time, Cal left and took her comforting aura with her. But just as Emry reached for the garden chairs again, a new figure appeared at the archway.

"Good morning!" Sage burst in with her usual enthusiasm. Emry steeled himself and turned around.

"Good morning—" he started, then the words dropped from his mouth.

It wasn't just her, but a gaggle of half the troupe—everyone who typically sat on Sage's side during rehearsal. They waved jovially to Emry and began to set up, as they usually did. Like everything was normal.

"I was thinking," Sage said, taking a pastry from the table and standing beside Emry. "If we're going to debut Aspen's magic partway through the concert, the set list deserves a second look. If we push 'Before I Leave' to later in the set—"

"Let's go, let's go!" Riley clapped as she strode into the garden. "Go big or go to the bar!"

A smattering of laughter rose from the musicians within the garden—and from those trailing behind Riley. The other half of the troupe, all filing in with their instruments, chatting, setting up their space.

He counted once, then twice. They were there—all of them were there.

"All right." Riley took his other side, rubbing her hands together. "We ready for this?"

He had to check himself to confirm this was all real. The grass under his shoes, the sun on his face. Aspen throwing him an overjoyed double thumbs-up from the back, half-hidden by Karlson's entire troupe.

No—*his* entire troupe. Just this once.

"Emry?" Sage nudged his arm. "I believe it's time."

He finally let excitement, not fear, take over his thoughts, and he bounded up to the front of the garden, where Karlson normally took residence. To his surprise and delight, lightning didn't strike him down when he stood there. Perhaps he could actually do this.

"Morning, everyone." He grinned. "And welcome to Spiritsong."

The next few days were filled with nothing but practice in every sense of the word.

First, Sage, Riley, and the others came by the garden every morning, filling the hedges with both music and light squabbling.

"You're singing too loud—"

"I wouldn't have to sing so loud if you weren't drumming the very grass out of the earth."

Then, in the afternoons, Emry and Aspen turned to their own sort of practice.

They started off with small, simple goals regarding the possession. First getting used to Aspen's presence, then regaining control of his senses without faltering. Next, after many healing flowers and somewhat improved moonflower tea recipes, they started walking. Straight lines, then turns, circles, around corners—

"Aspen, the wall, the *wall*—"

Aspen didn't balance out their control of Emry's legs in time, and his forehead smacked into the wallpaper.

Sorry, sorry!

Several days later, they practiced talking and singing—slightly easier, with fewer walls to worry about—then talking, singing, and simple motion. Emry surprised himself at how quickly he adjusted to the possession, how much easier it felt to take back control and move on his own. And Aspen surprised him at how smoothly they leapt to and from their lute, as if Emry were just another tree.

And if his daily pain was slowly growing more constant, steadier... He took his remedies and tried not to think about it too much. Surely it would fade once all this was over. With time, just like the doctors said. It had to.

The day before the concert, they sat down to their next test, a bit of motion practice: a teapot, a cup, and a small pitcher of milk in his room, all shadowed by a bouquet of flowers—one of three that had arrived that morning.

"Tea." Emry cleared his throat. "We can pour tea, right?"

Right, Aspen said confidently.

"It's simple."

You do it every day.

"Of course," he said, hoping no one out in the hallway was overhearing his one-sided conversation. "Here we go..."

He reached for the tea and poured without issue. Aspen's presence in his limbs, which had their own instincts on when to dip the pot and how much to pour, was easy to override now with his own intentions. He set the teapot down with confidence, then picked up the milk.

A twinge of pain—barely more than a brief prick—made his finger twitch, and he dropped the pitcher. He gave a small yelp and scrambled for it—

But the ceramic never struck the table. It floated below his fingers, and when he pulled his hand away, he found a vine holding the handle for him, stretching out from the nearby flower vase.

Emry stared at it. "Aspen, you can do that while you're possessing me?"

Well, I created a shield when possessing you the first time, didn't I? Aspen shrugged. *Comparatively, this is much easier.*

"Of course. But we've been..." Emry carefully took the pitcher from the vine, set it down, and checked his pocket watch. "We've been practicing for almost an hour now. Aren't you tired?"

Another thoughtful pause. *No, not really. You?*

Emry stretched his fingers. The pain disappeared as quickly as it had come, and though he knew it would circle back to him later, he felt...fine, for now. Normal. "Not tired at all, no."

He poured a splash of milk without further incident and stirred it in, watching the spoon clink against the cup. But Aspen wasn't focusing like he was, their thoughts stirring like a rustle in his chest.

What if I did that onstage? they asked.

Emry tilted his head. "Pouring milk?"

No, growing flowers. Aspen reached out, and the bouquet began to grow, its greenery spilling over the vase and trailing on the table. As it grew, so did Aspen's excitement.

It would be so pretty if I grew some in the theater, they said. *Pigeon might even be able to hear the music through them. She's been talking to the other spirits, too, and she really wants to—*

"Em?" Cal knocked on the door. "I'm going down for some tea. Would you like to come with me?"

Cold fear washed over him. Cal knew about the concert, of

course. He just...may have failed to tell her about the possession aspect of it all.

"Oh, gods." He stood up and knocked the chair over. "Out, Aspen, out—"

I'm going!

Aspen leapt into their lute, and once the glow of possession had retreated from Emry's hands, he opened the door with a casual smile.

"Yes, happy to come with," he said too quickly. "Tea would be lovely."

Cal looked over his shoulder at the teapot on the table. "Oh, but if you've already had some—"

"No, no, I'd love to join you. One moment, let me get my coat."

As Emry ducked back inside, Aspen handed him a healing flower, eyebrows raised. "Are you going to tell Cal about the possession now?"

Panic rose in his throat, a terrible sensation against the bitterness of the flower. He had avoided telling her about it for days now. At first, it was easy to excuse—she had been so alarmed by the poison incident that he didn't want to worry her more. Then when Damir came by with his suspicion that Halleson had indeed sent the poisoned wine, well...there was no use in upsetting her further in that moment.

But now that they were a day out from the concert, there was no getting around the simple truth: she wouldn't like their possession plan. She'd hate it, in fact. She'd be angry and upset, and all he could think of was the last time she'd been angry and upset at a secret of his.

And when he'd finally told her back then, when everything had come spilling out, it had landed them in different cities, apart and silently miserable.

His throat closed. He couldn't do it. He couldn't tell her.

"Not yet," he mumbled.

"But she'll be at the concert—"

"And I'll tell her before, just...not now." He consumed the last orange petal, the taste burning the confession from his mouth. "Please."

THE REMAINING HOURS WHIRLED PAST, and in a blink, Emry had stepped out of the carriage and into the shadow of the Trellis.

The Trellis, the oldest and most venerated of Matlock's concert venues, was an outdoor amphitheater built on the city's western slope. From the road, Emry could hardly see anything other than its massive wooden shell, shielding the stage and projecting its sound to the seats built into the hill.

He almost laughed when Damir opened the backstage door at its base—under the shadowy structure, his formidable manager looked like an ant.

"In you get," he said, waving them inside. "Flowers are all set. If you have any issues with where we placed them, do me a favor and don't tell me."

"The flowers?" Aspen leapt out of the carriage. "Did you set them up already?"

They bolted through the door, leaving a trail of dust in their wake. Emry stood rooted to the spot with a nervous smile. "Whatever you did, I'm sure they'll love it."

Damir shrugged. "And if they don't, they can grow whatever they rotting like themself."

Emry had been trying to keep both his anticipation and his anxiety in check all day—but the moment he stepped into the Trellis, he lost the fight against both. He felt too small in the space. The wide doors, the soaring, scaffolded ceilings, the sprawling wood stage beyond the curtains... It was all meant for large set pieces, elaborate drops, grand troupes a dozen strong.

Not for *him*. He was just a person. Just a man with a lute and a misplaced gold pin.

He tried to move forward but couldn't take another step. Damir stopped and turned at the side curtain flanking the stage, and for once, a hint of softness appeared on his face.

"Go on," he said, gesturing to the stage. "And don't forget to breathe."

Emry braved his way to the end of the side curtain's shadow. Peeked out into the daylight bouncing off the worn wooden boards. Nodded to Damir, took a few more steps.

He made it to the middle of the stage and forgot to breathe.

The seats before him appeared endless—stretching out and up into a wooden semicircle, cradled by rows of trees and hedges. In the aisles of the floor seats, the venue's crew had placed dozens of bouquets of flowers. Wildflowers, hothouse flowers, greenery and ferns and everyday houseplants in mismatched pots. Raucous, colorful affirmations that spectators were going to come here, were going to sit in those chairs later that evening.

Because they were coming to see *him*.

"If you could move that bouquet over there..." A voice floated out from the seats, where Aspen pointed a poor stagehand this way and that. "No, wait, maybe here..." The spirit waved to Emry and bounded up to the stage. "Isn't it pretty? I'm trying to balance out the colors, but I think it'll... Emry?"

Emry couldn't see them properly, not through the tears—but they could feel the spirit's hug, tight and warm around his waist.

"I'm very proud of you," Aspen murmured.

Emry hastily wiped at his cheeks before his eyes could overflow all over again. "It's your stage too, Aspen. Just as much as mine."

Hara take him, it sounded strange to even say it.

"Hope you like the flowers." Damir wandered out behind him, drawing him back to reality. "I think you sold out every florist in the city with that request."

"They're excellent," Aspen said, then resumed their survey of the space. "But I think I might fill that corner there. And perhaps that one. And that one back there, if I have time."

Damir let out a long, slow breath. "After this concert, I'm quitting," he mumbled and shuffled offstage, hands in his pockets. "Two weeks' notice. No, one week. A day. I don't care."

But even as he waxed poetic on what he was going to do upon his early retirement, he held back the curtain to allow two more people onstage: Sage and Riley, with all of Emry's emotions reflected across their faces.

"My gods," Sage mumbled, her fingers drifting to rest on her lips. "It never gets old, does it?"

She floated across the stage, looking out at the seats as if she were counting each one. Trailing her, Riley could do nothing but grin at the view, bouncing on her heels as if she wanted the concert to start right now.

"I almost feel bad that this is your first venue," she said, clapping Emry on the back. "It'll ruin you for all the others."

Damir gave him a precious few more seconds to soak it in—to understand where he really was—before coming back and breaking the silence.

"Well," he said, his voice echoing across the stage. "Get ready for rehearsal, but don't play too hard. You'll need your fingers intact for all the handshakes."

The Guild's standard meet-and-greet parade of handshakes and small talk came directly after the troupe's rehearsal, invading their plush, relaxing back room with hot air and empty words. At first, it was all Vidanyan Councilmen—eager to glad-hand with the newest Guild members, invite them to soirees, and wax poetic over Aspen's flower-filled lute.

"Are you really going to play that?" one of them asked.

"Oh, no," Aspen said. "I'll be—um, singing."

Once there was a break in the endless train of pleasantries, Sage sat Emry firmly on a stool and opened up a velvet bag.

"All right," she said with an air of authority. "Do you have any sensitivities to makeup?"

"To what?" Emry blinked at her. Sage blinked back.

"It's a stage, Emry," she said. "A massive one. In order to look like a person to the back row, you're going to need to wear makeup."

The implication that the place was going to fill to the back row made Emry dizzy—too dizzy to protest when Sage started sorting through brushes and holding little pots of powder up to his face. "I don't want to hide the freckles, but I do need to emphasize your eyes..."

Somewhere off to Emry's left, near the table of food, Riley snorted. Sage side-eyed her.

"Don't laugh, you and the others are next."

"I can do my own, *thank* you."

As Sage worked, Aspen stood next to her and slowly morphed their face to match her work. Through their changing appearance, Emry watched as Sage applied something black to his eyes, something shimmery to his cheekbones...

Toward the end of Sage's elaborate process—as the brushes were making Emry's nose itch yet again—another knock rattled the door.

"Not another one," Riley muttered. But instead of a Council member, Damir's blond head popped in.

"You'll thank me for this one," he said. "Thought you all might like to see a friendlier face before the Forsgren Quartet warms up the crowd."

He pushed the door all the way open, revealing Karlson. His posture slouched and shadows weighed down his eyes—but his smile was as warm as ever.

"My brave musicians, venturing into the world without me," he said in a scratchy, barely-there voice, and leaned against the doorway. "How are you all holding up?"

The troupe burst into a mix of cheers and weak reassurances.

"Just fine—"

"*So* excited—"

"Totally not about to throw up, no sir."

"Better than me on my first night at the Trellis, then," Karlson said. "I think I was vomiting for most of the day beforehand." His grin softened. "Mr. Karic, a bit of advice for you."

Emry's heart began to pound in his ears. Karlson held up a finger.

"You only get one chance to play the Trellis for the first time," he said. "Do have fun, won't you?"

Emry grinned. "I will."

"I look forward to celebrating you all," he said, then disappeared into the humming backstage darkness. Emry looked at Damir and gave a silent nod of thanks. His manager gave an imperceptible nod back, then stepped aside to clear the doorway.

"Well, you heard the man," he said gruffly. "Your opener starts in fifteen. Be ready."

The troupe scrambled to grab their instruments, checking their tuning and scurrying out into the backstage area. The humming had grown to a strong thrum now, a low sound that Emry could feel through the ground, shaking energy out of the floorboards and into the air. He dared one peek out from behind the side curtain. There was the audience—packing the floor alongside the massive bouquets, their faces obscured beyond the footlights. Behind them, the sun had nearly set beneath a clouded sky, covering them in a cool blanket of dusk.

A perfect evening for a concert.

"Em?"

Emry jumped and whirled around. Cal stood behind him, hands clasped in front of her, nervously tossing a glance over her shoulder. As she turned, the footlights caught a hint of the glittering embroidery in her dress. "I'm sorry, I just—Damir said I could stop by before the opener, but only for a few seconds..."

"Hey." He took her hands without thinking, only realizing then how much his hands were shaking. He regained his breath, then tried to steady his fingers. "Thank you. I...I wouldn't have gotten here without you. You know that, right?"

Cal gave him a wide, proud smile. "On the contrary—if you had left Tazlo with me years ago, I may have taken you away from all this." She took in the vaulted backstage and the shimmering footlights. "No. This was entirely on your own merit, sir."

"Sir?"

"Look around you. Look at this place," Cal said, her eyes sparkling even in the darkness. "This is all yours tonight. *Sir.*"

A hundred emotions—love, guilt, fear—ripped through Emry's chest, and he tucked a curl behind Cal's ear with a hand that shook even harder than before. He hadn't told her yet, but he couldn't tell her now, he couldn't—

"No matter what happens tonight, will you trust me?"

Cal's expression faltered. "What do you mean?"

Emry opened his mouth, but then the Forsgren Quartet passed him on their way to the stage, and Damir appeared behind them. "Ms. Breslin, it's time."

Emry took in a ragged breath and kissed Cal, the gesture warm and insistent and loving and scared.

"Trust me," he whispered. "Please."

Then Damir guided Cal back into the shadows, leaving Emry standing at the edge of the light.

CHAPTER SEVENTEEN

CAL

C<small>AL</small> <small>RETREATED</small> from backstage up to the observation deck, her face tingling with the alarming sensation of Emry's last kiss—the shaking hands at her cheeks, the unsteady breath that had brushed her lips. She glanced back at the Forsgren Quartet onstage, knowing he stood somewhere behind the curtains. She couldn't fault him for being nervous, not for a concert like this—but stage fright had never bested him before. He was comfortable onstage; he *belonged* onstage. No, something else had to be going on. Another threat to his life, perhaps. Another poisoning? An attempted attack backstage? Her breath hitched, and she turned around. She could sneak back into the shadows, around Damir, and insist that Emry tell her what was going on—

But as she gripped her skirts to navigate the stairs back down, she spotted someone inside the observation deck: Dev, flanked by both Halleson and Zeke, his smile thin as he entertained a rotating crowd of admirers. He turned to bow at a newcomer, and the edge of his notebook flashed in his hand. All of Dev's information right there, with the man himself distracted...

Cal silently cursed and released her skirts. There was nothing for it now—she had to trust Emry like he had asked. She glanced one more time at the stage, then opened the door to the observation deck and slipped inside.

In her opinion, the deck was a rather clunky addition to the Trellis. The long, looming span of half-enclosed rooms hunched at the back of the amphitheater, looming over the seats while keeping the toast of society safely tucked away from the common audience. The deck furnished them with everything they could possibly want—food, drinks, even cigar and card rooms in the back if they grew bored of the theater. When she passed the luxurious seats at the forefront of the deck, she wondered how such boredom could be possible. The view of the stage was stunning, the evening air perfect. She trailed a hand over one of the seats with its lustrous wood and plush cushioning. She wanted nothing more than to watch Emry's debut in such a place.

But apparently, no one on the deck felt the same way.

The seats around Cal were entirely empty. Instead, everyone milled about in their usual gossip circles, laughing and chatting and sipping from little glasses. They were hardly glancing out at the stage, much less paying attention to the opener's music. Cal snatched up a glass of her own from a passing waiter, taking a vengeful sip and hating how good it tasted. If any of these nitwits tried to utter a single word during Emry's performance, she would take their drinks and pour them directly onto their expensive headdresses.

While the Forsgren Quartet continued their serenade onstage—as beautiful as a sunset, if anyone happened to be *listening*—Cal pinpointed her target. Dev had currently gotten himself stuck between two gossip circles, but Halleson and Zeke still flanked him, like one imposing and one half-crumbling column. Dev maintained a thin veneer of social decorum, but Zeke had lost it entirely. He barely uttered a word in the conversation, glancing frequently at Halleson's tall figure casting a shadow over Dev. Cal couldn't blame him for his anxiety—Damir's leading suspicion was that a man in Halleson's employ had sent the poisoned wine to Emry. But Zeke's constant shuffling made his own situation very clear. Whatever bargain Dev and Zeke had struck with Halleson, whatever they had promised to deliver from the depths of their dig—they hadn't delivered on it yet.

Comforted by this, Cal focused on the notebook in Dev's hand. He had it on him so frequently that it appeared to be a mere extension of his wrist at this point, the black leather blending in with his black-cuffed coat. She couldn't depend on Dev to let slip anything more about his plan, but that notebook had no such qualms. If she could just find a way to page through it quickly... She swallowed. She'd have to steal it, if only for a little while.

So much for upholding decorum as a Council representative.

But she couldn't target the notebook yet—Zeke had broken off to approach her, his gait stiff.

"Ms. Breslin," he said, giving her a short bow. "We never got the chance to speak at the theater the other day."

It was easy to see why his tone was so stilted, his actions puppet-like. Dev and Halleson both monitored him from across the room—and by extension, Cal. She stiffened, recalling the letter and the poisoned wine. They wouldn't dare do something to her in such a public place, but she didn't dare risk it, either. For now, she'd have to play along with the charade.

"I apologize on behalf of Aspen's actions," she said with a mask of politeness. "I'm sure it was a misunderstanding."

Zeke nodded in gracious acceptance of the false apology. "Of course. I can assure you that all of Mr. Gray's research is entirely above board, and nothing he's doing is impacting the local ecosystem. He's made sure of that."

His eyes tightened. Words from a puppet, and just as sincere. At least he knew they were lies—his pleasant demeanor was thinner than an eggshell, betraying the anger simmering underneath.

"Absolutely," Cal said, then continued in a genuine undertone that Dev and Halleson wouldn't be able to catch from across the room. "If you need any assistance, you'll reach out to me, won't you?"

A hairline crack ran through Zeke's facade.

"I will," he said, his tone deeper. "I truly do have the highest respect for your expertise. And..." He leaned forward. "For what it's worth, I am actually looking forward to watching the Karics perform. I don't think anyone else here quite understands the privilege of seeing them onstage."

Finally, someone who understood.

"I'll be sure to pass that along," Cal said, giving him a true curtsy. "Have a good evening, Mr. Whitlock."

Zeke slipped away, the charade complete, and Halleson's attention drifted elsewhere. Cal wandered in the opposite direction, eager to get out of his eyesight and consider her next move. People would soon be taking their seats for the main act, and so would she—she'd need to grab Dev's notebook before he sat down. But he remained in a tiny social fortress of tables and people. There would be no quick sleight of hand here. Not that she was very good at that, anyway...

Then she saw it—the perfect opportunity, delivered to her by a wonderfully ignorant source.

James, walking toward Dev with two drinks in hand, one of them overfull and sloshing.

Cal set aside her glass. It was time to make James' ambition useful once more.

She maneuvered closer to them as James approached, successfully infiltrating Dev's fortress with his winning smile and pompous determination.

"As we discussed at the garden party," he said, wasting no time in launching his assault, "I'm very much preparing to be a leader like yourself, and I was wondering..."

As James blathered, a group of women passed behind him. One of them stood tall and haughty in a feathered headdress and an old-fashioned gown—one with a wide bustle and a conveniently long train.

On Cal's part, all it took was a bit of timing and one single step.

The train snagged; the woman stumbled. Only a little, but just enough to bump the woman next to her, who bumped into James, who stumbled forward—

—and let the wine spill all over Dev's ostentatiously gold waistcoat.

Cal nearly laughed. He looked far more normal now with a stain on his clothing.

But she couldn't tarry to enjoy the display—she had to duck away as soon as the first woman stumbled. By the time the wine had spilled and the damage was done, she was standing back behind the tables, nowhere near the minor scuffle.

"Oh my goodness, I'm so sorry!" The old-fashioned woman clapped a hand over her mouth. James began dabbing ineffectually at Dev's shirt with a handkerchief, his face the color of the spilled wine.

"Such a waste of a good drink," he tried to joke while Zeke rushed off to find a towel. Cal tensed, waiting for her moment.

"Quite all right," Dev grumbled and set aside his notebook on the table behind him. "I'm sure Mr. Whitlock can top you off once he's returned..."

"No need, my good sir."

James turned to flag a servant for assistance—and his gaze briefly left both Dev and the table, leaving the notebook unattended. Cal held her breath and dove for it.

She grabbed the book, shoved it in her pocket, and ducked into the empty cigar room nearby, freezing once she reached the shadows. She let one second go by, then two, waiting for footsteps or an indignant cry from Dev...

Nothing—just the usual chatter and James' loud apologies.

She exhaled and began flipping through the notebook.

The writing was reminiscent of the Dev she had met months ago.

Immaculate notes, figures, and calculations, all strewn about stained and torn papers. Not having time to parse the calculations, she flipped through another few pages and found maps, their edges dotted with drops of wine.

At first, she thought she was looking at a copy of Lydia's drawings from her office—concentric half-circles, all spanning out over the sketched outline of the province. Just like with Lydia's map, the circles shrank around the border, around the city of Matlock.

So, Lydia had been on to something, after all.

She flipped hurriedly through the other notes. There were many that didn't make sense to her, scribbled in a shorthand already obscured by atrocious handwriting—but there were other maps, too. Maps of tunnels, paths leading into chambers and into more paths. All of them led down to chambers that Dev consistently labeled *wells*, each a mile wide and hidden under a thick layer of crystal. Then on the next page, descriptions of mining equipment, theories about how to break through the crystal and harvest the energy within...

But when it came to the spirits' health, the dated logs of the dig were the most damning. The frequency of the logs aligned perfectly with how often Pigeon and her friends suffered—Dev's crew ventured deeper several times a week, relentlessly discovering new chasms and digging new tunnels without any regard for safety, consequences...or the torment of the spirits above them.

She had been right. It was all Dev and his reckless, ambitious digging, upsetting the rivers and slowly killing the spirits day by day—and what's more, he didn't care. She flipped through more pages; the logs went back for months. He would have been in the city as soon as the gardens were showing signs of blight. He had dug several times since Cal had first come to him at the opening ball.

She was tempted to throw the book in the fire, to curse what Dev had become—but had he really changed all that much? Of course, the man who had once scrambled across rooftops for a few jars of spirit energy would want access to an entire well of it. In other, safer circumstances, so would she. The amount of research that could be done on the origin of spirits, the strides her field of study could make—it would be just as Dev had said at the party. It was nothing but pure potential.

And to him, it was well worth more than a few lives.

Out on the deck, the chatter grew louder, reminding her of her precious time limit. She ripped out the pages describing the maps and the mining attempts, then slapped the notebook closed and hurried back out.

"No, no, I insist that I cover the cost of a new shirt," James was saying heroically, as if the very thought of it saved the day. "And allow me to fetch you another drink myself. I've been meaning to chat with you about your research, and if you'd be willing to hear about my own plans—"

Cal slipped the notebook back on the table just as Dev grasped for it, his false smile still directed at James.

"Ah, I see," he said uncertainly, picking up the notebook and slipping it into his pocket. "Well, perhaps once Mr. Whitlock comes back..."

As much as Cal would have liked to watch Dev suffer under James' conversation, she couldn't stay and keep the proof to herself. She snuck out of the observation deck and back down the stairs. Damir would let her backstage again, once she told him she had the information—then they could shut down the dig site and get themselves out of the city. Emry and Aspen would do one simple, pleasant concert, then let Karlson have the stage again and retreat to safer ground—

But she was too late. Onstage, the Forsgren Quartet gave a final bow, and the crowd began to cheer for Spiritsong.

CHAPTER EIGHTEEN

EMRY

As the Quartet left the stage, they grinned and clapped Emry on the back, not reflecting even a fraction of the nerves he felt. Emry couldn't imagine it. How were they not collapsing in relief after their performance? How could they go on with their lives, when he was standing here, his debut jitters about to engulf him—

Aspen bounded past him and peeked out at the audience, who were hardly more than loud shadows beyond the edge of the stage.

"Look at all of them," they breathed. They regarded the crowd not with anxiety but joy, like a child spying presents on their birthday. "You think Pigeon'll be able to hear us through the plants? Do you think she'll have fun?"

Their excitement sent a deep crack through Emry's jitters.

"I know she will." He nudged them. "Are *you* ready to have some fun?"

Aspen nodded fiercely and rushed up to Sage and Riley. "We should do a count."

Sage frowned. "A count?"

"Yes. Humans do that, right?" They held a hand out. "One, two, three, go?" They raised their arm, then stared at the musicians. "Do you...not do that before concerts?"

Riley pushed up her sleeves. "We do now." She jerked her head to the others, drawing them into a rough circle. "One, two, three..." She looked to Aspen for the final word.

"*Spirits*, obviously," they said. Emry nudged in between Riley and Sage and placed his hand atop theirs.

"Thank you," he murmured to them. "Both of you."

Riley bumped his arm. Sage flashed him a smile and squeezed his fingers.

"One, two, three, spirits!"

Then the circle broke apart and strode onto the stage.

For a moment, everything was footlights and darkness and cheering, an abstract form of a concert that gave Emry precious few seconds to paddle upstream against his nerves. He grabbed hold of what he could sense—Aspen beside him, his troupe members behind him, his audience before him.

He wrestled his lungs back into a rhythm. It was too late to go back now. He could only give them what they wanted.

So, he pulled his energy from the stage, from the very floorboards, and gave the shadowed audience an easy grin.

"Evening!"

The shadows cheered back.

Their first few songs passed by in a blink—all familiar pieces to both the troupe and the audience, with quick tempos and lyrics that everyone knew by heart. Their carefully curated progression made it easy for Emry to settle into the stage and pretend like he actually belonged there. These wooden boards were no different than any other stage, he told himself, and his audience no different than some friends at a tavern. He and the rest of the troupe were there to entertain, to make their people laugh and clap and sing, and that was that.

But no one at any tavern had seen what they were about to do.

"We've got something special for you tonight," Emry said. His voice threatened to warble, and he forced himself to take on a casual air—one he adopted at his smaller venues, tiny pubs and dusty inn corners.

"In case you didn't know, we have a forest spirit in our midst," he continued, gesturing to Aspen beside him. Deafening cheers from the amphitheater—Aspen laughed and bowed.

"And we thought," Emry said, shifting his lute strap as the applause died down, "well, we can't have a proper concert without letting Aspen show off a little, right?"

Aspen set aside their lute and lined up next to him, flowers already blooming in their hair. Emry dared one glance up at the observation deck, where he knew Cal was watching.

He sent up a silent prayer to any god listening that she'd forgive him once this was over.

"So, without further ado"—he nodded to Sage—"this is 'Before I Leave.'"

Sage started the first verse entirely by herself, in a slow, heavy version of the normally upbeat song. The inversion had been her idea, and Emry had loved it from the start. The contrast jolted the audience to attention while her lone voice danced across the air, high and sweet, laced with an endearing hint of roughness. She could have carried out an entire concert by herself like this if she had to.

> *I know the road is calling me back home*
> > *It says I must be on my way*
> > *But before I leave, I want to believe*
> > *That your heart is begging me to stay*

Emry joined in at the chorus, careful to maintain her tempo and balance her voice. Their voices needed to weave together, not drown each other, and in a venue like the Trellis, such a feat was effortless. Their duet twirled all the way to the back seats, intertwining with the flowers dotting the aisles.

> *So tell me now*
>   *'Fore the road drags me down*
>   *That in your pulse you hear a vow*
>   *That you love this runaway*
>   *Say it out loud and I'll stay*
>   *Oh, please, 'fore the road drags me down*

Aspen's voice flitted over the second verse, their ethereal song bearing echoes of Emry's tone, and by extension, his sisters'. Emry's heart skipped—for a brief, intense moment, it felt like his family was behind him, singing like they used to do at Sada. He held tight to that feeling—the love, the familiar homesickness—before holding out his hand to Aspen.

As soon as he moved, the other troupe members tensed, leaning in for their moment. Sage watched him closely. Riley held her drumsticks poised. They were all set to begin the moment Aspen disappeared, the moment Emry's hands began to glow.

But Sage and Emry had to repeat the chorus one more time first.

> *So tell me now*
>   *'Fore the road drags me down*
>   *That in your pulse you hear a vow*
>   *That you love this runaway*
>   *Say it out loud and I'll stay*
>   *Oh, please, 'fore the road drags me down*

Aspen looked at Emry, green eyes dancing in the footlights, and took his hand.

His vision plunged into darkness, as it always did, flooding him with fleeting panic. The possession had to be instant this time. He had to align with the rest of the troupe, he couldn't pause or stumble or stutter even for a second—

Then his vision opened again, and his glowing fingers flew swiftly, automatically along with the burst of music from behind him. Riley led the charge now, releasing the tension Sage had so carefully crafted into an upswing of floor-pounding energy. And within the riot of sound, Aspen's magic danced, infusing the very air with the bright echoes of a hundred voices. They weren't just a troupe—they were a whole choir, an entire orchestra, full and fierce and overflowing.

But Aspen wasn't done yet.

Slowly, the flowers began to change. They were pinpricks of light, at first—blue, green, purple fireflies amidst the shadowed faces. But with each verse, the bouquets bloomed farther outward, spilling over seats and into the aisles, until the audience floated in a sea of perfumed beacons. All throughout the seats, people leapt to their feet, gasping and craning their necks to take in the endless stretch of beauty.

The troupe couldn't help but bask in the awe, both celebrating and encouraging the ethereal growth. Sage whirled around onstage like a cloud, skirts flowing around her ankles, her voice filling every crack the light hadn't touched. Riley's arms were a blur behind the drums, grin wide, eyes blazing, sweat dripping down her forehead.

A wild bliss stirred in Aspen and poured into Emry. This was what they had promised, wasn't it? An unfamiliar bard, a forest spirit, and a virtuosic troupe putting on the best concert they had ever seen?

The forest spirit had done their part. All the others had to do was keep playing.

The music kept tumbling forward in raucous waves, and when the audience began to sing along, Aspen tugged Emry off the stage and through the aisles. Flowers and vines blossomed around them, and Emry's voice wove through the crowd in a way that had been impossible, unthinkable, in any other performance he had ever done.

As he looped back onto the stage, fingers flying along the neck of his lute, he bravely sought the gaze of one person standing in the front row—Karlson. Those around him had stood up to follow Emry's path, gaping and singing and clapping. Karlson stood with them, observing the spectacle with a more professional grace.

But as Emry passed, he grinned and gave one single, approving nod.

Emry leapt back onto the stage with unrestrained joy.

He lost track of how many songs they sang afterward. He knew there were two more in the set, but there must have been an encore, and perhaps another. His makeup was smudged with sweat and at some point, his waistcoat had come unbuttoned—but it didn't matter. He could stay on these floorboards forever, tangling flowers and magic and song. And within him, Aspen didn't want to stop, either. He could feel them reaching for more vines, growing more flowers, soaking up the cheers and the fragrance of thousands of blooms—

But when the last song ended, Sage looked at Emry and froze in fear.

What? Aspen asked. Emry narrowed his gaze at Sage in a wordless question. She raised a hand to just under her nose; Emry mimicked her motion, then pulled his hand back.

Blood, warm and dripping, stained his fingers.

"That's all we have for tonight!" Sage called to the audience, bounding forward to wave to the shadows and block Emry from view. Out on the floor, the lights within the flowers began to flicker out. "Thank you all *so* much, this has been an incredible show, and you're the best audience we could have possibly asked for—"

Aspen pulled Emry toward the curtain, alarm now coursing through them both. He managed one last nod to the audience before everything went fuzzy and tilted, and a strong hand veered him into the backstage darkness.

"Steady," Damir's voice guided him further into the black. As soon as the footlights left Emry's peripheral vision, his legs collapsed.

Aspen—

I'm trying, get me closer—

His tilted sight locked on the flowering lute sitting against the wall. He tried to stagger toward it, then fell back to his knees, Damir's hands grabbing his shoulders. His breath came in shuddering waves, and stars crowded his eyes.

"Karic," Damir hissed, his voice full of fear. "I don't have an antidote for this!"

But Emry couldn't respond—it was all he could do to keep breathing and reaching for the lute.

This is as far as I can—

Aspen leapt out, sending him fully to the floor. He caught the ground with his hands, the wood blessedly cool against his palms, then reached out to steady the rocking lute.

"Aspen?" He coughed. "Tell me you're in there."

"I'm here," they said, the lute vibrating against the wall. "I'm all right. But you—"

"I'll be okay." Emry lowered his forehead to the wood, relishing the coolness of the planks and letting the stars filter out of his vision. Then he slowly pushed himself to his knees, stabbing pain jolting with every tiny movement, lightheadedness muddying his thoughts. He screwed his eyes shut and felt around for the healing flower Aspen had set aside. Even with the bloom, he'd feel this one for days, he was sure of it.

"Here." Riley staggered in and handed a handkerchief to Sage, who pressed it to his face. He took it and nodded to them both.

"Thank you," he murmured. "Really, I'll be okay. I..." His troupemates' silhouettes briefly went double, and he dragged himself to lean against the wall. "I think I'm okay. Just need to take the flower and rest for a—"

"What in Shiro's name was that?"

They all turned. Cal stood in the backstage doorway, tears streaking her face.

"What were you rotting *thinking* up there?" she shouted, her voice both trembling and radiating fire. "You could've—you could've *died*. I thought you were going to die right in front of me. What were you thinking? What were *any* of you thinking?"

Emry broke, his guilt and shame increasing his pain tenfold until it throbbed deeply in his arms. If he'd cut his own heart out, it would have hurt less.

"I'm sorry," he said, the words coming out fractured and raspy. "I'm sorry, I should've told you—"

"Told me?" Cal repeated, stepping forward. "You shouldn't have done it in the first place!"

Aspen's lute shook with their voice. "It's my fault, too!" they tried to shout back. "Look, I agreed to do it!"

Damir stepped between them, hands raised.

"Don't care who's to blame right now," he said. "Give him space. He's still bleeding."

But the stage wasn't done receiving visitors.

"Mr. Karic?" one last voice called out, slicing through the chaos. Everyone except for Damir turned around to face the source. Emry weakly craned his neck to look at the newcomer.

"Hello, Karlson," he wavered.

Karlson regarded the assortment of people around him—Cal's tear-stained face, the blood dripping from Emry's nose, the guilty looks on Sage and Riley's faces—then stepped back and raised his hands.

"So..." he said slowly. "I suppose this a bad time to congratulate you on the best concert Matlock has ever seen?"

CHAPTER NINETEEN

CAL

THE BACKSTAGE AREA devolved into chaos. Between troupe members rushing to talk to Karlson, the Trellis crew attempting to close the stage for the night, and the terrible, blood-soaked standoff happening by the wall, the very air hardly had space to get a word in.

"Out," Damir finally said, shooing Sage and Riley away. "I'll ensure they make it back to the hotel, but right now they need space." He turned back to Cal. "Ms. Breslin, I completely understand your concern here, but please allow me to get them both back home and settled."

"No," Cal found herself saying, her voice still ragged and brittle. "I'll accompany Emry back to the hotel myself. If you would please escort Aspen separately and have a doctor meet us at the room?"

"Cal." Aspen scrambled up their lute in mouse form, their silhouette guttering in the shadows. "Please don't be too angry with him—"

"Don't think I'm only angry with *him*," she said sharply. "You played your part. I would just like to..." She took an unsteady breath. "Talk to Emry on the way there."

Talking to Emry alone in a carriage did require a certain skirting of the rules, but as Cal helped him stumble into the vehicle, she gathered a few facts to reassure herself. The narrow road beside the Trellis lay dark and empty, and if anyone truly cared to gossip about her in the morning, it would be overshadowed by gossip of the concert itself.

Emry's performance, at least, had made sure of that.

The carriage finally rolled into the street, with Emry lying down on one seat and Cal sitting ramrod straight on the other. She couldn't bring herself to relax an inch nor push her memories of him—eyes glowing, white veins pulsing in his arms and up into his neck—out of her mind.

The last time she had seen him like that, he had almost stopped breathing.

"I'm sorry," Emry croaked weakly from his corner. He still held a bloodstained handkerchief to his nose, his inhales slow and heavy. But his eyes were shining with anxiety as they searched her face. "I'm so sorry, I truly didn't mean to scare you."

"Why did you do it?" she asked, her words cracking.

"Karlson couldn't perform. Damir was going to cancel the concert if—"

"If what? If you didn't endanger yourself onstage?"

Emry lowered his handkerchief. "If we didn't bring something different, something that would draw them in. It was that or throw away our debut. Aspen and I made that decision together."

Cal had to look out the window, her throat tightening. Everyone had known for days—everyone except for her. "And why didn't you tell me?"

"I meant to. Aspen wanted to, I just..." He hesitated. "I knew you'd be angry."

"Of course, I'd be angry!" Her tightly coiled rage began to unwind, whipping her words louder and faster. "You nearly threw your life away and didn't deem it necessary to even *warn* me. So, I stood there, watching you, feeling like an utter fool for ever—"

She looked at Emry and cut herself off.

He had unconsciously curled deeper into the corner, his entire body stiff, his inhales uneven. He was preparing for loudness, for anger and insults. He had received it before, hadn't he? Years ago, with his family.

Years ago, with her.

She weighed her own barbed words on her tongue, sharp, angry rebukes aching to be unleashed...then swallowed them. It took effort —the anger was still there, simmering behind her teeth—but letting it take over now would only ensure that he never told her anything again. She had almost lost him, yes, but if she shouted at him now, if she unloaded all her resentment, she would lose him in a different way.

She took one more deep breath, then reached for his wrist and held it gently.

"Look. I don't want you to feel like you need to hide anything from me," she said quietly, trailing her thumb across his wrist. "Whatever you're worried about or afraid of, we can talk through it. Even if it does make me angry." She met his gaze and placed her other hand on top of his. "You can trust me. I'm not going anywhere, all right?"

The fear in Emry's eyes gave way to exhaustion, and he sank bonelessly into the corner. Cal could almost see his anxiety unwinding in invisible spirals around him.

"I love you," he said, the words coming out as a raspy sigh. His hand moved to hold hers, even as he winced through the motion. "I'm not going anywhere, either. As much as it...might've looked it like onstage." He exhaled. "I'm so sorry, and I won't hide anything like this from you again, I promise."

She linked her pinky finger with his. "Truly?"

With effort, he lifted the back of her hand to his lips. "Truly."

CHAPTER
TWENTY

CAL

THE PEEK OF THE SEASON

If you were not in attendance at the Trellis yesterday evening, may Hara have pity on you, for you have missed a concert that the goddess herself would have applauded.

I am afraid poor Karlson is all but forgotten, and all the season longs for is another appearance by Spiritsong. Not even this writer can pay proper tribute to Mr. Karic's talent and Aspen's magic—and I do mean that in a literal sense. You simply must see them for yourselves to believe it. If I tried to describe their artistry to you without such observation, I daresay you would send me to the seaside for my health.

THE FOLLOWING MORNING, Cal woke to a headache, a pounding amalgamation of fear, anger, and restlessness from the night before. She dressed with slow, weary movements, less than eager to begin the day, step into the sunlight, search for some tea—

But when she opened the door, she found a little patch of sunlight waiting at her feet.

Someone—or, rather, someones—had stacked a dozen flower crowns in front of her door, a card balanced atop the petals. She picked up the card and read it first.

I know flowers won't fix anything, it said in Emry's unmistakable scrawl, *but try telling that to a forest spirit*. Then, surrounded by scribbly circles, hearts, and underlines in a different, messier hand: *We love you.*

Cal brought the stack inside and set the crowns on her bedside table, where their perfume wafted around her. Fighting against her residual anger, she looked through each one. There were no red roses here. Instead, Aspen had woven in daffodils, white tulips, hyacinths...all perfectly crafted symbols of regret and apology.

She ran a finger over one of the soft tulip petals. She hadn't shaken the previous night's events, of course. Visions of glowing veins and unmoving hands had followed her into her dreams, contributing to the headache that now haunted her.

But those nightmares weren't real, she reminded herself. Emry and Aspen were alive and well only one room over. They were alive, and they loved her, and she still loved them.

Terrible mistakes and all.

She set down the flowers and opened the nightstand drawer, where Dev's stolen plans lay. Her chest tightened again, but her anger shifted, directed at someone different, someone far less apologetic.

Yes, she loved Emry and Aspen—and someone out there was trying to kill them both.

"We need to take down the dig site," Aspen said. "Now."

The trio stood in Pigeon's garden the following day, forming a huddle with Lydia and Damir to share Cal's findings. Aspen took no form today—to save their energy, they were invisible, their lute leaning up against a tree. But there was no mistaking the rage in their voice. "We have to destroy it as soon as we can."

No one in their little circle could blame them. It wasn't just Dev's stolen plans that had incensed the spirit—the garden they stood in was a far cry from what they had seen weeks ago. Rosebushes openly withered and browned, hay-like grass crackled under their feet. There was no hiding the state of the garden anymore, and its patrons whispered in fear, shoving fruit and coins into the fane in a desperate bid to heal the place.

Cal desperately wished that it would work. Dev was single-handedly waging war against the Matlock spirits, and right now, he was winning.

"And we're sure this dig site is doing...*this* to the spirits?" Damir asked, toeing the dead grass with his boot.

"S'not just the spirits anymore," Lydia said, her usually loud voice closer to a low grumble. "The problem's spread to other gardens, too. You see that cypress patch on the way here?" She handed Cal a smudged map. "Completely dead, and no spirit's ever lived there. Aspen confirmed it for me."

Cal grimaced at the map, a drawing of Matlock increasingly covered in frantic red circles.

"Without seeing the dig site myself, I only have theories, but..." She passed the map to Damir. "Based off Dev's mining pattern, I believe what we're seeing is a sort of defense mechanism on the well's part, like a flinch. Every time he tries to mine it, it pulls energy from above to protect itself. It started with the spirits"—she pointed to Pigeon's garden on the map—"but clearly that's no longer enough."

From his spot on the bench, Emry leaned over to inspect the map in Damir's hands. He sat with a hunch and leaned heavily on his cane, his Guild pin stowed away and a hat shading his face to avoid attention from the public. After a full day of rest, he looked far better than he had immediately after the concert, but his unsteady movements and lethargy remained.

"Look, I agree with Aspen that the site needs to be taken down," he said, his voice scratchy. "But are you sure there's no one we can go to about this first?"

"We shouldn't risk it." Damir folded the map. "I told you, Halleson has far too much of a presence in this city. We lay a finger on his reputation, and we're the ones who will get jailed. If we can find and destroy this dig site, it'll be the quickest solution to..." He waved at the garden with the folded paper. "All this."

"Then we'll find it," Aspen said. The lute rocked a few times, and Pigeon's red rhythm blooms began to grow around the instrument. Damir stared blankly at the display.

"What are they doing now?"

"Bartering," Emry said.

Aspen had come up with the idea this morning. The stolen notes hadn't specified the location of the dig site, and the northern forest would take weeks for them to comb through on their own. But if the city's spirits could reach out and sense it, help them narrow down the search...

Yellow flowers soon joined the red flowers, followed by purple, then blue. Cal tried to recall which spirit each color represented. Willow had been orange earlier in the week—or perhaps they were purple? She dug out her notebook. Gods, it would be so much easier if the spirits could simply talk out loud...

The flowers all furled and unfurled in rapid succession. Damir frowned at the movements. "And what are they doing now?"

Cal compared the colors to her notes. More than five spirits were all talking now, and quickly, if the pattern was anything to go on. "It seems they're debating."

Minutes passed—then the flowers all withered, and Aspen

appeared as a mouse perched on the head of their lute. A heavy sigh came out of their little body.

"She says they can do it," they said, "but they want music."

Emry tilted his head. "Music?"

"They heard our concert and now they want one of their own."

In the branches above them, a barely visible pigeon began to hum wordless fragments of "Before I Leave," the same half melody she had memorized earlier.

"Well, we"—Emry glanced nervously at Cal—"we can't exactly do a full concert with all of the, um, trimmings, but...I suppose we could have a special sort of rehearsal here?"

He looked at Damir for approval, whose tired eye circles overrode any other emotion he may have had.

"Look," he said. "I'd rather the spirits not have learned collective bargaining so fast, but if it's just a few songs they want..." He slumped. "I suppose we can fit it into the schedule."

"Good," Aspen said, cleaning their whiskers in satisfaction. "A few songs, and my friends will find us the spirit well."

CHAPTER
TWENTY-ONE

EMRY

THE PEEK OF THE SEASON

I must admit that the letters from my column's admirers have been perplexing as of late. I profess myself to be knowledgeable of the social goings-on of the city, of its various shocks and disturbances—but I am afraid I know very little of the biological goings-on of its gardens.

If one is concerned about the distressing state of our groves—and indeed, many of you are, as you have written—might I humbly suggest a prayer to your preferred spirit? One can only trust that they know what is best for their domain, and that their illness, whatever it is, flies away as quickly as these last few weeks have.

AFTER PIGEON'S SUCCESSFUL BARTERING, Emry rested for the remainder of the day. Though many were eager to see and speak with him after the concert, he couldn't bring himself to remain standing for much longer than what the garden visit had required. He spent the afternoon and evening alternating between sipping moonflower tea, grumbling about pain, and debating with Aspen on how to make it up to Cal.

"I can do better than flower crowns," Aspen said, the lute sitting beside Emry in bed. They sometimes curled up in terrier form at his feet, but they were invisible now, just as tired as he was. "What if I expanded her garden in Vornik?"

"That would be nice, but she needs something now, not weeks from now." Emry flipped his pillow to the cool side and buried his face in it, pretending like that would help with the pain. Not only did the heavy, oppressive aches keep him bedridden, but his thoughts had thickened into mush, turning his brainstorming into a piddling little shower.

"She needs something nice," he continued, weakly waving a hand. "You know, not a *thing*, but time. She deserves a break." He paused and lifted his head from the pillow, his squishy thoughts solidifying. "She deserves a break."

TWO DAYS LATER, when Emry could finally stand and walk again, he took a breath and knocked on Cal's hotel door. It wasn't a good look, being alone and knocking on a young lady's door like this, but he'd risk it. He'd risked many other things on this trip—what was one more?

"Yes?" Cal's voice floated into the hall.

Emry cleared his throat. "It's me."

When the door opened, he couldn't help but feel a twinge of fear, as if he didn't quite believe she was done yelling at him for his blunders. He tightened his grip on his cane and pushed the feeling away.

Cal wasn't yelling at him—she merely stood there in her dressing gown, her hair already up in twists for the night.

"I thought you'd be at the rehearsal for Pigeon," she said with a frown, peeking out from behind the door.

"I'll be leaving soon, yes, but..." He held out his hand with a jolt of anticipation. "There is something I have to do first."

Cal hesitantly took his hand, not moving from behind the door. "Em, I'm not exactly dressed to go anywhere—"

But he didn't pull her into the hall. He kissed the back of her hand, then stepped into the doorway, lowering his voice to a husky whisper.

"At the risk of sounding like an utter rake," he murmured, "get into bed."

Cal's confused frown shifted into an utterly befuddled smile. "All right, then..."

He closed the door and let her lead the way to the bed, where she slipped under the covers. Once she was in, he leaned forward, gave her a soft kiss...

And tucked the covers tight and snug around her.

"Footman, if you could?" he called. Aspen entered the room on cue, bearing several trays with exaggerated aplomb. They carefully laid the trays all around Cal—steaming tea, cookies, a stack of chocolate cakes Emry had convinced the hotel kitchens to send up...

"I'd have brought them in myself, but, well." Emry gestured sheepishly to his cane. "I had to employ some assistance."

But Aspen didn't mind—they were greatly enjoying stoking the fire, fluffing the pillows behind Cal's head, and nudging the lavender on the tray, making the decorative stems grow a little more purple.

Cal's confusion melted into a laugh. "What is all this—?"

But they weren't done. While Aspen buzzed about, Emry stacked books all around Cal—first the ones she had brought with her, then new ones he had sent for, each with its own ribboned bookmark. He had gathered any and every bit of reading material he thought might interest her: newly published theories on the stars, titillating romance novels... He had even thrown in a book on pirates, silently marking that one to borrow later for himself.

He stepped back to appraise his bookish handiwork and stifled a laugh. Between the trays, blankets, extra pillows, and stacks of literature, he could barely see the recipient of all his affection. She beamed and lifted a stack of books so she could see him.

"Em, truly, what is all this?"

"Only the very least you deserve." Emry held out a hand to Aspen. "Excellent work, footman."

"Thank you, sir." Aspen shook his hand. "I will await my tip outside."

They bowed and ducked out, giving Emry a few more seconds alone with Cal.

"Are you comfortable enough in there?" he asked, taking a seat beside her on the edge of the bed.

"Very." Cal sank into the pillows and hugged one of the books to her chest. "Thank you for all this."

He grinned; he hadn't seen her so relaxed since before they left Vornik. He would have to pull this stunt far more often.

"Thank you for everything." He kissed her on the forehead. "Have a good night, love."

He started to stand, but Cal reached for him. "Wait," she said, pushing herself to sit higher. "The night of the concert—I'm afraid I made a blunder of my own."

"Cal, I'm sure you didn't—"

She took his hand in both of hers.

"I never congratulated you on your performance. No matter my... feelings on it at the time, it was a triumph." Her voice softened. "Please don't think I didn't notice."

A knot formed in Emry's throat. It didn't matter what the papers said or even what Karlson said—this was the highest compliment he could have received.

"Thank you." He squeezed her hand and began to pull away— but she didn't let go just yet.

"And one other thing?"

"Yes?"

She reached up, pulled on his cravat, and kissed him, knocking the breath out of his lungs. When she finally released him, her beaming smile had gone wickedly sharp.

"A bit of rakishness suits you."

LATER THAT EVENING, Emry set off with Aspen, Sage, and Riley in tow, his thoroughly good mood untarnished. Not by the pain in his knees, nor the cold chill in the night air, nor even by the argument currently happening behind him.

"You know," Riley grumbled, shifting her drum in her arms and looking around at the deserted street. "After the Trellis, I didn't think this is where we'd end up performing next."

Emry hid a grin; he and Aspen had thought up a quick lie to encourage the ladies to join them for this special rehearsal. Music healed spirits, Aspen asserted. And so, the spirits needed some music.

"I think it's nice," Sage said, trying to sound encouraging. "Even if the music doesn't help, I'm sure the spirit will appreciate the, um… show of support."

Emry ushered them into the garden and let Aspen instruct them on where to set up. The spirit bounded from one tree to the next, finally landing on a cherry tree by the balcony railing—not Pigeon's normal tree, but the healthiest one in the garden.

"This one," they said. "Set up here."

They did so, forming a small band underneath the boughs. As they prepared, flowers of all colors sprang out of the ground—spirits taking their seats, as it were. Emry elbowed Aspen. "Your friends are here to see you."

Aspen grinned and touched the grass, sending light blue flowers of their own into the fray.

They played through the first several songs on their Trellis set list. The garden was no amphitheater, but Emry enjoyed the sound anyway. It reminded him of the Sada festival, not in Tazlo but in Senne, where they sang in the forests through the evening. He wondered how many silent spirits had been listening to him then, deep in the trees, absorbing the music.

He knew there were several listening here—but once the songs finished, there was no further evidence they had heard the music at all. Just a breeze rippling through the flowers, weakly filling the silence left behind.

Emry shifted. Like his first visit, the garden unsettled him, particularly in the gloomy quiet. Though the grass around him had grown a little greener at the music, he could still feel how weak the grove was, like it mirrored the aches all through his body. And beside him, Aspen frowned as well, their gaze roving across the garden in concern.

Riley was the first to break the silence. "Listen, the garden's real nice and all, and I hope they liked it, but I'm starting to get cold and—"

"Wait!"

Riley froze. "Who said that?"

A pigeon hopped onto the branch above them, materializing out of the darkness. It was nothing remarkable—not until one caught its wispy edges and the sunset-like patch of iridescence at its neck.

Before anyone could blink, Aspen had shifted into a pigeon, too, fluttering around in a tizzy of questions.

"How are you feeling?" they asked. "Did you like the songs? Did you have a favorite?"

And Pigeon responded—not with silent looks, nor hummed melodies, but with actual words.

"Lovely?" she said, testing out the sound. "Lovely...music. Beautiful, thank you much."

Emry stared in wonder. Here she was—the first Matlock spirit to talk to humans. Drawn out by Aspen's friendliness and a bit of music.

If he'd had full use of his legs, he would've sprinted to pull Cal out of bed for this.

Then Pigeon swooped down to a lower branch by Sage and tilted her head. "Another? Please?"

Sage gasped in delight and grabbed Riley's arm. "Yes," she said, scrambling to pick up her instrument. "Yes, absolutely, little one."

They gladly began another song—but as the night wore on, it wasn't just spirits that came to listen. People meandering by the garden peered in, then slipped past the gates and took a bench to watch. They gradually waved over acquaintances who were walking by, who hailed their own friends. And before long, the garden was full of people—not disinterested society folk dripping with silk and jewels, but normal people off the street, just as eager as Pigeon for some music at the end of a long day. Emry felt a warmth he couldn't attribute to the night air—it wasn't all that different from his old musical haunts, the inns and taverns and pubs.

At first, he feared Sage and Riley would be unimpressed by this audience—but they were more relaxed than he had ever seen them before. Riley started taking recommendations from the crowd, ensuring everyone heard their favorites. Sage urged Pigeon to sit next to her so the spirit could see how the hurdy-gurdy worked. And Aspen couldn't decide which form to take—sometimes a pigeon, sometimes a human to sing with Emry. All around them, more flowers bloomed, and more spirits listened in. It wasn't easy for them—Emry could see how weak the stems were, how the leaves already drooped—but they did it all the same, their petals standing in rapt attention.

Once the last song ended, Emry gently touched one of the vines on the balcony, home to a rainbow of colors. The vines thickened and grew greener, a small show of appreciation for him. He smiled; they should come back to perform at the garden more often.

When he voiced as much to Sage and Riley, they heartily agreed.

"Can we do this again tomorrow?" Sage asked eagerly as they packed up for the night, the moon hanging high in the sky. "Should we go to this garden again or another one?"

Riley perked up—not to dash the idea, but to pile on. "Can we bring drinks to the next one? Spread the word a bit? If we can find a bigger garden, we could fit more people, really get something going."

Emry laughed. "I don't know if the garden's neighbors will want us out here every night," he said. "But we'll come back soon, I promise."

Sage and Riley wandered out of the garden together, still planning the next venture.

"You know, if we get some hand pies to go with your drinks..."

"We'll need the full troupe for the next one, obviously. They'll be on board if I tell them there's pie. You think Karlson'll come and watch?"

"Oh, he'll be terribly jealous we're doing this without him..."

But they weren't the only ones eagerly planning something.

"Helping," Pigeon said to Aspen, her words light on the breeze. "Finding the dig soon."

"Thank you." Aspen bowed to the bird. Emry bowed as well.

"Pigeon," he said. "Do take care of yourself, will you?"

Pigeon bobbed her head and cooed. Then they made their way back to the hotel, Aspen bouncing with energy the entire way.

"Pigeon says they've already got that spirit searching." They pointed to another garden as they passed. "And one up there on that tier. And a few down on the lower level, but I can't see those gardens from here. I'll try to visit all of them later tonight and see if they could hear the music. I hope they did."

Emry ruffled Aspen's hair; a few flower petals fell out. "I'm glad you've found friends here," he said. "Just give them a few days, and we'll make sure they're all healthy again."

Aspen gave a happy hum that sounded a little like a pigeon coo.

CHAPTER
TWENTY-TWO

CAL

Upon hearing of the successful rehearsal in the garden, Cal held on to a childish hope that Emry's music would sustain the spirits a little longer—that their boosted morale would somehow translate to more energy, greener grass, rosebushes that actually bloomed.

But several days later, she woke up to a grumpy, translucent Aspen perched on the balcony railing. Instead of waking up excited to talk about what they had learned from the city spirits overnight, they were quietly working on their embroidery, stabbing the fabric with far more force than was necessary. The needle kept slipping out of their wispy fingers, and all around them, the balcony flowers had furled.

"The spirits are afraid this morning," they explained when Cal asked after their mood. "Jasper's not answering, Willow's barely talking. Pigeon thinks they might not last the week."

A chill went through Cal. Jasper and Willow weren't the only spirits bearing the brunt of Dev's continued escapades—half of

Aspen's shoulder wasn't there at all. Just sunbeams streaming through thin air.

"And the spirits haven't found the well yet?" she asked.

"They're getting close." Aspen dropped the needle again and shook out their near-formless hand. "I could miss the regatta today and stay with Pigeon, so she can tell me as soon as she knows."

Cal bit her lip. Damir had business on the other side of town today and had insisted they remain in a public place, where high-profile crowds could shield them from any threats. To help, she had secured an invitation to the annual regatta, where Lydia and her associates had gone in on a tent together. The riverside would be packed, Cal reasoned, and Emry liked boats. It would keep them safe for an afternoon, at least—and let her keep an eye on Aspen's flickering.

"I'd prefer you stay with us," she said, trying to keep her tone positive. "It's only a few hours, and we can check on Pigeon the moment we're done."

In an attempt to lift Aspen's mood, she explained the regatta to them as they traveled down to the riverside, pointing out the observation tents along the river and where the rowers would start the race. Despite Aspen's wariness, it was a clear, lovely day, and the sunshine gradually brightened Aspen's mood.

But when Cal arrived at Lydia's tent and found Emry and his troupemates already present, she found that the sunshine hadn't improved everyone's outlook. Though Emry stood without a cane today, he still wore a frown, his eyes fixed on the river.

"Georgie, Mar, and I could take 'em," he muttered and folded his arms, his voice heavily tinged with homesickness. "We'd beat them by half a minute, easy."

"I'd bet on you." Sage nodded confidently. Riley sipped her wine.

"I'd bet Sage's money on you."

The three of them stood at the edge of the tent with an excellent view of the grassy slope, the pathway, and the river's edge below. On the opposite side of the tent, Lydia and her researchers huddled in tense, hushed conversation. There were no boats yet to distract them—at the moment, there was only one safety officer in a kayak lounging by the riverside.

Aspen set down their lute and joined Lydia and her team, but Cal gravitated toward Emry first. She could allow herself half a moment in the sunlight before being dragged back into worrisome scientific discussion.

"What's the prize for this race, Cal?" Emry asked her as she approached. "A decent spot in the social papers?"

She gave a hum and mimicked his pose, looking to the water. "Five hundred gold, I believe."

Emry choked. "Five hundred—?" He pointed to the safety officer. "Forget my sisters, just put me in the kayak. I can do it."

She laughed. "I don't believe that entirely follows the rules of the race."

"Never mind the rules," Riley said. "I want to see it. Emry, I'll give you three hundred of Sage's gold if you steal the kayak and show them all up."

"Excuse you," Sage said—but she smiled behind her wineglass. "I'd put in two-fifty at most."

"Deal." Riley prodded Sage. "I'm going to need more snacks for this."

They turned and trotted up the hill, leaving Cal and Emry behind.

"If he wins the gold," Riley said, "we could get more hanging plants for the next concert. You know, the ones with the really big leaves."

Sage gasped. "What about trees onstage? Real, actual trees..."

They wandered deeper into the tent, and Emry sighed.

"What about it, Ms. Breslin?" He gave her a sidelong glance, his grin going crooked. "Wouldn't you like to see me win out there for you?"

Heat rose in Cal's cheeks as she recalled Emry rowing in the past.

Sleeves rolled up, strong arms fully on display. And the way his arms were folded now...

She looked down at his arms, then caught herself. Oh, no. She was staring. Gods, she shouldn't have flirted with him the other night. The moment had stuck in her brain ever since, and all she could think about now was him making more low, rakish comments behind closed doors—

"You don't need to win to please me," she stammered, knowing immediately it was the wrong thing to say. Emry leaned closer to her, his breath brushing past her ear.

"Then what do I need to do to please you?"

His hand skated the small of her waist, and to anyone else, it would have looked as if he were simply making a quiet comment to her about the weather or the state of the water. But to Cal, the simple touch sent shockwaves through her, and she found herself staring at his cravat, silently willing it to undo itself.

Emry drew away, his grin wicked. "Well, I'm off to get a drink. Do inform me once you have an idea, yes?"

He wandered off, whistling her favorite melody. Cal cleared her throat and tried to remain as stoic as possible. Stupid men, stupid bards, stupid societal rules against kissing them silly in public...

She checked the river, looking to see if the boats were going to pass by soon and distract her. There were no boats yet, but her gaze did catch a few people at the neighboring tent. It was far more extravagant than Lydia's. Someone had gone to the effort of carrying rugs and armchairs to the shoreline—and it only took a second to see who was hosting.

Halleson, surrounded by people, his back turned to Cal. She quickly ducked back behind the fabric of the tent, but pricked her ears to catch a scrap of his conversation.

"No, I'm afraid the new art gallery won't be finished by the new year," Halleson was informing his admirers, "but I am indeed hoping to unveil something...*different* to you all before the year is out. I trust you will find it quite special. Another great boon to the city, I believe."

Cal briefly curled her fingers into a fist. A great boon to the city, indeed.

Halleson's voice faded away, and she dared a peek to see if Dev was in the tent as well. She saw no sign of him, and Halleson's back was still turned to her, thankfully—

But one of the man's guards briefly glanced in her direction, and fear latched in her throat.

"Ms. Pietri?" she called, eager to hurry out of the guard's line of sight. "Do you know when the race will begin?"

She tucked herself safely into the researcher huddle, only to find that their conversation echoed the tension Aspen had felt earlier.

"Gardens nine through twelve are entirely dead as far as I can tell," Mr. Spencer said, his face pale. "Dry as tinder. Visitors were in a panic, but I hardly knew what to tell them. Wish I could just"—he waved his hands in frustration—"*talk* to the spirits. See how they're feeling, tell them we're trying to help..."

Lydia turned to Aspen. "Have you spoken to our friends? How are they doing?"

"Not good." Aspen's gaze unfocused as they silently checked on the other spirits. In such concentration, they faded even further—Cal could see the river through their form, and the rowers beginning to pass the tent. "There are...at least two spirits I can't find anymore, and—"

"Hello, hello!" another voice stepped in jovially.

Cal stiffened. James had appeared at the edge of the tent, as sudden and jarring as if she had chanted *pomade* three times over a ring of lit candles. He smiled, undeterred by the group's serious expressions.

"Ah, our spirit experts. Just the people I wanted to see," he said, continuing inside.

The huddle stared at him.

"What do you need, James?" Cal said flatly.

"Absolutely nothing," he soldiered on. "Only your presence. I know we're all worried about our dear spirit gardens, so I've taken it upon myself to throw a charity ball at the end of this week at the Oakvale Grand. Invitations to come shortly, but I wanted you all to be among the first to know."

He paused, clearly expecting fanfare of some kind—praise or applause, perhaps.

He only received a few confused nods in return.

"A charity ball?" Lydia repeated with a frown.

"I'm organizing it with Mr. Halleson," he said proudly. "He was able to pull a few strings to make it happen at such short notice."

Cal pursed her lips. So, James was on friendly terms with Halleson now. Lovely.

"Will Mr. Gray be in attendance?" she asked. As she suspected, James lit up at the name drop, a shiny toy dangled in front of him. He pounced on it accordingly.

"I've spoken at length with Mr. Gray, and while his business carries him out of town that day, he expresses his full support for the venture."

Cal nodded. That meant Dev would be digging at the end of the week. If they wanted to destroy the dig site, they had to do it soon, before the day of the charity ball—

Someone outside the tent gave a yelp, and Cal turned to look at the water.

At first, she thought she was seeing things—the river had flown into a tumult in a matter of seconds. The once placid water now tumbled over itself in angry swells, brown with silt and drowning branches. Cal blinked, and its rage only grew. Waves rose and pummeled the shoreline, quickly overtaking the sidewalk. Observers close to the water rushed back up the slope in a panic, while the poor rowers scrambled to beach themselves as fast as they could.

"River's flooding," Cal breathed, then whipped back to Emry. "The river's flooding!"

The tent broke into chaos. Lydia tried to guide people out in an orderly fashion; James pushed a few people out of his way to get to higher ground. Emry ran to Cal instead, his hand at her elbow.

"Where's Aspen?"

They looked at the river. Aspen's form was nowhere to be found.

But Aspen's lute sat in the hands of Halleson's guard, who stood at the edge of the tumbling water.

"*Hey*!" Emry stumbled forward, but it was too late.

The guard threw the lute into the churning waves and ran.

CHAPTER
TWENTY-THREE

EMRY

Cal's scream rang in Emry's ear. He staggered forward, reaching for the attacker—but the man had already darted up the hill, and behind him, the lute spiraled away on the frothy water.

"Aspen!" Cal yelled, but the rushing water muffled her voice. "Oh, gods—"

"What is it?" Sage ran down, her gaze swiveling. "Where's Aspen?"

"Get to higher ground, all of you. I'll..." Emry ran toward the water on instinct, his path fruitless—until his gaze landed on the abandoned kayak at the edge of the river, caught between a branch and an armchair that had tumbled down the hill.

"Meet me at the docks up ahead!" he shouted back to them, then shrugged off his coat and started for the kayak. Cal tried to reach for his arm.

"Emry, no—"

But he had already splashed into the water, raw fear suppressing his protesting joints. "Go, I'll meet you there!"

He leapt into the kayak and paddled out with a panicked grip, ignoring the puddles inside the vessel and the riverweed draped over the bow. He had no time to settle in—the water had already turned into an unpredictable cluster of rapids. There was no avoiding whip-sharp branches in the debris, nor the other abandoned boats spinning wildly without occupants. He saw no other humans caught in the water—for that, he thanked Hara—but there was no sign of Aspen, either.

"There!" Cal shouted from the banks. She and Riley pointed downriver, where the lute flashed above the waves. Emry looked beyond it to the docks ahead. Dirty, churning water spilled over them, turning the wooden platforms into a line of dangerous undercuts.

He had to get to Aspen before either of them reached that point.

Cold spray pelted his face as he struggled to get closer, fighting every rapid until his arms trembled. And beyond him, the maddening loop of the current threw the lute this way and that in crazed indecision. Closer to Emry, then farther away, then closer still—close enough to count the lute strings, to stretch, to reach for it over patches of slick riverweed—

The attempt sent a sharp jolt of pain through his aching limbs, and he reeled back before he could tumble into the water.

"Emry *Karic*!" Cal's fear shot her words across the river. "I swear to Hara, if you fall in—"

He wiped water from his eyes, shoved aside the pain, and reached again, eyes darting between the lute and the looming docks. But his arm was still a foot away, foam freezing his shaking hands, waves threatening to yank him into the muddy depths. He was almost there—gods, if he could just close the distance between them—

Below his hand, a strand of riverweed shot out toward the lute and wrapped around its neck. He leapt to catch the soaked vine and pulled in the instrument like a struggling fish.

THE SPIRIT WELL

"You did it, Aspen!" he shouted, slinging the lute over his shoulder. "Hold on for me, I'll get you back on shore."

With all the remaining strength in his screaming arms, he forced the kayak to shore and careened into the banks with very little grace, mud and water spraying in every direction. It was all he could do to stumble out and escape up the hill before the rushing waters claimed the vessel again. As soon as his feet struck the higher walkway, he dropped the lute onto the grass and fell to his knees beside it.

"Aspen?" he rattled, then coughed out water. The taste of mud wasn't going to leave his mouth for a week. "Please tell me you're in there."

He desperately fumbled with the mess that was the lute—pulling leaves out of the sound hole, rubbing dirt off the wood, cleaning up the spirit's drenched flowers. One of the flowers, a simple daisy, opened up to the sunlight, eager to dry off.

"Don't bother cleaning it out," Aspen said weakly. "I'll—I'll get it all sorted..."

Emry hugged the lute to his chest in relief, not caring about the water pouring onto him. "Oh, thank Hara. You scared me to death back there." He kept cleaning the lute despite Aspen's words, his voice still shaking. "You really came through with that riverweed, though."

"Riverweed?" Aspen echoed. "What are you talking about?"

"The riverweed—you made it move. It wrapped around your lute and everything."

"That wasn't me."

Emry's hands stopped moving.

"Another spirit, do you think?" He looked at the churning waters. "In the river?"

"There aren't any river spirits here."

He kept staring at the water.

"Emry?"

He didn't answer. He was too busy trying to rebuild the moment in his head. Seeing the slick riverweed below his fingers, wanting so desperately to reach out and grab the lute—

It hadn't been...*him*, had it?

What a silly idea, he tried to tell himself. But his thoughts became jumbled, his chest tight—and the patch of grass around his hand began to shrivel.

He yelped and pulled his arm back...and the grass regained its color.

Oh, gods. It *had* been him.

As he knelt there, staring at the patch of grass, the wispy shape of a mouse formed on the back of his hand—barely there, the shadow of a shadow. But Aspen mustered the strength to place a tiny paw on Emry's knuckle, their bright black eyes focused on his face.

"Emry?" they said again, their voice shaking as much as his hand. "Was it you?"

Emry met their gaze. "I—I don't know. Maybe." He let out an unsteady breath. "Yes. I think so."

Aspen scuttled up to his wrist, their form weighing hardly more than a feather—but whatever they wanted to say next was drowned out by approaching voices.

"There they are—"

"Is Aspen all right?"

"Someone get a medic!"

Aspen disappeared. Emry held the lute to his chest and staggered to his feet. He wanted to dismiss the call for a medic, but he couldn't fault them for the concern. He was completely soaked, spattered in mud and stray leaves from head to toe. As he wiped at his forehead, smears of blood came back on his hand—no doubt due to the many branches he had rowed through.

He blinked, and Cal was in front of him, embracing him without a second thought for the mud that would stain her clothes.

"Thank the gods." Her voice rattled through his ribcage. "I thought I was going to lose you both. Aspen, do I need to find you more soil?"

She took a handkerchief and frantically dabbed at both Emry's cheeks and Aspen's lute, doing nothing but smearing more dirt around. Behind her, Riley tried to shoo away the growing crowd.

"Nothing to see here! Go on, go about your business!"

"Oh, don't worry," Aspen said bitterly to Cal. "I've got enough mud in here to last me a lifetime." A pause as water sloshed out of the sound hole and onto the grass. "Do I have permission to kill the man who threw me in?"

"Yes," Emry said.

"No," Cal corrected, then turned him toward a nearby bench. "Sit. Both of you."

She guided them to the bench and graciously accepted a few offerings from Sage—a blanket and a mug of something hot and watery. Emry sipped on it, but it did nothing for the muddy taste in his mouth.

"Thank you, Sage," he said, smiling weakly to reassure her—but she looked as unsteady as he felt.

"Cal said someone threw Aspen in," she said, her eyes wide. "Who would do that? Who would..." She took a breath. "I need to find Damir. And Karlson. And get you more blankets. Riley!" She picked up her skirts and dashed off to the other woman.

Cal watched her go, then lowered her voice. "Your attacker was one of Halleson's men. Though whether the attack was ordered by Dev or by Halleson, I can't be sure."

She rolled up Emry's sleeve to check his pulse. Some of the more stubborn onlookers gave her scandalized looks and whispered amongst themselves. Emry rolled his eyes—it wasn't like she was undressing him in public—

Then she started untying his cravat.

"Cal?" he tried weakly. She shot him a look and set two fingers at the pulse above his collarbone.

"If they think it's wrong for me to take care of you, they can all be dragged to dust."

She checked the pulse at his neck, then resumed cleaning his wounds in earnest, her hands blissfully warm against his river-chilled skin. When she blotted a thin cut along his jaw, he was sorely tempted to take her fingers and kiss each one, crowd be damned—but she finally drew away, her handkerchief too muddy to be of further use.

"You're freezing," she said, taking one of his hands in both of hers to warm it up. She wasn't wrong—in her grip, she felt like a hearth against his skin. "You need to change. Come on, let's find you a carriage."

Cal hurried them through the hotel lobby and up the stairs—a sight to be sure, as they dripped water and mud across the marble—then parted with them both at Emry's door.

"I'll send for someone to get a fire going," she said, then was off just as quickly, leaving Emry to stumble into the room with Aspen's lute.

He struggled to change into dry pants and a shirt, his arms complaining with every movement—but even so, he couldn't keep his thoughts off the water and the riverweed. He could still feel it against his fingers, cold and slimy and—

And leaping to save Aspen. Because he had wanted it to.

"Would you like to be out on the balcony, Aspen?" he rambled before the spirit could say anything. "The sunlight might help you recover faster."

"We should talk about—"

Emry hurried onto the balcony and placed the lute on the stone floor, making sure it caught the full sun. "And really, if you need any more soil or anything, I'm happy to—"

An invisible force applied pressure around Emry's waist. A hug, he realized, from the spirit too weak to take shape.

"Please," they said. "Please just sit in the sun with me."

Emry sat cross-legged next to the lute, then rested his head back against the railing and closed his eyes. The sunlight soon wicked away the river water and eased his thoughts. A maid soon came by to stoke the hearth, but he had all the warmth he needed out here. Perhaps he could doze off until Cal came back and pretend that everything had been a bad dream...

"I can feel it," Aspen said. Reality broke back into his thoughts.

"Feel what?" he asked. Beside him, the lute slowly regrew its leaves, water leaking out of the cracks. Seeing such a waterlogged wooden instrument would have given Emry a heart attack if the thing weren't already shattered and bursting with flowers.

"What you did," Aspen continued. "The connection you have." An invisible presence settled in front of Emry. "Your magic."

Emry's heart stuttered at the word *magic*.

"Oh, please, I don't," he fumbled, "it was a—a *fluke*, I can't do—"

"Here." A tiny branch from the balcony's flowers broke off and floated to the floor in front of Emry. "We can test my hypothesis. Try making this grow."

Emry narrowed his gaze at the space in front of him. "I regret introducing you to Cal."

"No, you don't." Aspen's smile came through in their voice. "Try it."

Emry exhaled and faced the little branch. He wasn't like Aspen—he couldn't feel it growing, or not growing, now that it had been snapped off its vine. But he could sense its general presence, just like he had known the garden flowers were dry and known the forest at the border was different. The *knowing* of it was hard to grasp, like trying to describe the sensation of knowing a musical note was too sharp.

But it was there all the same.

He held a hand out over the branch and thought about it growing longer. There was no desperation or urgency here, no life hanging in the balance, but he willed it all the same. He wanted it to drink in the sunlight, to reach higher into the sunbeams and away from the hot stone—

A leaf poked out of the node under the break. Then another. Then a tiny new branch, green and delicate, grew toward the sky.

Emry started laughing.

The sound was both disbelieving and bitter, joy and fear clattering against the stone walls of the balcony. He had a fraction of what Aspen had—he had *magic*, such a simple, pleasant, green thing—

But at the same time, he had magic, something no other human had. His family had only just accepted that he was a bard, and he had only just made headway in courting Cal—what would they think of him now? Would he be a fascination or a repulsion, a brother or a son or a science experiment? Would society turn him into a party trick like Aspen? Something to be gossiped about, gawked at? Gods, he wanted to belong both on the stage and off it, was that too much to ask—

Two invisible arms wrapped around his waist to hug him, and it didn't matter that Aspen had no form—he knew their green eyes were looking up at him, wide and worried.

"Does it hurt?" they whispered, their voice broken. "Is this my fault?"

Emry returned the hug fiercely. "It doesn't hurt," he reassured them. "And it's not your fault."

"But all the possessions and—and the flowers, they must've—"

"Done something, yes." He set a hand on Aspen's hair and could still feel a few tiny flowers there, the petals tickling his fingers. "But it was as much my doing as it was yours. I won't have you blame yourself, not for a second."

Voices echoed out in the hallway—Cal, Damir, and Karlson, their words slowly growing louder. Aspen pulled away in the faintest of human forms, but their hands gripped Emry's with their full strength.

"You have to tell Cal," they said.

Emry opened his mouth.

"You *have* to," Aspen repeated, their grip tightening. Emry looked at the door, excuses and lies bubbling up in his throat. He'd tell her once this was over, or when they were back in Vornik, or maybe never—

But he had promised her, hadn't he? If he went back on that now, he didn't deserve someone like her.

"All right." He nodded. "I'll tell her."

ONCE THE DOOR OPENED, the afternoon blurred. Cal ushered Emry straight into bed and dumped three new blankets over him. Damir swept in and began to pace about the room in a wake of curses, promises of revenge, and renewed oaths to quit his job after the season ended.

"And you're absolutely sure I can't wrap you all in duvets and send you back up the river to Vornik?" Damir muttered by the hearth. The trio stared flatly at him. "Was worth a shot."

"There is one thing we can do," Karlson said. "We can cancel the next few concerts."

Emry's heart seized, and he tried to sit up under all the blankets. "No, please—we only just started, it'll cut the debut—"

Karlson leaned against the hearth next to Damir. "I don't like it either, but I've had enough experience with knives in backstage shadows to know you wouldn't be safe there. We should cancel them for now, until this problem is sorted."

"Until the problem's sorted?" Damir repeated. "Halleson's throwing my musicians into the river. Who says he's going to stop once we ruin his little spirit murder project?"

"We'll figure that out." Karlson raised a calming hand. "But we need to ruin his little spirit murder project first."

"Dev will be back at his dig site at the end of the week," Cal jumped in. "If we could try to find the site before then..." She looked at Aspen's lute, which still sat in the sun on the balcony.

"My friends are working as fast as they can," they said sharply, then relented. "But...I'll check with them tomorrow."

Damir nodded and ran a hand through his hair. "Tomorrow, then we sort out how to take it down." He gave a tight-lipped smile and clapped Karlson on the back. "Just like old times, isn't it?"

Karlson's nose wrinkled. "Can't say I missed it."

The pair soon left, and Aspen's presence retreated back onto the sunlit balcony. Emry flopped back onto the pillows with a groan. After only one concert, his debut had been summarily cut off at the knees.

"I'm sorry about the concerts." Cal took his hand. "You'll get them back."

"Shouldn't be worried about those," he mumbled. "Between Aspen and the other spirits..."

But he could hardly finish the sentence due to his growing exhaustion. He closed his eyes, a puddle of weariness, disappointment, and pains from his effort on the river. Gods, he was so done with sleep and bedrest. If he just had a garden of those orange flowers...

Cal squeezed his hand, drawing away some of his frustration. Slowly, he shifted his free hand to cover hers.

"Thank you," he said, eyes still closed, his voice hardly above a murmur. "Appreciate you being here and helping me. Even if sitting on the edge of my bed is a scandal in itself."

Cal sighed. "You're right. I suppose I should go."

But she made no move to leave. He cracked one eye open; she stared out the window, eyes unfocused over a worried frown.

"Here." With effort, he opened his arms. She fell into him, curling against his chest and hugging him tight. Relief settled over both of them like a blanket—tension unwound from Cal's spine, and the comfort of her weight pressed Emry into the pillows.

He hummed and kissed the side of her head, hugging her tighter. He needed more time with her like this. Not just to tell her about the magic—though that needed to happen—but simply to *be* with her.

And besides, he had followed all the stiff rules of courtship so far. Every boring event, every tedious guideline. But they were only going to do this once. Cal deserved more than that, didn't she?

"Join me in the garden tomorrow," he said, the thought tumbling out before he could fully consider it. "Just us."

She pulled away. He tensed, expecting her to decline, to maintain a semblance of logic and social decorum.

Instead, she smiled.

"Just us?" she said, her eyes brightening. "What time would you suggest, Mr. Karic?"

Emry grinned. "Is midnight romantic enough for you?"

She kissed his hand. "Midnight it is."

CHAPTER
TWENTY-FOUR

CAL

CAL EMBARRASSED herself by how much she looked forward to the garden rendezvous.

She tried to sort out her thoughts as she sat down to breakfast in the tea room. Logically, she shouldn't have agreed to it. It was a foolish idea—couples trying to sneak away during a social season rarely got away with it, and the scandal that ensued was never worth the trouble. And to get caught while in the city on Council business? It would ruin her career. James would become the lead, and she would have to spend her days getting him coffee and writing his reports and calling him *sir*—

"Can we please go to Pigeon's garden today?" Aspen begged from their chair beside her. Despite being told to relax, they had insisted Cal bring their lute down to tea so they could guard her. She tossed them a sideways glance.

"Aspen—"

"I promise I won't take a shape or anything," they said. "But I need to see if they've found the dig site yet."

Cal relented and carried their lute over to the garden in the afternoon. The instrument felt unwieldy and strange on her back, like she was somehow imitating Emry and failing. But Aspen never complained, not even when she went to put it down on the garden bench and dropped it too quickly on the stone.

"So sorry, Aspen!" She rubbed the back of the lute with her sleeve.

"It's fine," Aspen said. "The lute's already broken, you know."

"Oh." Cal paused, then set the instrument down again in embarrassment. "So it is."

Aspen dove into conversation immediately—not just with Pigeon but with the other spirits as well. Rhythm blooms of several colors formed around their bench, their blossoms tiny and frail. After a few minutes, Pigeon herself swooped down in a form that looked more like a gust of wind than a bird.

"Hello?" the spirit started, then looked at the lute and spoke more confidently. "Hello...Cal!"

Cal withheld a gasp. Emry had told her Pigeon had begun to talk, but the delight of that discovery couldn't compare to hearing the spirit's voice herself. It was both startling and welcoming, just like when she had first heard Aspen speak from the lute. But Pigeon's voice was distinctly less human than Aspen's, a discordant mix of pigeon coos and the Matlock accent that surrounded her every day.

"Hello, Pigeon." She curtsied, then sat on the bench and angled herself away from the rest of the garden. If the other patrons overheard the bird talking to her, she'd have an inconvenient crowd on her hands. "Have you had any luck finding the dig site?"

Despite Aspen's determination, she didn't expect much from the ailing spirits on that front. Pigeon's bird form barely held together, and the flowers from the other spirits were missing several colors.

Pigeon tilted her head at the question, then began to hop and peck at petals on the ground.

"I...see," Cal said. An unusual response, but then again, Pigeon was only just entering the world of human language. She supposed she needed to be patient. "Aspen, if they don't have it yet, we shouldn't bother them too much." She reached for the lute. "They'll need all their strength for—"

"Wait."

An invisible presence formed next to her; it would have been unsettling if it didn't give off the distinctly Aspen scent of honeysuckle.

"Look at what she's doing," Aspen continued.

Pigeon continued hopping, and a sketch made of petals slowly came together before them. A jagged horizontal line, a line pointed upward—then slowly bending right, waving around rocks and acorns on the ground...

"Do you see it?" Aspen asked eagerly. "That's the northern edge of the city. And that's the path out, and a turn right, then left..."

"Oh." Cal blinked. Then: "Oh, thank Hara, they *have* got it."

Before the petals could blow away, she whipped out her notebook and copied down the map, drawing arrows and labeling strange markers that Aspen had to translate for her.

"That one's a boulder..." They paused. "Wait no, *that* one's the boulder. The leaf over here is a burned tree."

Once Pigeon had finished, Cal could hardly make sense of it all. They had to go down the deer trail, past a stream—if they reached the gully, they had gone too far...

She supposed this was what she got for asking spirits for a map.

"Pigeon says that's as much as she can provide," Aspen said while Pigeon hopped happily around their bench. "She thinks I'll be able to feel it, though. Like it's..." They trailed off as they parsed the spirit's words. "Home?"

"Home?" Cal repeated. Aspen's presence wavered, and Cal got the distinct impression of a frown.

"Not exactly," Aspen said. "*Memory* is closer. Like the past, but familiar. If you push all those words together, that's what she's trying to say." Their presence rippled with newfound energy. "So, when can we go?"

Cal tucked her pencil behind her ear. Aspen needed no special equipment to take down the dig's tunnels themselves—they were insistent on that part—but there would be no ambling up to this part of the forest in a carriage, not with these sorts of directions. And walking on foot was out of the question, given Emry's state. No, they'd need horses of some kind, hired discreetly...

"Very soon," she said, closing the notebook. "I'll sort this out with Damir."

As soon as she returned to the hotel, she caught Damir slouching his way across the lobby, glaring at a member of the Quartet.

"Look, if you accidentally ordered twenty bottles of wine," he said, "that cost is on you, not on the Guild—ah, Ms. Breslin." He waved off the musician and turned to her. "Please tell me you have cheaper news for me."

Cal handed him the map. "Are three horses cheaper than twenty bottles of wine?"

Damir's look flattened.

∼

After discussing the approach with Damir—the route, the horses, the time—there was only one element left to plan out: her midnight rendezvous with Emry.

Before the sun set, she ventured into the garden and ducked around the dry hedges, trying not to chide or laugh at herself as she considered the evening's tryst—gods, she had agreed to a *tryst*—from every angle. Holding a lantern would surely get her spotted at night, so while there was still light out, she memorized every bench and blight-withered hedge path. Afterward, she assessed what her dress should be—something simple and dark, with slippers that hardly made a sound, but not too simple, lest she look frumpy for her midnight garden dalliance...

Cal sighed at her wardrobe. How did those women in her romance novels manage it? She was blushing and having heart palpitations just thinking about the whole ordeal. She shouldn't have agreed to it. She should have been sensible.

But then midnight struck, and she found herself sneaking out of her rooms anyway, adorned with her navy shawl and softest slippers.

Whether Emry had planned for it or not, midnight was a perfect time to access the gardens. A private function in one of the ballrooms was winding down for the evening, with most of its guests deep into their cups. While the hotel's staff was busy wrangling those guests into rooms and carriages, Cal slipped past them, heart beating wildly as she tried to maintain a quick but innocent stride. Through the halls, then onto the patio, then out into the—

"Ms. Breslin, good evening!"

She slowly turned around, her breath stuck in her throat. James Edwards stood behind her, dressed in his finery for the private event and just as flushed as the other guests.

"What fine luck!" he said, his words overly brightened by drink. "I was going to ask you a question at the regatta before the…" He frowned. "You know, the whole…"

Cal stiffened. "Flood."

"Flood!" James snapped his fingers, then narrowed his gaze. "What are you doing out here, anyway? I didn't think you were attending the ball."

"I am…um…" Cal glanced back at the balcony. The door was so close, she could almost taste the cool night air beyond.

She could talk her way out of this, surely.

"Research." She took on a brisk, professorial tone. "You see, I'm documenting the strength of spirits at different moon cycles, and it's imperative that I take the data exactly at midnight, or else all my findings will—"

As expected, James' eyes glazed over.

"Sure, yes, absolutely," he said, waving away her answer. "About my question. I was meaning to ask you about those, ah, spirits Aspen was talking to."

Cal stopped in confusion. James had never once asked about anything related to spirits—not even for work. "I beg your pardon?"

"The ones they mentioned at the regatta," he said. "Fascinating, really. Where do they usually go to talk to them?"

Cal wanted to scoff. Surely, he didn't *actually* find it fascinating—that must be the drink. But she didn't exactly have time to probe his line of questioning—the garden lay behind her, dark and inviting.

"The closest is Pigeon's grove," she said vaguely. "Just down the street."

James' nose wrinkled. "Pigeon?"

"Yes, at the corner of Linden, but..." Cal edged away from him. "I really must go. For my research, you know—"

"Yes, of course, of course." James gave an off-kilter bow. "Have a good evening, Ms. Breslin."

She gave a hurried curtsy and fled onto the balcony, not stopping until she was deep into the crisp air of the hedge garden. She took a refreshing breath, then steadied herself and waited for any footsteps, any grass crackling underfoot.

Nothing so far. Good.

"Emry?" she whispered, squinting into the dark. The moonlight was weak tonight, and the hotel lamps far away, deepening the shadows she crept through. "Em?"

"Cal?" a whisper returned to her. "Over here!"

A soft blue light flickered beyond her, half-hidden behind branches. She checked the hotel balcony once more, then picked up her skirts and carefully ventured deeper.

After several turns, she came across a part of the garden that hadn't been in her memorized map of corners and pathways. This was supposed to be a simple hedge wall, but at some point, it had transformed into an archway with a thick curtain of hanging vines. She tentatively pushed a hand through the vines, then continued through to the blue light beyond.

What she found was a little nook between the hedge and the stone wall bordering the garden. The wall spilled over with flowers and ivy until hardly a brick was visible, releasing a generous perfume into the air. She stepped farther in, expecting her slippers to meet with grass—but they caught on the edge of a blanket instead. And down there on the throw, surrounded by a dim ring of glowing blue flowers, was Emry lounging with a wine bottle and two glasses.

"Thank goodness you found me," he said, his cheeky grin illuminated by the tiny field of lights. "I can't drink all this by myself."

She knelt down and pressed her lips to his, not giving him the chance to put down the wine or say anything else. The flowers' perfume had settled everywhere—on the blanket, in his clothes, in his hair. She drank it in wherever she could, delighting in the simple fact that they were alone together. No scrutiny, no danger, no expectations—just Emry and the grin she could trace through their kiss.

When she finally pulled back to catch her breath, his smile only widened.

"Wine later, I suppose?"

And he set the bottle aside.

∼

When they did finally get around to pouring the wine and watching the stars overhead, they spoke of anything but the current state of the city. They spoke of dancing, of summer, of when they were going to visit friends in Tazlo and Senne and Etris. As the night wore on and the stars moved along their path, Cal breathed easier and more slowly, entertaining the fantasy that she could simply fall asleep there and wake up next to him in the morning.

But Emry was growing more and more restless.

"Wonder if Aspen snuck out to visit the spirits tonight," he said, sitting up and running a hand through his hair. The flowers that Aspen had laid out for them were slowly dimming, but they still highlighted his collarbones through his half-open shirt. Cal reached up and toyed with his collar.

"I wouldn't worry about them," she said. "We don't need to leave yet."

"No, it's not that, it's..." Emry didn't lie back down, but he didn't meet her gaze, either. "There's—there's something I should tell you."

Cal sat up immediately. She knew that tremor in his voice, when the words were difficult to get out. She set a hand on his shoulder. "Is everything all right?"

"I think so," he said. "I mean—yes, I'm all right. At least, I think I'm all right. I just..."

He paused, then turned around and took her hands. "I need to show you something, but please know that no matter what, I love you."

Worry gripped her, ripping away all sense of relaxation the garden had provided. What could he possibly have to show her? What was he hiding now?

Her thoughts prepared to spiral, but she reeled them in. He was coming to her, after all—let him show her what he needed to show.

She gave him a wordless nod and sat back. He knelt on the blanket, holding his fingers out over the grass beyond the wool. One of the flowers there had wilted, its blue glow all but gone.

Emry closed his eyes, took one slow, controlled breath...and the flower perked back to life.

Cal stared in disbelief. The petals had bloomed back larger, glowing twice as bright. She dared to touch them—velvety soft under her fingers, delicate and sweet. A real flower, a very real flower, that Emry had made grow before her eyes.

Not Aspen. *Emry.*

She looked up; he had sat back on his heels, his gaze already teary and afraid as he rushed into his words.

"I only discovered it during the flood. But I—I think it may have started earlier. And I don't know why, and I don't know how, and I don't know what's happening to me—"

She pulled him close, hugging him as tight as she could. "You're all right," she said, clutching his back as his shoulders shook. "You're perfectly all right, Em."

She let him regain his breath, then drew back and took his hands in hers, examining his palms. They looked and felt the same as they always did, despite the power now living within them.

"Does it hurt?" she asked.

"No," Emry mumbled, wiping tears from his face. She reached up and brushed one away.

"How does it feel?"

"It feels..." He took a breath. "Easy, actually. Like...singing, I suppose."

A hundred other questions spilled into Cal's mind—how had he discovered it? How much could he do? Was it only flowers, or did it extend to other plant life?

She tamped them all down. He didn't need her questions. He wasn't a subject to research.

He was her future husband, and he was afraid.

She ventured only one more inquiry. "Does Aspen know yet?"

"They do." Emry ran his hand over the grass, the blades thickening at his touch. "They knew as soon as I saved them from the river. But no one else—I wanted to tell you first."

Cal kissed his cheek, tasting salt from his tears. "Thank you. I'm honored."

"Honored?" Emry gave a humorless laugh, still not able to look her in the eyes. "Are you sure you're not...not upset? Repelled?" He gestured to the hedges. "Every eligible bachelor in that hotel is—is perfect and rich and *normal*, and I'm out here singing songs and getting possessed and growing flowers like some sort of *plant*—"

A surge of affection went through Cal, and she wanted to take his shoulders and shake him.

"Em, look at me," she said. He hesitated, then met her gaze. She gently took his face in his hands, her fingers tracing the freckles on his cheeks.

"I don't care how perfect or rich or normal those men are," she said. "They aren't you. You were magical before, Emry Karic, and you're magical now. None of that changes who you are or what I think of you." Another tear fell down his cheek, and she wiped it away. "I love you, and I don't care if you can grow flowers or thorns or—or bubbles."

That got a true laugh out of him—broken, but true—and she smiled.

"Do you understand me?"

He turned to kiss her palm, then pulled her into a tight embrace, one filled with relief and joy and love.

"I love you," he murmured into her hair. "I'll try to work on bubbles next."

CHAPTER
TWENTY-FIVE

EMRY

DAMIR SIGHED, the energy sinking out of his slumping shoulders. "Karic, when I said that the Guild used to be spies, I truly meant *used* to be." He gestured to the horse before him. "I don't have the joints for this sort of work anymore."

To amplify his complaints, he maneuvered his way onto the horse with a loud grumble and a wince, one hand pressed to his back.

"Do you need a moonflower?" Aspen held a small gray flower up to him. It wasn't one of their best, given that they were still recovering from their impromptu journey down the river; the petals were too pale, the stem thin and brittle. Damir eyed it with suspicion.

"No, thank you."

While Damir shifted in the saddle, Emry tried to rebalance himself on his own mount. He couldn't claim to be comfortable on a horse, either, particularly not with his current aches. He had largely grown up on boats as his method of transportation. They could capsize, sure, but they'd never kick him in the head or rear at the sight of a tree branch swaying.

Cal, however, sat perfectly at ease in a plum riding habit she had borrowed from Lydia. She took one look at Emry's stiff posture and Damir's wincing, then gestured to Aspen. "Dearest, I'll hold the lute for you this time."

They set off down a rough dirt road in the forest, their eyes straining in the blue light of dawn. Aspen flitted in the form of a translucent bird, keeping pace with them in the boughs above.

Earlier that morning, they had reached the edge of Matlock by carriage, then acquired horses on the premise of taking a day trip out of the city. It was Damir's hope that the dig site wouldn't be active so early in the morning, allowing them to safely access the place.

"We don't need to linger," he reminded them, his eyes constantly monitoring the trees on either side of the narrow path. "Get in, collapse the tunnels, get out."

Aspen landed on a branch ahead of them, rustling the leaves. Damir jumped at the sound, his hand unconsciously moving toward the flintlock pistol at his side. Emry grimaced; an unusual sight, but unsurprising given the circumstances. It paired well with the antidote swinging from Damir's watch chain. Clearly, his manager hadn't truly left his days of danger behind him, no matter what he claimed.

Aspen hopped between a few more trees, then flitted down and landed on Cal's shoulder. "It's up ahead," they said. "I don't think anyone's there."

The road quickly opened up into a clearing, the grass pounded flat by the travels of horses and wagons. But even if the grass hadn't been pummeled, it still would have been flat and brown—the entire forest was similarly dead in this area, withered and bleached and blighted. On the other side of the clearing, the entrance to the dig site yawned at them—a ragged cave in the side of the mountain, blasted open to make room for people and equipment.

And equipment Dev had no lack of—off to the side, a large shed squatted between two pines, its towering doors almost as intimidating as the deep black cave. Emry dismounted and took a peek through the slats—the shadowy space was filled to the roof with tools. He could make out neat rows of shovels and pickaxes near the doors, then larger wagons and who knew what else in the back...

He stepped back to survey it all. No wonder Dev had paired with Halleson to pay for all this—on his own, he could have afforded perhaps two shovels and a wagon wheel.

"Time to go in," Damir ordered, eyeing the cave warily. "Just the first few chambers need a good shake, right?"

"Right." Aspen approached the edge of the tunnel, a vine already curling around their fingers. With their free hand, they pushed lightly on the wooden scaffolding at the entrance, as if gauging its strength. The spirit had pored over Cal's notes all night, and Emry had gone through it with them until the maps were burned into the back of his eyelids. But the core of their plan was simple: a few targeted pulls on some scaffolding, then the tunnels would collapse, Dev would be ruined, and the spirits would be safe.

Emry joined Aspen at the entrance. "And you're sure you don't need me to help—?"

A warning shiver shot up his spine, and he immediately reeled back from the darkness. Something rumbled like silent thunder in the deep—he couldn't hear it, but the tremor shuddered through his bones all the same.

He glanced back at Cal and Damir, who had taken no notice, then at Aspen, who still had one hand fixed on the scaffolding.

"It's really down there, isn't it?" Emry said quietly. "The well?"

Aspen nodded, their gaze unwavering. Emry squinted at them—the edges of their form shifted toward the tunnel, like a light breath pushing a candle flame.

"If it's hurting you to be here—" he began.

"It isn't," Aspen said. "It doesn't hurt, it feels..." They bit their lip. "Like what Pigeon said. Familiar, home, past, all of that."

"Maybe it *was* your home once." Cal stepped up behind them, peering into the darkness. "If this truly is where spirit energy originates, then I daresay you and your friends have all been here before." Her voice softened in reverence. "Whatever is down there was your first grove, in a sense."

Aspen regarded the darkness once more, ears pricked to the silent thunder—then they set their shoulders back, and all around them, the grass withered and curled.

"He shouldn't be down there," they said through gritted teeth. "*None* of them should be down there. What if they destroy it? What if they—?" The vine in their shaking grip grew long, sharp thorns. "I'm taking it down now, all of it. The tunnel, the equipment, the shed—"

The sound of hooves and muffled chatter floated in from the forest path. Emry's heart stuttered, and behind them, Damir let out a low curse.

"Get back, both of you. We have to hide—"

"No," Aspen hissed. "I can still do this." The vine in their hand shot out and wrapped around the scaffolding, dirt showering the ground. "I can still destroy the entrance."

Emry reached for them. "Aspen, no—"

The spirit pulled, and as their form flickered, all the vines on the scaffolding went taut. One of the beams cracked, its snap echoing like a gunshot through the clearing.

"Who goes there?"

Damir rushed toward the horses. "Quick, behind the shed!"

They led their mounts behind the structure, their movements cramped and frantic. When figures appeared at the head of the pathway, Aspen made a gesture toward the sky. A breeze sifted through the dry canopy above, and the dead leaves rustled loud and long. Emry dared a peek from around the shed—Dev, Zeke, and Halleson were dismounting in the clearing while a burly man in somber clothes checked the tunnel. Behind them, workers filed in, bleary-eyed and already speckled with dust.

Emry silently swore. Between the visitors and the workers, there was no getting into the tunnels, not now.

"No one here, sir," the burly guard said to Halleson, who glanced up at the moving canopy.

"Just the wind in the trees, I suppose," he muttered. Even here, the man had insisted on wearing his understated finery. The silk lining of his riding cloak flared around him while he smoothed out his coat, ensuring each button shone brighter than the morning sun. And he failed to hide his look of disdain as common workers sulked around him, kicking up dust and dragging around muddy equipment.

"Now, about that crystal layer you mentioned." Halleson finally straightened. "I want to see it for myself."

Damir carefully crouched at the corner of the shed. Emry imitated his posture, his fear numbing the cracks in his knees. Once Halleson disappeared into the tunnel, they could mount the horses and make a run for it as soon as they were gone—

"Yes, about that," Dev said, making no move to guide his visitors into the cave. "You may observe the well, certainly, but I must warn you, I am still determining how best to harvest the energy underneath the crystal floor."

Halleson waved his hand. "I can provide you with more tools, if that's what you need."

He and his guard approached the cave, but Dev wouldn't be dismissed so easily.

"A standard digging implement will not suffice," he said sharply. "The mechanism must be fully inorganic. Anything wooden, even so much as a handle, will soak up the energy." His words sped up. "And the workers can't stand near the device, lest the energy attach to *them*. I need something fully metal, something that can be operated from a distance and handle the energy without sustaining damage—"

Halleson stared blankly at him. "Then invent something." He scoffed, and Emry could have sworn his very mustache ruffled. "You are the great Mr. Gray, are you not?"

"A new tool like that will take time, even for me." Dev looked at

Zeke for support, but the poor man only managed a silent, hesitant nod. Dev soldiered on. "If you grant us only a few more months—"

"A few more months?" Halleson whirled away from the cave. His shadow now fell sharply over Dev, and the more his tirade spiraled, the more the shadow loomed. "You promised me an unveiling during the season. I have promised *others* an unveiling during the season, of proportions as great as what you promised me." He pointed one thick finger to the cave. "I will *have* my name on this energy of yours, and I will have it before the season is out."

Dev bristled, his eyes reflecting back Halleson's anger in force—but there was no denying who held the purse strings here. Who had paid for the equipment that surrounded them, who had salvaged Dev from the mess of his own shunned research.

Dev finally stood down, a whisper of thorns in his tone.

"And you will have it, of course," he said. "Now, you wanted to see the well for yourself?" He turned and strode toward the tunnel. "I have lanterns within."

Their footsteps and voices began to fade into the tunnel, and Emry tensed. The clearing wasn't all that large. It would only take them seconds to run around the workers, minutes to fully disappear down the road...

Then Dev's footsteps paused at the entrance.

"Mr. Whitlock?" he asked. "Were these here yesterday?"

Emry peeked out once more. Dev reached out to one of the broken vines hanging around the scaffolding. Zeke cleared his throat.

"I—I don't believe they were, sir."

Dev whipped back around.

"Fan out," he snapped. "Someone was here."

As the group spread out, Damir stood up, a hand hovering over his pistol—but Aspen grabbed his wrist.

"Don't move," they whispered, then knelt and put their hands to the ground. Damir stared at the spirit in incredulous anger.

"Tree-kid, you're going to get us *killed*—"

Heavy footsteps tromped closer to the shed.

"Hoofprints over here," Halleson's guard called out. "Looks like they're fresh."

Damir pulled out his pistol. "That's it," he said. "I'm going to cover you, you three make a run for it—"

A red rhythm bloom appeared before Aspen's hand. Then a yellow one, then a blue one. The spirit grinned.

"That won't be necessary." They looked up at Damir. "I called for some help."

Shrieks rattled the clearing. Damir leaned around the shed and swore.

Thorns had shot up from the flattened ground, holding everyone in place—Dev by the cave, Halleson and Zeke near the pathway, the guard three steps from the shed's corner. They all tried to kick the thorns away, but the thin, pointy vines wrapped stubbornly around their torsos and arms.

"Go!" Aspen shifted into wolf form. "The spirits won't be able to hold them for long!"

They mounted their horses and burst out from behind the shed in a panicked heap. The guard tried to reach for the pistol at his hip, but the weapon was encased in vines.

As soon as Dev saw them, he spat a curse and struggled harder against his bonds.

"I knew it, I *knew* it was you—"

Aspen skidded to a halt before him and growled.

"Aspen!" Emry twisted around in the saddle. "Not now!"

The spirit gave a huff, snapped their jaws once at Dev, and lumbered off down the path.

CHAPTER
TWENTY-SIX

EMRY

THE PEEK OF THE SEASON

For all the colorful promise of this season, I am afraid it is turning out to be far grayer than anticipated.

Karlson has canceled his next concert, with no mention of Spiritsong swooping in to rescue us from our doldrums. We have yet to hear of an exciting engagement in days, and our poor gardens continue to reflect our despairing moods.

Though one small glimmer of hope is ahead—the upcoming charity ball at the Oakvale Grand. It is a surprise, yet a welcome event, given the circumstances, and this writer looks forward to both mingling and supporting our dear spirits.

They didn't stop for breath until they reached Matlock again, where Damir quickly diverted them to an inn on the opposite side of the river.

"You're not going back to the hotel," he said after depositing the horses with a confused stablehand, tipping generously to ensure no questions were asked. "Not right now, at least. We need to ensure our lovely acquaintances don't try to follow us with their pistols."

They snuck inside and hurried into their new rooms, where Damir closed the curtains immediately. Relief settled over Emry and his groaning limbs, sore from the panicked escape. They were firmly out of view now, tucked in a nondescript little place whose red stone blended in with all the other red buildings around it. Even the room itself was bland—no rug, no artwork, no carvings on the furniture. He could happily recover from the chase here, in the unremarkable chair next to the unremarkable hearth, and wait until no one was actively trying to kill them.

But beside him, Aspen bristled.

"How long do we need to stay?" they asked, stubbornly peeking through the curtain at the other side of the city. "I need to check on my friends."

"I realize we owe a great debt to the other spirits, but you must stay here," Damir ordered. "I need to go retrieve Ella right away. She'll know how to handle Halleson."

"But—"

"I mean it, tree-kid." His expression softened, and he rubbed his forehead. "Look. All three of you have done...extraordinarily, given the circumstances, but I'm afraid this calls for far more support than I intended. I'll send for your things and inform Karlson of what happened. If anything else happens in the city, tell him immediately." He made for the door, then paused. "I realize it's difficult for you, but...please stay safe."

Emry nodded. "I will wrap Cal in a duvet and not let her leave."

"Wasn't talking about her."

∼

As safe as Emry initially felt, the tiny room soon turned into an infuriating confinement.

After a day, they all grew restless, a heavy feeling of defeat soaking into the monotonous wooden corners of the room. There would be no more concerts, no more courting, and no more communication with friends—not while they were cooped up in here.

And out there, the spirits still withered.

"They're wondering why I'm over here," Aspen said that afternoon, looking out at the sun rippling over the river.

"It's so you don't die," Emry said, an open book covering his face; he had long since given up on reading it. Aspen fiddled with the curtain.

"I'm not going to let *them* die so I can stay safe in here," they said. "We have to do something."

Emry glanced out at Cal from under his book. She frowned at her own novel, trying hard to look like she was content in her reading—but her eyes weren't scanning the page at all. Emry nudged her.

"We know Dev is struggling to get to the well's energy," he said. "What if we tried to get to the dig site today, before Dev has the chance to figure things out?"

Cal's gaze didn't move from the page. "Today is James' and Halleson's charity ball, which means Dev is at the site. Unless you have a good idea of how to sneak around him and all his workers, we'll just get caught again."

Aspen released a low growl. "Then we go to the ball and threaten Halleson."

"And have his guard shoot us?" Cal shot them a look over her novel. "You're the only one here who's immune to bullets, my dear, and I don't think your flowers can heal such wounds."

Emry tapped his fingers on his book in thought—perhaps the ball wasn't such a bad idea.

"It won't be just Halleson there." He sat up. "Karlson and Lydia are going, aren't they? If we join forces with them, maybe they can help us finish this."

Cal shut her book. "But Halleson—"

"Won't hurt us if we stay in plain sight with the others. Not even he can get away with such public violence, not there."

"He can't throw me into the river from the hotel," Aspen offered. Oddly enough, this didn't satisfy Cal, and she wandered over to the window with her lips pressed into a line.

"We're still safest here," she said. "If Damir takes the river routes back down like you told him to—oh, no." She yanked the curtain closed. "They're looking for us."

Emry leapt out of the bed, cracking the curtain open just enough to peer at the street. Zeke stood in front of the inn, talking to the stablehand Damir had bribed the other day. Emry held his breath—but the stablehand shrugged and pointed farther down the road.

Zeke gave the inn one long, suspicious look, then thanked the stablehand and continued down the street.

"Safest here, are we?" Emry mumbled. Cal gave a long sigh and looked at Emry.

"Plain sight?" Her gaze swiveled to Aspen. "*No* fighting?"

Both of them nodded. Her arms fell to her sides in defeat.

"Then by all means, let us be off to the ball."

WHEN THEY ARRIVED at the Oakvale Grand Hotel, Emry tried to take encouragement in the number of people swarming both the lobby and the outer plaza. With half of all society here in their dizzying attire, there had to be some sort of safety in numbers.

But then again, Damir had been convinced the regatta would be safe, too, and that had ended in an unfortunate adventure downriver.

"Any sign of Lydia or Karlson yet?" Cal murmured.

"Not yet," Aspen said, gaze swiveling across the crowd. Their form barely held water now, their lute dangling dangerously off one shoulder. Emry had offered to carry it for them, but they had staunchly refused. "Wait, is that—?" They made a face. "Oh. Never mind."

Emry followed their gaze to the ballroom entrance, where James greeted everyone with a delicate balance of welcoming charm and sobriety appropriate to the occasion. Cal groaned.

"Is there any other entrance?" she tried, but it was too late. The flow of the crowd swept them across the lobby and straight into James' receiving line. He extended a hand to them, eyes lighting up when he saw Aspen.

"Welcome, welcome. Lovely to see you here." Then, to Aspen directly: "We do hope this endeavor will help your little friends."

Aspen barely suppressed a glower. "I hope so, too."

They left him behind as quickly as possible, sticking close together as they waded into the fray of small talk and pleasantries. At least the venue was something to be admired—the Oakvale Grand's ballrooms were perfect for such an occasion. Chandeliers sent warm light scattering over marble flooring, and a line of pillars guided the eye to a low stage at one end of the room. James had even lined up the Forsgren Quartet to entertain, and the center of the room filled with swirling dresses and tailcoats.

But the reason for the event cast a strong shadow over all the glamour.

"It's not just the spirit gardens that are dying," one woman whispered in a huddle near the pillars. "Ms. Pietri said that over three hundred gardens are almost dead."

"Even the one across from Rose Street looked awful when I passed it," her friend said. "So terrible. It was my mother's favorite, you know…"

Emry searched for the knowledgeable Ms. Pietri and found her back by the door, hemmed in by James and a journalist.

"Thank you for your comments, Ms. Pietri." The journalist turned to James. "And how exactly do you and Mr. Halleson intend to use the funds from this ball?"

James nodded somberly along with her question. "Well, many of the gardens require extensive revitalization, and as a rising leader in my department, I will *personally* ensure we bring in the best and the brightest to assist..."

Emry wrinkled his nose, but Cal had stopped listening to the man's drivel—her eyes were locked across the room instead, refusing to turn away from the danger.

Though Halleson wasn't basking in the attention of journalists like James, he was just as surrounded, holding court of his own at the other end of the ballroom. Emry tried to pull Cal and Aspen behind a pillar, but it was too late—he caught sight of them and immediately leaned over to whisper something to the man on his right.

"Come on," Emry murmured to Cal, "let's go get Lydia and find Karlson—"

A hand touched his shoulder.

"Gods!" He leapt and twisted around. Behind him, Sage raised both hands.

"Sorry!" she said, eyes wide. "It's just me!"

Emry sucked a breath, a hand on his racing heart. "What are you doing here?"

But Sage wasn't alone—Riley stood beside her, just as eager to pounce on them.

"Where have you all been?" she pressed. "We thought Damir had kidnapped you from the city after what Karlson told us about the regatta. What in Shiro's name is going on?"

"Why are people trying to kill you both?" Sage joined in with her demands. "And what on earth is happening to the spirits?" Her eyes narrowed. "You know something about it. Don't try to tell us you don't."

Emry opened his mouth to form some sort of excuse—but beside him, Cal grabbed Emry's arm in a vise grip. He looked over his shoulder.

Halleson was approaching, calm and swift, easily parting the crowd as he went.

"Look, it's a lot to explain—" he tried, but his troupemates weren't letting go so easily.

"You've known about the blight this whole time, haven't you?" Sage urged. "If you just tell us what you're really doing here, maybe we could—"

"Good evening, Halleson," a man in the crowd called. Emry lowered his voice to an urgent whisper, his heart pounding in his throat.

"I will tell you later, I promise," he said. "But right now, we're trying to stay alive. So, if you could *please* just stay close—"

They didn't need further prompting. Sage linked arms with Aspen, and Riley lined up next to Emry, forming a firm perimeter around the trio.

"I can't say I understand," Sage murmured. "But I *can* say that no one is dying today."

Riley cracked her knuckles. "Can't guarantee no injuries, though."

Halleson's shadow fell over them.

"Ah, my dear Karics and Ms. Breslin," he said, as if he had been merely wandering by, rather than making a direct line for him. "Are you enjoying the ball?"

The crowd moved a respectful distance from their conversation. Not too far away to eavesdrop, of course—only far enough away to give Halleson the deference he was owed.

Sage and Riley, however, stood their ground with stony looks.

"Of course." Emry gave Halleson a short bow, holding tightly to Aspen's hand. Even without his modicum of magic, he could feel Aspen's energy winding in anger, ready to leap on Halleson the second they had a good excuse.

That energy only grew hotter when Halleson's men casually filled the space between them and the rest of the crowd, swiftly and silently outnumbering their little band. Emry stepped closer to Cal. If any of them made a move toward her, it wouldn't be Aspen who attacked first.

"Thank you for arranging the event," Cal added, her voice tight. "I see you are as supportive of the spirits as you are of the sciences."

Halleson's eyes flashed, but he maintained his composure.

"I am always supportive of my city's health," he said. "It's merely part of good business to care for it and ensure all its *natural* resources are put to good use. No stone unturned, as they say. I am so very fortunate to have associates like Mr. Gray who understand the importance of that."

Then he lowered his voice, the glint in his eye filing to a sharp point.

"And, as for what's next," he said, "you must forgive me. It's merely part of good business."

The faint smell of smoke struck Emry's nose, and the building fury in Aspen's energy halted—not in restraint, but in distraction, in confusion...in fear.

"Pigeon," they whispered.

Before anyone could catch them, the spirit bolted for the door, shoving anyone and everyone out of their way. Emry tried to run after them, but other hands shot out and grabbed him, locking both him and Cal in place.

"Unhand me—" Cal tried yanking herself away. Sage ripped her own hands out of one guard's grip.

"You heard her!" She shoved Cal's captor. On the other side, Riley fiercely elbowed the man holding onto Emry, sending the guard reeling and clutching his nose.

"We've got them," Riley shouted at Emry. "*Go!*"

Emry took Cal's hand and rushed out the door, blowing past Lydia, James, and the journalist. Lydia leapt out of the way in confusion.

"Cal—?"

But there was no time. Aspen wasn't in the lobby, nor were they out in the plaza. And all around them, the smell of smoke poisoned the air.

"Oh, gods." Cal grabbed Emry's sleeve and pointed. A dark, billowing plume rose from a familiar corner down the street. "Pigeon's garden."

They sprinted along the cobblestone, the smoke ahead growing thicker and more acrid. As they ran, the crowd in the street slipped into chaos—some people running away from the flames, others scrambling for buckets and water.

But up ahead, Aspen ignored all of them. They stood alone, silhouetted against the garden's flames, their arms raised to the sky.

Emry dragged Cal under a balcony just in time. A burst of rain fell in a sudden deluge, splashing their ankles and sending a great hiss from the garden. Those approaching with buckets had to veer away, shielding their faces from the angry, defeated wave of smoke. The gray enveloped both Aspen and the garden gate, and the flames died as quickly as they lived.

"Thank Hara," Emry muttered, but Cal was already back out in the street, trying to squint through the stinging haze.

"Halleson—" she started, then coughed and turned away from the smoke.

"Yes?" Emry guided her into clear air, keeping one eye out for Aspen as she spoke.

"Halleson didn't stop Aspen," she finally managed. "He stopped us, but he didn't bother trying to stop them. Why did he—?"

A carriage careened around the corner, taking the turn at a sharp angle without a care for anyone else on the street. Onlookers shrieked and scattered apart once more, giving it space to charge recklessly ahead. Emry and Cal dove back under the balcony, and the carriage missed them by mere paces. But it didn't stop—it dove straight into the smoke, grinding to a halt in front of the garden.

A discordant mix of a squawk, a roar, and a human shriek shattered the air, then the scuffling of boots and slamming doors filled the cracks.

"We've got them, let's go!" a familiar voice shouted.

"Dev," Emry breathed, then charged into the clearing haze, fists clenched—

But the fight was already over. Red flowers were strewn about the cobblestones, mixed with splatters of soil, ivy, greenery—everything that had been in Aspen's lute, except for the lute itself.

And down the street, flying like a drunken arrow, the dark carriage headed north.

CHAPTER
TWENTY-SEVEN

CAL

U̲n̲t̲i̲l̲ t̲h̲a̲t̲ n̲i̲g̲h̲t̲, Cal never thought the sight of flowers could make her sick.

"Did they—?" She couldn't finish the sentence, tears already stinging her eyes along with the smoke. "They didn't..."

Emry took her hand with a shaking grip.

"The lute isn't here," he said. "Dev weakened Aspen, but he didn't kill them. If we can catch up to them..."

He ran for the nearest carriage stop, and Cal frantically searched for another way to follow—a cart, a horse, anything—but all she could see were people converging on the black, soggy mess of a garden. Most of them were passersby, setting handkerchiefs to their faces against the lingering smoke.

But some of them had run straight from the hotel, pushing the curious locals aside.

"Cal?" Lydia rushed in, flanked by Sage and Riley. "Are you—?" The blood drained out of her face when she saw the garden. "Pigeon. Is she still there?"

Something glimmered at the top of the garden wall—a flash of a beak, a hint of a feather. Lydia touched the stone in relief.

"Oh, thank Hara..."

"Pigeon, what happened?" Sage asked, holding a sleeve over her mouth.

Panicked, angry words floated down from the invisible bird. "Men. Ran in, threw fire."

"A trap, then." Cal swallowed and turned to Lydia. "Dev set the fire and took Aspen."

"*Took* them?"

The crowd rumbled at the news, but Cal's swirling thoughts blocked out their chatter. The fire in Pigeon's garden had been intentional, set specifically to draw Aspen out—but how had Halleson or Dev even known about Pigeon? Cal had never mentioned that particular spirit to Dev, and she couldn't image Halleson visiting the gardens or speaking with a local...

"Ms. Breslin!"

She turned and stiffened. One of the latest onlookers was the last person she wanted to see right now—and one of the last people she expected to be running into the fray. "James?"

He skidded to a stop before the garden gate. "Good gods, what happened?" he panted, his gaze flitting between her and the wreckage.

"Aspen's been kidnapped." She glanced impatiently back at Emry, who had waved down a carriage at the corner. If that carriage wouldn't take them all the way north, she could always demand James let them use his...

"Kidnapped?" James repeated. "*Here*?"

Then something highly unusual flashed across his face. Something Cal had never seen there before, or even thought him capable of.

Guilt.

"My gods..." He took his hat in his hands, his voice suddenly weak. "Why—why would someone do that?"

Then she remembered. The brief conversation with a drunken James on her way to the garden. A simple question about spirits and a garden on Linden Street...

She rounded back on him, her gaze piercing—or, at least, she hoped it was. She wanted it to be sharp enough to hurt. "What did you do?"

"Nothing!" James held up a frantic hand. "Nothing, I swear!"

"What did you tell Mr. Gray?"

"I—I, um..."

Under her stare, his resolve collapsed like a soft pudding.

"I asked him for a letter of recommendation," he said miserably, "and he said he would write one if I told him where Aspen spends most of their time. He said he needed to talk to them alone, so I"—he gestured to the garden—"I told him there was some rooster spirit here that they liked to talk to at the corner of Linden—"

"Rooster?" Pigeon screeched over by Lydia. "*Rooster?*"

Her silvery outline of feathers inflated until she was a round, angry puffball, ready to take form and fight—

But Cal was too fast.

She slammed her heel down on James' boot with all the strength she could muster. James yelped and whipped his foot away, hopping up and down on his good leg. While he was unbalanced, she hooked her foot around his knee and pulled, sending him to the ground in an undignified heap.

"You loathsome dolt!" she shouted. "Was that your plan? Selling out Aspen so you could get a promotion?"

James tried to wriggle away from her. "I didn't know Mr. Gray was going to—"

She set her heel firmly on the edge of his tailcoat, grinding it into the grimy cobblestones. "You don't know much of anything, do you? You should've brought an aide to do the work for you. Perhaps you would have gotten away with it then."

"Cal!" Emry ran up from the waiting carriage, his glare raining fire down on James. "Is he—?"

"He sold out Aspen," she hissed. All around her, the crowd's buzz whipped into anger. Riley rounded on James, and Emry rolled up his coat sleeves, looking about ready to turn into a wolf himself. And part of her wanted to see it—wanted to see them lay into the stupid man like he deserved—

"Wait." She reluctantly held out her arms, stopping both of them from advancing. "Save your energy and detain him. We need to follow Aspen first."

Though Riley grumbled, she and Sage immediately took hold of James' arms.

"We'll fetch Karlson, too," Sage said, then nodded to the waiting carriage. "Go get them back."

Cal took Emry's hand and made for the carriage.

"The northern city gate," she ordered the befuddled driver, then slipped in alongside Emry.

"What do we do once we get Aspen back?" Emry asked, anger still curling around his voice. "We can't just let Dev and the others go."

Through the window, Cal caught the silhouette of the hotel down the street and Sage and Riley dragging James toward it.

"We'll bring Dev back here, too. He wants his time in the limelight, does he not?" She gave the hotel a cold smile. "We shall ensure he gets it."

CHAPTER TWENTY-EIGHT

EMRY

Emry bounced his leg restlessly on the seat. His growing aches hated the motion, after all the running he had done, but he couldn't help it—he had to do something, lest the slow amble of the carriage tear his mind apart.

"I swear, pushing this thing myself will get us there faster..." he mumbled. He kept wondering how far ahead Dev's carriage was. If they were beyond the gate yet, approaching the dig site, sweeping Aspen away somewhere he couldn't reach—

To distract himself from his thoughts, he took Cal's hand and intertwined their fingers. But she didn't respond right away—she was too busy looking out the window, trying to catch something that had gone by.

"Are you seeing this?" she asked. Emry leaned around her shoulder. At every garden they passed, flashes of red burst in the grass, like scarlet fireflies hovering low.

"Pigeon," he said. "Those are her flowers."

Then other colors joined in, frantic and fast. By the time they reached the northern gate, he counted over a dozen different hues flying through the gardens, across every tier of the city he could see, all blinking in their hurried, silent language.

"What do you think they're saying?" Cal said. Instinctively, Emry turned to where Aspen would have sat, eagerly translating for them, the colors reflecting in their delighted gaze. They were responsible for the spectacle, after all. Without them, the gardens would still be dark and quiet.

His heart sank, and he kissed the back of Cal's hand to reassure them both.

"If I had to guess," he murmured, "they're telling this carriage to go faster."

To Emry's dismay, their horses moved even slower.

After paying a painful amount of gold to rent mounts at such a late hour, they set off down the dirt path, eager to gallop away and catch up to Dev—but caution forced them to slow their pursuit. Their rented lanterns barely punctured the gloomy night, and the close press of trees formed a natural defense for the dig site. Anyone could be hiding behind the branches, waiting to ensure they never reached their quarry.

So, they crept forward, praying the horses wouldn't stumble over a root and they wouldn't stumble into an ambush.

"We're getting close," Cal finally whispered to Emry, breaking the monotony of the crickets and rustling branches around them. "Douse the lanterns."

Emry did so, throwing them to the mercy of the half-moon above. A few paces later, his growing unease forced him to dismount.

"Let me check up ahead first," he said, then crept along the tree line, his eyes straining in the darkness. A pinprick of light both eased his sight and confirmed his fears—up ahead at the clearing, a figure stood in front of the cave, a lantern perched on a crate beside them.

And all around, a scattering of workers moved tools and crates, hunched and shrouded in the mist.

Emry bit back a curse. He had no easy way of getting past such a blockade. Not unless he served as a distraction while Cal—

Then the figure turned to survey the clearing, and the lantern briefly illuminated the man's nervous expression—Zeke, holding a shovel in a tight grip and jumping at the movement of the shadowy figures around him.

Emry crept back to Cal, who dismounted and crouched behind a wide oak tree.

"He sees more reason than Dev," she murmured, pulling her shawl tighter against the cold. "Let me try to talk to him. And if he won't budge..."

Emry rolled up his sleeves. "I don't have an oar, but I'll do my best."

Cal straightened and strode into the clearing.

"Mr. Whitlock—"

The man shrieked and dropped the shovel he was holding. "Ms. Breslin!"

Around him, all the workers rounded on her—but Zeke quickly dismissed them.

"She's with me!" He rushed up to Cal, a hand on his heart. "Thank the gods you came! I've been looking all over the city for you."

Cal stopped in her tracks. "Beg pardon?"

"Dev's gone out of his mind," Zeke rambled, pointing back to the tunnel. "I tried to keep him from kidnapping Aspen, but—"

Emry stepped out from behind the tree. "Why did he do it?"

Zeke yelped and jumped once more.

"He"—the poor man had to catch his breath here—"he wants Aspen to retrieve the spirit energy for him. None of our workers can, but he thinks Aspen will be more resistant to the energy."

"Resistant?" Cal snapped. "What if it kills them? What if it releases a surge?"

Emry's hands curled into fists. "It doesn't matter. Aspen would never help him."

"Of course, they wouldn't," Zeke said. "But—but Dev's got a torch to the lute, you see, and—"

Emry's heart dropped to the ground. He grabbed both the shovel and the lantern, then nodded to Zeke.

"Lead the way," he said. "Now."

They hurried into the darkness, Emry the only one cognizant of the well's rumbling far below. He half-expected the ground to shake under his feet, but the tunnel remained jarringly steady. So, he steadied himself and tried to adjust to the low thrumming in his mind, letting it fade into the background until it became more like lapping waves than looming thunder.

But as soon as he gained confidence in wrestling the sound, their bold adventure stopped short at the elevator.

"Of course," Zeke muttered, holding up a rope attached to the crank shaft. Its severed edge splayed over his palm, already fraying.

"I don't understand," Cal said, holding the lantern up while Zeke inspected the rope. "How does Dev plan to get back out?"

"There's another exit farther down the mountain," Zeke said. "Close to the actual well. We only just managed to finish digging it last week." He sighed and regarded the path behind them. "We could try to walk all the way around, but this path is so much faster..."

Emry followed his gaze outward and spotted Aspen's vines from the other day, still swinging from the cracked scaffolding.

"Hold on," he said. "Let me see what I can do."

He tugged down one of the vines, held it next to the rope, then focused on extending it, pleading for the vine to grow as thick and strong as the rope. Once it began to obey, he placed them closer together, weaving the vine into the fibers of the original structure until they were one.

He handed Zeke the rope and wiped sweat off his forehead with a shaky hand.

"Not sure how Aspen does it, honestly," he said.

Zeke stared at him, his jaw slack. "How did you—?"

Cal pushed the lantern back into his hands with a sharp glare. "You didn't see anything."

Zeke cleared his throat and stepped into the elevator. "No, ma'am. Nothing at all."

They descended carefully, Emry keeping both his hands and his thoughts on the vine to ensure it wouldn't come undone. But the farther they went, the more his arms trembled, and they all released a tense breath when the elevator finally touched down.

"Perhaps we, ah, use the lower exit on the way out," Zeke said, his smile faltering.

"Happily." Emry shook the exhaustion out of his arms, then tugged the vine loose and wrapped it around his wrist. So far, Zeke's lantern illuminated a path of nothing but gray ahead—it wouldn't hurt to have a plant or two, even if just to strangle Dev with. "Lead the way, then."

But it wasn't just Zeke guiding them through the cave. Their footsteps followed a fragmented trail of petals and leaves—small, but reassuring proof that Aspen's lute had come through here recently. Cal kept her worried gaze on the petals as they moved.

"Mr. Whitlock," she said, "what does Halleson mean to do with the spirit energy from Dev?"

"I try not to think about it," Zeke said, then reconsidered. "Dev is...very good at speeches, as I'm sure you know. He convinced Halleson—and me—that the energy has potential to be anything and everything. A tool, a healing draught, a weapon...anything that got Halleson to want his name on it first."

"And what will it actually be?"

Thunder rumbled through the tunnel. Not the spirit well's deep growls, but true thunder, punctuated by loud, sharp cracks in the ceiling. Zeke gulped.

"Hopefully not our deaths."

They continued on for a few paces—then the thunder rolled in again, and a brief shower of soil dropped down ahead of them. Emry threw a protective arm out in front of Cal.

"Zeke," he said in a warning tone. "How stable is this area?"

The lantern light jostled—Zeke's hand was shaking. "I can assure you, this area is quite stable. I've inspected it myself many times. But..." His gaze traveled nervously over the dark ceiling. "We should keep moving down. We haven't reached the keep yet."

"The keep?" Cal repeated. Zeke opened his mouth, then paused.

"You'll understand once you see it."

Emry had half a mind to inform him that he was actually rather done with mysteries for a while, thank you, and he wanted to know what such a *keep* was right now—but once they descended down the long slope, the words dissolved on his tongue.

This new chamber was filled not with stalagmites or curtains of rock but a forest of shining crystal. Giant translucent pillars jutted out of the ground at all angles, some piercing both floor and ceiling, others forming short clusters of sharp points. Each one stood as thick as a barrel and half as tall as the Oakvale Grand, their angles forming bridges and archways and obstacles all at once. And every single one sparkled with reservoirs of spirit energy.

Zeke's voice lowered in something akin to admiration.

"Most of these have been here since the start of the excavation," he said, raising his lantern to better showcase the display. The light bounced and played amongst the facets, warm against the cool glow of the crystals. "But more have grown in our paths since we first discovered them, particularly near the well itself. A few of the more irritated tunnelers began calling it a keep that continues to rebuild itself."

"Its self-defense mechanism," Cal said in awe, placing one hand on the nearest pillar. The bracelet on her wrist dangled by the larger stone, a pitiful sight compared to the massive structure. "It truly is trying to protect itself."

"Yes, it tried," Zeke said grimly. "It wasn't able to stop Dev."

Cal's face darkened with an angry shadow not even the crystals could chase away.

"Look at all this." She gestured to the chamber. "Think of all the studies that could have been done on this if it had been uncovered properly."

Zeke raised his free hand. "I completely understand—"

"And now he's gone and ruined it!" she snapped. "Potential years, *decades* of discovery and knowledge, and we're going to have to just—lock it away, because he insisted that a few spirits could die for his—!" She huffed and swiped the lantern. "Give me that."

She marched forward; above her, thunder rolled once more, a distant reflection of her anger. The crystals closest to the path rose and sharpened a little.

"Ms. Breslin...?" Zeke ventured, then looked back at Emry, who raised his eyebrows and gestured to the path with his shovel.

"Well," he said. "Best do as she says."

As they continued into the depths, the crystal forest only sharpened, threatening impalement if they took so much as one step off the path. And it wasn't only the crystals that loomed—the silent thunder of the well grew with each step, becoming harder and harder to ignore. Even Cal and Zeke started to wince.

"What is that?" Cal rubbed her forehead. Emry carefully guided her away from a jutting pillar.

"I think we're getting close to the well," he murmured.

"Mr. Karic is right," Zeke whispered. "Douse the lantern, if you'd be so kind."

Cal doused the lantern, turned the corner, and stopped in front of the most unusual tunnel Emry had ever seen.

It wasn't made of the usual imposing rock but pure crystal, like rippled glass undulating in large, blue waves around them. Dev's tunnelers had hastily sanded a narrow path on the floor, forcing them into the depths single file, Zeke in front. He kept his steps careful and silent—then pressed himself against the wall and motioned with his head to the next chamber.

"They're here."

Emry peered over Zeke's shoulder. Beyond him lay a glowing crystal sea, frozen under a ceiling that vaulted twice as high as the hotel ballroom. Dev and Aspen faced off in the center of the glowing floor, and under their feet swirled what the scientist wanted so dearly—raw spirit energy, floating in vast, roiling spirals.

Emry crept to the edge of the crystal layer, dizzied by the endless whirlpools and their significance. The origin of all spirits and the source of last year's destruction. Life and death, a spinning starfield just under his heels.

The silent thunder of the place deafened him.

"Do it," Dev commanded, gaze locked on Aspen. It didn't matter that the spirit stood in front of Dev with their back to the tunnel—Emry could see straight through them, to the scientist holding a torch to Aspen's half-empty lute. As he spoke, he brought it closer to the wood, his hands shaking.

"I said, *do* it," he repeated, gesturing to the metal contraption beside them, its points facing down into the crystal layer like teeth ready to sink into a meal.

"I won't," the spirit hissed back, flickering in rage. "I'm not letting you kill an entire city of my friends! I'm not letting you mine our future!"

But Dev's eyes were wild, the torch throwing ragged shadows across his crazed grin.

"Just a sample, my good spirit!" he said. "If you leave me to keep digging on my own, more of your spirits will come to harm, won't they?" The torch's shadows deepened. "Best end all this now and save what's left of them."

Aspen snarled, and their form tried to change—to a wolf, to a bear, to an eagle—but nothing stuck, and they crumpled back into human form in frustration. In their weak state, they looked like a mere illusion formed by the light of the well.

"I'll go get them," Emry whispered to Cal, reaching for the vine around his arm—but she set a hand on his wrist.

"And the well?" she asked. "If we leave the tunnels intact, Dev will just come back."

"You could..." Zeke steadied himself. "You could take down the two entrances." He nodded to the pillars near their own tunnel, then to the ones by the dark exit tunnel beyond. "If you collapse those, the well will grow crystals back over them for protection within weeks. Days, perhaps, if no one's digging. It's...not perfect, but it'll do."

Cal turned to Emry. "Can you manage it?"

He stiffened. The pillars in this chamber were nearly the width of a carriage. He could rush Dev and free Aspen, of course, but neither of them had the strength to take down anything like this, not even on their best days...

Thunder shot through the chamber one more time, sending debris showering over Dev and Aspen. A shadow flickered in the darkness above, and Emry threw himself in front of Cal again, preparing to shield her from falling rock—

But the shadow wasn't rock, nor crystal, nor dirt. It was a vine of thorns forcing its way down through the ceiling, crawling steadily along the wall. Rainwater soon followed it, dripping and splashing near their feet. As each drop sizzled and faded, a few precious glints of spirit energy twirled up from the splashes, and the entire chamber filled with a strange mix of scents: petrichor, flowers, cobblestones, iron fences...

And with each drop, Aspen's form began to solidify. Emry grinned.

"Aspen and I can do this." He turned back to Cal. "I just need to get the lute back."

"Understood." Cal grabbed Zeke's shovel and weighed it in her hand. "Well," she sighed, "it's not an oar, but it will have to do."

"What—?"

Then she sprinted into the spirit well.

"Devrin Gray, you drop that torch right now or so *help* me Hara—"

Perhaps it was the thunder, or the guttering torch casting light off her shovel—or perhaps it was the murderous look in her eyes that came with dealing with men's egos day in and day out—but whatever it was, Devrin Gray took one look at Cal Breslin and dropped his torch.

It was all Emry needed.

"Aspen!" He ran forward and whipped the vine toward the spirit. Aspen whirled, caught it—and disappeared, their presence rushing through the vine and straight into Emry's arm.

I knew you'd come! The spirit threw his arm back in recoil. Relief spread through him—though whether it was his or Aspen's, he couldn't tell. *I knew you'd make it!*

Without missing a step, Emry kept running, grabbing the lute from the floor and skidding to a halt under the rain.

We're not the only ones.

Above them, the vines and rain expanded into a downpour. Flowers of all colors bloomed stubbornly along the vines, but Emry didn't need the markers to know the other spirits were there—he could feel their rage stowed along with their energy in every raindrop. And with each drop that struck the lute, Aspen's presence grew stronger and stronger.

Think you can take these pillars down? Emry asked. Inside him, Aspen grinned.

Dev did tell me to end all this now, didn't he?

The lute shuddered in Emry's hands—then greenery burst out of it, flowers and soil and wild curls of thorns stretching the cracks of its once-shattered body. It grew so heavy, Emry had to drop it, and Aspen leapt from him into the lute.

But the spirit didn't remain on the ground for long. Just like the thorns, they curled and expanded into a wolf form—first up to Emry's waist, then his neck, then his head. A massive wolf soon towered over him, teeth bared, tail lashing, vines expanding outward to slither up the pillars. They placed both paws on either side of Emry, sheltering him from the thorns with their mass of flickering fur.

Emry supposed he should have been terrified, being flanked by claws the length of his shin, a wolf's hot breath snorting over his head. He had never seen Aspen so large, so menacing, so vengefully sharp.

Instead, he grinned. Dev had angered a forest spirit, after all. This was what he deserved.

This was what *Aspen* deserved.

The spirit bared their fangs at Dev, who had staggered back from Cal and now stared up at Aspen in horror.

"No," he croaked as tendrils writhed past his feet, snaking over the well and closing off its energy to him. One particularly thick vine wrapped around the metal mining contraption and crushed it with a screech. "No, you can't!"

Aspen laughed, a mix of a high, victorious shriek and a deep rumble that mimicked the well below them. In desperation, Dev sprinted forward—but Zeke yanked him back, and he fell to his knees in a flailing, useless struggle.

"*Please!*" he tried wildly. "You can't do this to my—"

"Yours?" The surrounding thorns all sharpened at the word. "No, I don't think you understand. This never was and never will be yours. This is theirs. This is *ours.*"

All around them, the spirits' flowers bloomed stronger, a rainbow of angry fireflies shivering down the walls. Aspen lowered their head, fur brushing Emry's shoulder, until their teeth were level with the scientist's stricken face.

"You're in our grove, Dev," they said softly. "Get out."

The sound of snapping crystal filled the air.

CHAPTER TWENTY-NINE

EMRY

THE CHAMBER WHIRLED into a chaotic blur. As the crystal pillars shattered, Emry joined Cal in rushing to the exit, one arm raised to shield her from jagged shards. Together, they slid on rainwater and dodged hissing clouds of spirit energy until they stumbled into the narrow tunnel.

"Aspen!" Emry staggered to a halt in the safety of the shadows. Zeke and Dev tumbled past him, but he paid them no mind—his gaze was fixed on the spirit, whose fur now glittered with broken pieces of crystal.

"Go!" they ordered, pounding their way toward him. With every beat of their paw, the crystal floor shuddered and flashed. "I'll be right behind you, *go*!"

Emry tried to stay rooted to the spot, to ensure Aspen made it out —but above them, the weak wooden scaffolding gave a horrible shudder, and he pressed on with a terrified curse.

There were no lanterns or crystals to guide them in this final tunnel. Only inky darkness, the groan of collapsing soil, and Cal's terrified shouts bolstered them onward.

"Zeke?" she yelled, holding a sleeve against the growing clouds of debris. Above them, the soil groaned. "Where are you?"

"This way!" Zeke shouted. "Follow my voice!"

They followed his echoes, from shadow to dust clouds to weak gray light, until they finally staggered into a moonlit clearing. Emry fell to his knees with a shuddering cough, the grass dewy and cool against his palms.

It would have been a refreshing reminder of his survival, if it weren't for the lack of Aspen behind him.

"Did you see them?" he asked Cal, wheezes marking every word. "I should go, I should go back—"

A lute crashed into his chest and tumbled into the grass behind him, knocking out both his breath and his fear.

"Did you see?" Aspen gushed, their gasps vibrating the lute strings. "Did you *see* that? You came, and my friends came, and I took it down, all of it—"

Cal grabbed the lute and hugged it, crushing it against her chest.

"Forget about wrapping Emry in a duvet," she said. "Once we get home, I'm planting you in a garden."

"Hey!"

"She's right." Emry pulled them both in with weary, trembling arms, resting his head against Cal's shoulder. "Straight into a tree for you. I'm thinking a nice poplar."

"You know I don't like poplars—"

"Ms. Breslin?"

Zeke cautiously cleared his throat behind him. Emry reluctantly released them and stood up. Zeke was crouched next to Dev, whose hands he had clumsily tied with a stray vine. Dev, for his part, could do nothing but glare at his former assistant and cough out puffs of dust. All his desperation and wildness had melted, leaving the man muddy, disheveled, and half-bent with exhaustion.

It should have been a gratifying sight—and it was, certainly—

but sadness fluttered through Emry right along with his anger. Before all this, before his terrible deals and reckless decisions, Dev had been on a golden path of his own making. He had shown the world his brilliance, propelled himself out of his lonely, neglected house. He had been destined for great things, genuinely great things —not the inside of a prison cell.

Now, however...

"I didn't want him running away." Zeke straightened, trying to keep his voice strong while it trembled. "We should face whatever consequences we must. Though"—he faltered—"I ask that if it involves leaving the city, we do so before Halleson learns of what happened."

Cal's gaze sharpened on Dev. "Oh no. There will be no leaving the city." She got to her feet, holding Aspen's lute with both hands. "Mr. Gray will speak fully and truthfully for the rest of the evening, lest Aspen be encouraged to bare their fangs again."

Zeke guided them to a carriage he had held near the cave exit, alongside a bevy of confused dig workers expecting barrels of spirit energy and not five dusty beings demanding a ride back to town.

"Excuse me, pardon me." He waved them all away and gave a nod to the equally befuddled driver. "To the, um..." He turned back to Cal.

"The Oakvale Grand."

Zeke's voice wobbled. "The Oakvale Grand, please."

When they arrived at the hotel, the ball was still going strong. The crowd hadn't yet forgotten their odd scuffle with Halleson—they fielded more than a few surprised looks upon their return—but Emry ignored them. That little tussle was nothing compared to what they were about to do.

He squeezed Cal's hand, then looked at Dev and Aspen. Dev's

bonds had been cut, but Aspen stood firmly next to him, their form translucent except for the long claws on their hands.

"With me, both of you," Emry said, then made a straight line for the stage, which the musicians had abandoned for a short break. Aspen poked Dev in the back to follow.

"Look, whatever you're planning," Dev hissed at both of them, "you're better off having Halleson on your side. He can pay you—"

"Oh, just what I've always wanted," Aspen drawled. "Human money."

Emry glanced across the ball. Halleson was watching them approach the stage with an increasingly blanched face, but he couldn't leave—Karlson, Sage, and Riley had surrounded him with wide, friendly smiles, with the rest of the troupe forming a wider perimeter.

He pushed away his exhaustion and stood as straight as possible. Aspen had done their part, Cal had done hers—even the troupe stood at the ready to do theirs.

All he had left was to do his part.

He locked eyes with Karlson, nodded once, then ascended the stage with Aspen and Dev.

"Evening," he called, as easily as if it were the start of a performance. The crowd turned to him and immediately began to buzz. Beside the stage, the Forsgren Quartet stood in confusion—he held up an apologetic hand to them. He only had a moment onstage, but that was all he needed.

"Aspen and I would like to thank you for coming out and supporting Matlock's spirits tonight," he said. "And I'm happy to say that Mr. Gray has good news for you all. Don't you, Mr. Gray?"

In the crowd, Halleson went from pale to scarlet. Dev swallowed and looked around him—but Cal, Lydia, and her colleagues blocked the stairs, and onstage, Aspen flashed him a wide, fanged smile.

"Yes." Dev faltered. "The...threat to the spirits has been neutralized."

The crowd cheered—but Emry wasn't done.

"And what was the threat, exactly?" he said, adopting a tone of professional curiosity. All around the stage, journalists scribbled. Dev's eyes widened in fear, even as he tried to mimic Emry with a passive, distanced air.

"There was an underground expedition that was...disrupting the spirits."

"Disrupting?" Emry repeated. "I have it on good authority that several spirits were killed."

The crowd's murmur sharpened, and Emry gave them a moment to let the words sink in.

"How incredibly fortunate it's all been stopped, then," he continued, setting a hand on his chest. "Who ordered that expedition in the first place? Who was responsible for all this?"

The crowd grew louder, more indignant. Dev stiffened, his face radiating the panic and anger of a cornered animal.

Out of the corner of Emry's eye, Cal grinned. Emry took a wicked delight in the satisfaction.

"I..." Dev stammered. "I'm—not entirely sure—"

Aspen growled. Emry leaned forward.

"Oh, surely you are," he said. "The people want to know."

Indeed, the people did. They all leaned forward—the journalists, the scientists, the sparkling gentry who for months had clung to his every word.

Dev broke.

"*Listen,*" he snarled, his tone ricocheting across the ballroom. "I wouldn't have had to mine so quickly if it wasn't for Halleson demanding results before the end of the season—"

He pointed one damning finger at the man.

And the accused, in all his finery and all his authority and all his riches, made a run for it.

The ball exploded. Karlson and his troupe leapt for him, only to scuffle with his guards instead. Halleson ducked and dodged, eyes on the doors—but Riley tackled him with a reckless yell. Taking advantage of the havoc, Dev shoved Emry aside and scrambled for the stairs himself—

But Lydia and her scientists were far too fast.

"That's for Pigeon!" Ms. Preston whipped her purse at Dev's head. He stumbled backward, right into Mr. Spencer's waiting headlock.

"I've got him!" he shouted, half in victory, half in disbelief.

"You're getting spot bonuses, all of you." Lydia grabbed Dev's arm and helped drag him to the growing contingent of hotel security, both eager to join the fray and bewildered by the largest fight they had seen in their careers. "If you could take this man away at your earliest convenience, good sirs."

"What do we...take him in for?" one of the guards asked hesitantly. Lydia ushered them all out of the room, her eyes ablaze.

"Don't think Matlock's got any spirit-murder laws written just yet, but I'm sure we can figure something out."

As both Dev and Halleson left in various stages of disarray, shame, and bruises, the crowd descended upon those still present—Cal, Aspen, and Emry. In a blink, they found themselves surrounded by reporters and gossipers, all eager for the details not spilled onstage.

"It was a terrible shame to investigate a former colleague for such an act," Cal told a reporter, struggling to raise her voice over the crowd. "But rest assured, I collaborated with Matlock researchers on this every step of the way. Our partnership was invaluable, and I look forward to working with them on future efforts."

The reporter nodded and scribbled. "And Mr. Edwards?"

"Who?" Cal said sweetly.

"Mr. James Edwards?" the reporter repeated. "The other aide here. Will he be leaving the department, now that his collaboration with Mr. Gray has been exposed?"

Cal's smile sharpened. "I'm sure he will find other employment. After all, an Edwards cannot languish at a desk for very long."

Emry started for the reporter, preparing to rattle off Cal's other accomplishments she hadn't yet mentioned—they needed to write an entire article about her, obviously—but others demanded his attention first.

"Are you all right?" Karlson rushed up to him and Aspen, his hair rumpled and cravat crooked from his scuffle. Emry thought he saw a growing bruise under the man's eye, which only lent him a rugged air. "Gods, if either of you didn't come back, Damir and Ella would have murdered me with a lute string..."

"We're all right," Emry tried to reassured him—but now that the satisfaction of dragging Dev onstage was wearing off, exhaustion seeped into his bones. He looked at Aspen, who, despite not having bones, appeared just as weary. A wink of sleep—oh, about thirty hours or so—would do them good.

"Tired, I think," he continued weakly. "But we're all right."

With Karlson came a new wave of attention, and it wasn't long until the journalists hounded them as well, surrounding them with questions and half-filled notebooks.

"My dear Karlson," one honey-toned woman with a plume of feathers in her hair asked, "we are devastated to hear of your canceled concerts. With the spirits now in recovery, is there any chance you and your troupe might reconsider? A bit of a celebratory performance, perhaps?"

Sage and Riley brightened, and Emry's weary spirits lifted—oh, just one more concert, one more to continue his debut before the season ended—

But Karlson shook his head. "I'm afraid we'll be returning home to Vornik soon."

Emry cut in. "But, sir—"

"Where..." Karlson clapped him on the back. "We will be rather busy. You see, Mr. Karic will be forming his own troupe for a very special Vornik debut and full provincial tour."

The woman gasped in delight. Emry had to grab a nearby pillar for support.

"*Sir?*"

Sage, Riley, and Aspen immediately crowded him with a whirlwind of squeals and whoops—Aspen hugging him around the waist, Sage bouncing at his shoulder, Riley shaking his arm.

"A whole *tour*—!"

"Emry, congratulations!"

But Emry was in a daze. He must have misheard, it must be the fatigue getting to him, muddying his ears—

"Sir." He looked up to Karlson. "Are you absolutely sure?"

Karlson's grin softened. "Mr. Karic, you never needed my help for your debut," he said. "I knew Senne only raised good men."

CHAPTER THIRTY

CAL

Two days later, Damir returned with Ella in tow, fully prepared to lock down the entire city with her if need be.

"Karic! There you are!" He met Emry and Cal in the lobby, blustering in like a dark, distressed raincloud. "What are you doing here and not at the inn? I told you to lie *low*. This isn't—"

"Oh, it's all solved," Emry said with a smile, leaning on his cane. Damir stared blankly at him. Behind him, Ella stepped forward, her travel attire perfectly in place, with no sign of having just hurried across the border to save a city.

"What do you mean, solved?" she repeated.

Cal cleared her throat in poorly hidden pride. "Mr. Gray and Mr. Halleson have been detained upon suspicion of injuring hundreds and killing at least ten Matlock spirit citizens." She gestured to the hotel's tea room. "If we could discuss further over tea?"

After the aforementioned tea, a hushed conversation, and surprised silence, Ella and Damir stared at their teacups, taking in all they had missed.

"I must say I'm disappointed," Ella began. Cal stiffened—until the singer stirred her tea with a mischievous glimmer. "I was looking forward to detonating the dig site myself."

"Oh, detonation is still on the table." Damir stuffed a tea cake into his mouth. "Halleson won't remain in custody for long, and he nearly killed my musicians. If he gets caught in, say, a carriage explosion a few months from now, I wouldn't mind."

Aspen eagerly threw in their support for the idea—but to their disappointment, Ella tabled the discussion of murder for another day.

"Ms. Breslin. My dear Karics." She stood, giving each of them a gracious nod. "I thank you for your efforts, and I daresay Matlock does, too. But..." Her imperial gaze landed on Emry. "I feel rather left out not witnessing Spiritsong's Matlock debut. Damir couldn't stop talking about it, and that is no small feat."

Damir reddened and shot to his feet.

"Time to go, Ella," he said. "We're quite busy, very rushed today, everyone wants to see you—"

But Ella remained in place. "Can I count on you for a riveting reprisal? So I may congratulate you myself?"

Emry grinned. "Only if Riley gets the fireworks she wanted."

"Oh, gods help me," Damir muttered. Ella's smile widened.

"After your efforts here, Mr. Karic, you may have as many fireworks as you like."

"And you promise you'll help Pigeon write to me?" Aspen asked Lydia, hands on their hips. They stood at their final inspection of Pigeon's garden, the grass and bushes still charred but slowly returning to life in weak, green patches. Lydia mimicked Aspen's pose and nodded solemnly.

"I'll visit every day and help her write to you whenever she wants," she said. Pigeon landed on her shoulder, and she gave the bird's neck a light stroke. "I've also got Mr. Spencer assigned to the four gardens to the left and Ms. Preston to the five gardens below. We'll get your whole network writing in no time, I can promise you that."

After Aspen took one last tour of the gardens and declared themself satisfied with their budding greenery, all Cal had left to do for the remaining days was say farewell to the other researchers and pack for the return trip. And when it came time to pack, she threw her clothing together with far less attention to detail than usual, her excitement too strong to properly focus. Despite the beauty of the city, she'd had more than her fair share of balls and posh gardens for a while. Let the carriage bear her back to a familiar place, brimming with familiar faces, a familiar pot of tea, a familiar reading nook…

As she closed the clasps on her luggage, a knock sounded from the hall.

"Ms. Breslin?" Emry's voice floated in. "An invitation for you."

Cal smiled and opened the door. "I didn't realize you were the new footman."

Emry stood at the doorway, hands clasped behind his back. He had no cane today—a comforting sign, a day without pain—and sported a mischievous grin.

"I'm afraid I don't have a letter. And if I did, you wouldn't want it anyway. My handwriting's atrocious." He nodded to the hall. "I was wondering if you'd like to take a turn with me?"

Cal looked around for Aspen. "Shall we be chaperoned?"

"I do believe they're busy communing with some spirits." He offered up his arm. "Are you willing to endure a bit of scandal?"

Cal didn't hesitate to wrap her arm around his. "I shall be strong and endure."

To her surprise, Emry didn't guide her to the hotel gardens but out into the bustling street.

"Such a public place," she said lightly. "You really do want to start a scandal."

"And besmirch your honor?" His hand flew to his heart. "I wouldn't dare. I merely wanted to show you something."

Emry led her down a tier and toward the closest plaza—but even before they reached the space, Cal could tell the city was in the throes of some sort of celebration. Instead of carriages, clusters of people filled the streets, wandering and laughing under canopies of bright tapestries. The sunlight streaming through the fabric cast their faces in hues of emerald and amethyst, colors swirling along with the scents of cinnamon and sugar.

"What's all this?" Cal asked in wonder, using the crowd as an excuse to press closer to Emry. He shrugged, a stripe of ruby light passing over his hair.

"I asked Lydia," he said. "She says these sorts of things happen all the time. But she thought it might be because the spirits are growing back."

The flow of the crowd bore them farther into the impromptu festival until they reached the plaza itself. Like in the streets, there was no shortage of celebrants or color here. Banners and tapestries rippled from the multistoried buildings, hemming in a great swath of dancers circling around the fountain. Their steps were as dizzying as the shimmering water, swinging round and round with a fervor entirely foreign in the social season's gilded ballrooms. Here, people talked and joked as they danced, some of them spontaneously switching partners or stumbling out of the fray mid-song to greet friends.

Cal let out a delighted, envious breath. *This* was what she had been missing in those ballrooms—a dance that wasn't for politics or posturing, but for pleasure. A simple act of unscrutinized joy with someone she loved.

Emry held out a hand. "Do you have space on your dance card?"

"For you?" Cal beamed up at him. "I believe I do."

Slipping in with the dancers was like leaping into a fast-moving current—toes were stepped on, shoulders brushed, hands clasped and lost and clasped again. Those around them laughed at the chaos, encouraging Cal to do the same, and she quickly lost herself in the whirl of music and cinnamon and Emry's touch. For two sets, he held her arms, slipped a hand around her waist, spun her around. She wanted it to go on forever, for them to keep dancing until night fell and the plaza was lit only by the streetlamps and Emry's smile.

But when the second set ended, he pulled her away, giggly and breathless and warm. They found a stone bench under an arched alcove and half collapsed there, hands still intertwined, shoulders still touching.

"Can't believe I didn't break someone's foot back there," Emry said, pushing his hair out of his face. "Or elbow someone into the fountain."

"See?" Cal squeezed his arm. "I knew your dancing had improved."

"Against all odds." Emry set his head back against the alcove wall and closed his eyes. But Cal wasn't ready to return yet—she remained giddy and lightheaded, as if she were still spinning with the rest of the dancers.

"Dance with me again?" she asked without thinking. Emry opened one eye.

"Wish I could, love," he said, then held up two fingers. "But I'm afraid we've already danced twice. I may not know all the rules, but I do know that one."

Cal bit her lip. A third dance always meant an engagement, of course. A bold, wordless declaration, to be so enamored with someone that they simply couldn't stop dancing with them for the world to see.

Emry closed his eyes once more, and Cal watched him for a moment—his loose, dark curls against the flowered archway, the sunlight splayed over his freckles.

She stood up.

"Dance with me," she said, holding out her hand. Her fingers began to shake, her lips wobbling into a nervous smile.

Emry opened both eyes, brows lifted in gentle entertainment of an assumed jest.

"Dearest." He took her hand in both of his. "It's the third dance. If I agree, your dance card might just burn up on the spot."

"Then let it," she said, excitement bubbling up with her words. "Dance with me a third time and a fourth. Dance with me for the rest of my life." She let out a breath. "Please."

Emry stared up at her, the smile dropping from his face. "Oh," he said softly. "You're serious?"

There was no turning back now. She squared her shoulders. "Quite."

Then his grin took over his face, his eyes immediately brimming with tears. "But—you—I was going to—" He scrambled for something in his coat pocket and held up a tiny notebook, laughing while sniffing back tears. "Look, I still had five things I had to do!" He flipped through the pages and held them up. "I was going to—to take you to a teahouse, and start writing you letters, and—"

Cal's broke into joyful tears, laughing through their salty warmth. Emry took her hands again, his face shining. "Can I—can I still kneel?"

"Of course, you can," Cal managed, wiping her eyes as Emry knelt before her, his hands trembling as they held hers.

"Ms. Breslin," he said, beaming up at her. "It would be the honor of my life to marry you."

CHAPTER
THIRTY-ONE

EMRY

THE PEEK OF THE SEASON

An engagement!

This is hardly the first of the season, but by far the most exciting (my apologies to Mrs. Albingdale). It has reached this writer's ears that Mr. Emry Karic and Ms. Calliope Breslin are to be married. And, to add a delicious shock, those same whispers are telling me that Ms. Breslin herself proposed! Gentlemen readers, be prepared—Ms. Breslin may very well have planted the seed of a trend for the season.

And regarding seeds, many of you have written to me reporting that your favorite gardens have vastly improved—and we have that same couple to thank, along with our dear spirit friend Aspen. We shall miss the spirit's absence, and regret that such efforts had to bear them back to Vornik so soon, along with Ms. Breslin and Mr. Karic. This writer can only hope that in a few months' time, she can report on every detail of the impending wedding. I do wonder what their flower arrangements will be like.

"When is Riley supposed to arrive?" Cal asked Emry, resting her head against the top of the garden chair. Emry scoffed and poured them both more wine.

"As if Riley ever follows the normal standards of time."

Weeks after their return to Vornik, they lounged in Emry's garden at sunset, waiting for Sage and Riley to arrive for a discussion about his debut. Behind them, Aspen made their rounds through the garden as they always did, doing one last check of their flowers and newly sown seeds.

"This one's doing all right." They toed a robust Matlockian rosebush—a recent gift from Lydia—and moved on to the neighboring hydrangea. "Wish this one would grow a little faster..."

"There's no rush, Aspen." Cal's eyes closed against in the warmth of the evening. "You only just got those seeds in the mail yesterday."

Ever since Matlock, the correspondence coming in for the spirit had grown exponentially. Some still wanted answers to their original questions, of course—could they grow Aspen's garden for them, could they make so-and-so fall in love with such-and-such—but others had far more interesting topics to discuss. Some were convinced the spirit in their orchard was finally beginning to talk to them; others wanted to know if spirits only lived in lutes. Could they live in clarinets? How about drums? If their spirit friend eventually wanted to travel like Aspen did, could they carry them around in something nonmusical, like an apple crate?

Aspen answered every question as best they could, with occasional assistance from Cal. No, it didn't have to be musical; yes, it did have to have space for soil and greenery. No, Aspen didn't know what a spirit a hundred miles away was saying. Yes, they were sure the spirit wanted to talk. Spirits were friendly, for the most part, they reassured everyone. Once you got to know them.

But the best letters of all were the ones they received from Pigeon.

"Did I tell you Pigeon sent me another note today?" Aspen abandoned their hydrangea, eagerly digging the paper out of their pocket. It was wrinkled and smudged with dirt, but they showed it off proudly all the same. "Lydia helped write it for her, of course. She said Lydia's team convinced a local troupe to play at the gardens now and then. They're thinking of building a stage there, if they can make room."

"If they set up a stage, can we play there?" Emry asked—then a knock sounded from within the house. He set down his wineglass and stood, eyebrows raised to Cal. "I take it back. Maybe Sage forced Riley to stick to a schedule this time."

Aspen pocketed their letter and eagerly bounded through the foyer. Sleepy from the wine and the calm evening, Emry and Cal followed at a more relaxed pace. How lovely, to drink non-poisoned wine and lounge in a garden that wasn't dying.

"Please do tell me if Sage bothers you too much with wedding questions," Emry said as they walked. "She wouldn't stop discussing bouquets with Aspen last time we met with her."

Cal took his arm.

"Please, if she wants to handle any of the details, she can be my guest. I'm afraid I'm far too busy to think about bouquets."

Emry kissed her forehead. She had been promoted shortly after returning to Vornik, while James quickly escaped to a new department with less paperwork and more handshaking. Cal's days were now filled not with piddling reports but important meetings, team expansion, research discussions...

Things like bouquets and candles were quite low on her list of priorities.

"If Sage does want to take over wedding planning," Emry said, opening the door for Aspen, "she'll likely need to fight Marley for a few of the tasks. Mar's already insisted that she help with the—"

He looked at their visitor and trailed off.

This wasn't Sage or Riley. He didn't recognize the woman at all. She had to have been about eighteen, a scraggly beanpole with mud on her boots and skirt. She nervously clutched a flowerpot to her chest, its soil filled with a riot of daisies in unusual colors.

"Beg pardon," she said. "I'm Jasmine Rackham—um, Ms. Rackham." She gave a hurried curtsy. "I hope I'm not intruding, but...is this the home of Aspen Karic?"

Aspen peeked over Emry's shoulder. "Hello?"

"Oh, wonderful—I mean, um..." Flustered, she curtsied again. "If you have a moment, my friend Daisy would like to meet you. Ask you some questions. That sort of thing."

"Daisy?" Aspen repeated. The daisies in the flowerpot all perked up at once.

"Hello?" A voice floated up from the soil, clear as day and bearing the same light accent as Jasmine. "Are you Aspen?"

Everyone blinked at the flowerpot—except for Jasmine, who continued with her nervous smile.

"He really wanted to meet you," she said, holding out the colorful pot.

Aspen's face brightened like sunlight, and they looked up at Emry with a wide, happy grin. Emry, knowing of no established protocol for impromptu spirit visits, looked at Cal, who gestured graciously to the foyer.

"Well, we can't let our new friends stand outside, can we?" she said lightly. "Please, come on in."

Aspen leapt into action, leading their new friends into the parlor in a tumble of bubbling chatter. "Of course! Welcome, come on in. Can I get you any tea? How about cookies?"

"I, um—yes, tea would be—"

But Aspen had already dashed off to the kitchen. Jasmine gave yet another nervous curtsy, then set the flowerpot on the coffee table and wandered around the parlor in fascination. Peering at Aspen's half-finished embroidery hoop on the armchair, then at the painting of a white-stoned city on the wall...

As she moved, Daisy's flowers swayed in observation, too.

"Hmm," he said. "Aspen has a very strange grove. Where are all the trees? The soil? The mushrooms?" The flowers bent down to inspect the rug.

"I don't know about mushrooms, but..." With effort, Cal picked up Aspen's lute from the couch. Since its suffering at the hands of Dev, the plants within had grown back tenfold, tumbling over Cal's arms—a vibrant garden in its own right. "Technically, they live in here."

The flowers recoiled in confusion. "What's that?"

"Oh!" Jasmine brightened. "It's a lute. Mr. Karic, does Aspen really play that onstage with you?"

But Daisy hadn't quite caught up yet. "A...lute?"

Cal looked at Emry; Emry grinned.

"Daisy," he said, "do you like music?"

WANT MORE?

Did you enjoy *The Spirit Well*?

Leave a review and spread the word!

∼

Want more Emry, Cal, and Aspen?

Sign up for my newsletter to get three *Stray Spirit* bonus scenes and updates on the next book:

https://rkashwick.com/newsletter/

∼

Coming up next in the Lutesong series:

The Spirit's Curse

Also by R.K. Ashwick:

A Rival Most Vial: Potioneering for Love and Profit

The Stray Spirit

ACKNOWLEDGMENTS

I'll say it—this book was an unruly middle child and I have a lot of people to thank for getting me through its growth.

First, to my beta and sensitivity readers: Joe, Emma, Amanda, Rynn Hunter, Rose, and Tessa. Thank you for slogging through the trenches of the early drafts with me.

To my editor Kim Halstead and my proofreader Stephanie Slagle: you both were so, so patient with my misplaced affinity for commas and dashes. May my future manuscripts be ever cleaner for you.

To my cover designer Patrick Knowles: I know it wasn't a small task to follow an already established look for a sequel, but you absolutely nailed it (and were a saint through my notes and drawovers to boot!).

To my husband Joe, who suffered from my long writing sessions on the couch: thank you for your endless support and patience. I am out from under the blanket now.

To my cat Leia, who greatly benefitted from my long writing sessions on the couch: stop chewing on the blanket.

And finally, to everyone who read and enjoyed *The Stray Spirit*: thank you for making my debut author experience more than I could ever have hoped for.

About the Author

By day, R.K. Ashwick herds cats in the animation industry. By night, she writes, bakes, and herds her literal cat around the living room. She lives with her husband (and said cat) in California.

For more information, visit rkashwick.com.

Printed in the USA
CPSIA information can be obtained
at www.ICGtesting.com
LVHW040152180324
774757LV00003B/26